FLEETING PROMISE

By Sherban Young

THE ENESCU FLEET SERIES

Fleeting Memory
Fleeting Glance
Fleeting Note
Fleeting Chance
Fleeting Promise

THE WARREN KINGSLEY SERIES

Five Star Detour
Double Cover

MORE BOOKS

Opportunity Slips
Dead Men Do Tell Tales

FLEETING PROMISE

AN ENESCU FLEET MYSTERY

SHERBAN YOUNG

Columbia, MD

Cover and illustrations by Katerina Vamvasaki

Editing services by Katherine Richards from *The Reading Panda*

ISBN-10: 0-9912324-7-X
EAN-13: 978-0-9912324-7-5

MysteryCaper Press
Columbia, Maryland

www.mysterycaper.com
www.sherbanyoung.com

FOREWORD

This is the fifth volume detailing the adventures of my friend Enescu Fleet, semiretired private detective. While not much has changed since Vol. 4, I feel compelled, this time, to offer a heads-up to new readers. You might even call it a spoiler alert.

If you like your mysteries fresh and untainted, you might want to read the previous installment before digging in here. (The publisher called that one *Fleeting Chance*, which I thought was rather clever.) In fact, you might want to read all of them in order. I recommend this for a couple reasons. One, the good folks at MysteryCaper Press knew what they were doing when they stuck the volume numbers on the book flaps. You'll get more out of these if you read them in sequence. I know this to be true, because I lived them that way.

The second reason is less subtle. In order to record the following adventure for your reading and sleuthing pleasure, I've had to talk pretty regularly about the murderer in *Chance*. At times, I couldn't shut up about the person.

Well—you know how it is when something has broken down your reserve. You become uninhibited, a little too forward with the info. Once I got discussing the killer in *Book Four*, all sorts of details from *Books One* through *Three* began gushing out. I don't reveal any major mysteries—but a few plot twists won't be quite as twisty if you read this book first. I even tossed in a handful of references to *Five Star Detour* (not a Fleet book, but a damn good read).

So there it is. Maybe you're like I am and figure you'll never solve the mysteries anyway, so what does it matter? In that case, off you go. But if you're one of those brainy types, like Enescu Fleet, and want a shot at fingering the murderers in the previous books using nothing but your insight into the criminal mind and a knowledge of obscure facts, then start at *Book One* and carry on from there.

It's what Fleet would do.

J. P. Hathaway

1 — Aperitif

I peered up from the floor.

For a moment, I just lay there, wondering what to do for the best. I could try to move—that was one way to go. On the other hand, I could remain sprawled out on the hardwood awhile longer and see what developed. Both had their advantages. I would have to give it some thought.

It was while I was still weighing my options—and making real headway, I might add—that I happened to notice something glimmering in the moonlight on the other side of the room. I had a sudden inspiration. With a determination that would have shocked anyone who knew me, I dragged myself across the area rug toward the back wall. I was making excellent time. Eventually, after three good belly strides, I arrived at a mahogany sideboard. I reached out and grasped an object from the lower shelf.

I had done all I could do. I flopped down on the rug once more.

There had to be a fair amount of blood by now. My host and hostess would never get it all out. Not from pure alpaca wool. And then there would be my corpse to dispose of. I was a terrible guest, really. Tightening my grip around the item in my hand, I lowered my face gradually into the fleece.

I began to pass out. My mind, previously racing, came to a rest.

They could always try a little club soda. That might work.

2 — Guest List

That all happened on a Saturday. The previous Thursday I enjoyed a lot more.

On Thursday, I arrived home from my honeymoon. With my wife. It still felt funny saying that. *Wife. Husband. Adulthood.* See what I mean—funny. (Maybe you had to be there.)

For now, the wife and I—you can call her Lesley—had moved into my small but serviceable townhouse down the road from Casco Bay. I say *for now,* because very shortly, if Lesley had her way, we were going to need more space.

It all began about a month back, after the wedding. Ever since then, the light of my life had become ever so slightly baby conscious. It was developing into a craze. On our trip, she hardly missed an opportunity to dig me in the ribs every time some adorable pipsqueak toddled past—as if having a child was a kind of catalog-shopping experience and all that was required was choosing the right model to fit your needs.

I hadn't tried to put her off the idea. I might have been new at this, but I wasn't that new. I did, however, advance several small (but serviceable) arguments from time to time. If I remember correctly, some of these included: *Did we really want to take on such an enormous responsibility this early in our marriage? Could we really afford a baby—financially, emotionally, geometrically?* And my personal favorite: *What had any babies ever done for us?* Lesley had appreciated each of these points in turn: in so far as she only heard every third word I uttered these days.

"We got a postcard," she said, as I carried in the luggage.

I had been stringing together an impressive commentary on babies and their lack of traveling savvy, when the future mother of my child interrupted to say all that sounded super and she would take green peppers on her half.

"It's from Mum," she continued, turning the card over. (Lesley didn't only speak this way to be quaint; she was English, so her inherent quaintness was all part of the package.)

"Yeah?" I answered. I knew all about Lesley's mum and her postcards.

"Reading between the lines, she still can't forgive us, mostly you, for eloping. She wishes us every happiness in our new life together, mostly me. She will be in Venice this week—"

"And wishes we were there," I said—"mostly me. At the bottom of a canal."

"Something to that effect," Lesley agreed. She glanced up from the card. "Funny, I would have thought Dad would have had more to say on the matter. He hasn't seemed that cheesed off about it, at all."

"That is funny," I replied. I gazed at her a moment or two. "He's probably just pleased not to have to pay for anything…"

She seemed to accept that solution. For now.

She furrowed her brow. I've always thought it a pretty cute brow, when furrowed. "This is interesting. Jill is meeting them in Rome so she can scout locations for *her* wedding."

Jill Darlington, as you may recall, was Lesley's younger sister—forever to be known as "The Good Sister," if I was any judge.

"Jill's getting married?" I asked. It seemed like a natural question, and yet somehow—

"Yes! And just like her too. A month after we get hitched and invite none of the family, she starts planning a huge, formal wedding for the whole family to attend. Knowing Jill, she'll invite the Pope just to show me up."

"Is the Pope part of the family?" I wondered.

Lesley wasn't listening. She was too busy prowling around the kitchen island: a petite, brown-haired she-cat. "I swear, if she gives them a grandchild before we do—"

And there we had it. Babies, babies, all the time babies.

"Have you looked at the book today?" she asked. (She meant the baby book.) "We really need to have some names in mind, Johnny, both male and female. When we do get pregnant, it's important that we have that aspect all worked out. I've been reading that picking a name early helps with the unborn child's psychological development and sense of self-worth."

I sniffed. It sounded like the sort of thing she would read.

"I'm about halfway through," I said. "I've just gotten to the part where Baby Girl Yvonne, which comes from 'yew wood' or 'brave archer,' has run off with Baby Boy Andrew—'warrior,' also brave. Baby Girl/Boy Aubrey—'Leader of the Little People,' I kid you not—is naturally conflicted. It's gearing up for a real cliffhanger at the end. I can't wait for the exciting climax."

"There's no call for cheek," Lesley commented, furrowing again. "Give it another perusal while I unpack, and then we can try again before dinner."

Like Baby Girl/Boy Aubrey, I was conflicted. On one hand, I felt like I should know my own mind before continuing to embark on an endeavor of such monumental importance—"monumental," that was another useful word. But, on the other—it never hurts to *try*.

"Looks like we also got some kind of invitation," she said. She tossed me the envelope.

This time it was my brow's turn to furrow. On invitations I am seldom conflicted. They never spell fun in my experience. (Witness last summer's banquet at the famed Pendleton Institute in Baltimore; poker night on *The Stacked Deck* touring yacht—there have been others.) My only thought, when I see one now, is how I can extricate myself from the upcoming merriment with the smallest amount of unpleasantness.

Turns out I had it wrong. This invitation I liked.

It was from my old friend Ditters Dittersdorf. No, seriously, that was his name. Actually, it was Walter Dittersdorf, but who wants to call a guy Walter when the nickname Ditters is there for your enjoyment?

Years ago, back in English boarding school, my closest friends were two Brits named Ditters and Hutton. They didn't even hold it against me that I was from across the pond and the nephew of a congressman.

Hutton I still saw most every day—sometimes too much, frankly. Ditters, sadly, I hadn't run across in years.

"It's from my old buddy," I announced. "You remember Ditters?"

"No."

So that was how far our relationship had come? "The weekend we met," I prompted.

"Oh, *that* Ditters," said Lesley.

I frowned. How many Ditters did she know?

I tried not to hold it against her. As I had been told several times on our recent honeymoon—once before parasailing and twice while tasting conch cooked in lime juice—dour did not wear well on me.

There was a time, I reflected, that Ditters, Hutton and myself were practically inseparable. I mentioned this to Lesley, and she said yes, she knew. She recalled everything I had ever told her about my youth. (Personally, I don't believe I ever told her anything of the sort, but I was glad she didn't ask me to *hold the anchovies* or something. Her listening was improving.)

"Looks like he and his wife bought a bistro. They would be honored if we would drop in for the soft opening."

"Delighted," said Lesley.

I nodded doubtfully. Delighted was a strong word. "If they have any decency, they'll give us more to eat than pickles."

The remark earned another frown from the missus. It seemed my wife didn't remember *everything*.

I could appreciate her confusion. In the US, pickles were small, briny cucumbers. In the UK, pickle was a strange, vinegar-laced relish used on sandwiches. In either incarnation, she couldn't fathom why it would be Ditters' sole menu item.

"Oh! *Those* pickles," she said, finally getting it.

We both frowned in culinary reflection.

Ditters Dittersdorf, if you haven't encountered his product in your local supermarket, was a prominent purveyor of pickles (the US version, in appreciation of his adopted land). At one time merely an amateur champion of the preservation arts, he went pro a few years back—*Ditters' Dills*—and still did very well at it.

One could only hope that his professional status had satiated his need to turn everyone he met into a cross between unofficial taster and hapless lab rat.

"It's not a long drive at least," I said, looking at the address and the bright side in one encompassing gaze.

Lesley said smashing. She could roll with the punches too. "I remember his wife. Veronica or something."

"Betty."

"Yes, that's it."

I chuckled, peering back into the not-so-distant past. "Funny—the last time he got in touch out of the blue, it wasn't quite so pleasant. For some stupid reason he left word for me as 'Walter'—"

"Isn't that his name?"

"Beside the point. Between the alien label and the cryptic wording the fathead used in the message, I thought I had received a death threat. It got me pretty gingered up, as you Brits like to say."

"I have never used the expression *gingered up* in my life."

"I asked my uncle for assistance. He was no help, so that's when I hired that Warren Kingsley character."

Lesley remembered him alright. "The bodyguard." She spoke the word with such a throaty significance in her voice that I had to give her a double look.

"Yes," I said, though the term bodyguard was pretty loosely applied, I thought.

"He was dreamy," said my spouse.

"Yes," I answered again. Very dreamy. Quite. "Anyway, no confusion about assassins this time," I went on, returning to the subject of Ditters. I peered down at the date. "He isn't leaving us very much notice. Freaking thing is in two days."

Lesley was in a more tolerant frame of mind than I was. "Probably sat in the mail for weeks while we were away."

"Perhaps."

"And it's not as though we have anything on right now."

"Perhaps not."

It was all agreed, then. We were RSVPing *Yes*. Not that we had time to RSVP properly.

Lesley grabbed one of her bags—one of the small ones—and paused before moving off. "I was about to call Ate. Should we invite her and her father?"

I didn't see why not. Ditters would probably enjoy meeting a world-famous detective. "You might want to invite Hutton as well," I suggested.

Once again I had confounded my wife. I was getting good at that. "I thought you said you, Hutton and Ditters were the new musketeers at one point?"

I had said that, and we had been. But things change. "I doubt Ditters even knows Hutton's in the country. He always liked me better, you see. He tolerated Hutton for my sake, and Hutton tolerated Ditters. But I was more or less the glue that held them together."

"I see," said Lesley. It always makes women hot to learn that you were glue. "I'll check it out, then. Back in a tick."

I had hardly taken a swig from a bottle of water and toyed with the idea of unpacking, deciding better not, before the tick had passed. Lesley returned to say that everything was all set.

"Turns out Ate's father already had an invitation. Enescu Fleet, plus one."

I said ah. I had a pretty good idea who that plus-one was going to be. I frowned (again). "Ditters invited Fleet?"

"Apparently his was one of the first cards that went out. He got his days before Hutton did."

I couldn't figure it. "And Hutton got one too, you say?"

"With knobs on. He received his gilded invitation in the mail a week ago. He's bringing our girl Ate, so that's everyone. Evidently nobody needed your glue."

I didn't know why she had to put it like that. It was definitely weird, though. About Fleet. He knew practically everyone, it was true, but when would he have met Ditters? It didn't make sense.

It kept me baffled for a full thirty seconds. All the way from the kitchen to the bedroom.

While I was still discussing Ditters with Lesley, and preparing to bend to her wishes on certain unrelated matters, Ate Fleet was coming in from Hutton's balcony on the other side of town.

She was a tall and slender young woman of half-Latin descent. (Her father contributed the non-Latin half.) She had a round face, intelligent eyes, and was all-around attractive in a smart, comfortable-in-her-own-skin way. She had started wearing her hair long again recently. It looked good.

She came inside and shivered. Even though I wasn't technically present at the moment, I understood that she had *frozen her ass off* taking Lesley's call.

"You must be a block of ice by now," Hutton said to her—or so I have been told. (I can't think why anyone would lie about such a detail.)

"It's the only way I can get any reception in this place," she retorted, nudging her man away from the fireplace. Reception and heat were two things sorely lacking at Hutton's house.

Unless I miss my guess, her nudge had thwarted him in his favorite new activity.

Recently, my friend had been spending an inordinate amount of time looking at himself in the mirror. This wasn't run-of-the-mill vanity, mind you. He had been watching his new beard grow in: the kindly nurturer urging on each hair with words of encouragement.

He liked to pay special attention to the leaders of the pack—the alpha strands. If they could make it, there was hope for the rest of the landscape.

Taking off his glasses and polishing them—I mean, he could have; why not?—he asked who was on the line.

"Lesley Darlington."

"You mean Lesley Hathaway now."

"I suppose I do."

"Little Lesley Darlington," he mused. He shook his head. "It seems like only yesterday that I was meeting my best friend's girl."

His companion at the hearth pointed out that it nearly was yesterday. "You only met her a little over a year ago, the same day I did, so knock off the Uncle Hutton routine."

Hutton knocked it off. "What was she calling about? Girly stuff?"

"Not that girly. She wanted to see if we were going to your other friend's restaurant opening."

"Ditters? Of course we are. Why shouldn't we?"

"How should I know? Hathaway seemed to think you might not have been invited."

"Now that is strange," said my friend. "If anyone needed to worry about getting stiffed, it would be he. Don't repeat this to Hath, but Ditters always liked me best. Two Britishers sticking it out through thick and thin. The kid practically worshipped me."

"That's spectacular," said Ate. "Anyway, I told Lesley we were coming."

"Sterling work."

"She also asked about Dad, but I told her he already had his invitation."

"Yes, about that," said Hutton—"why has he?"

"Why has he what?"

"Why has the great Enescu Fleet received an invitation to Hath's and my old school friend's gastronomic extravaganza?"

"I don't believe the invitation specified a reason."

"No, I don't suppose it would. Still, it's odd," he remarked.

Ate didn't see why. "People are always inviting Dad to things. I think the first card in a newly sealed pack says *Enescu Fleet is cordially invited…* and then a space for you to scrawl in the name of the event. It's like those attractively posed people you get with new picture frames."

Hutton nodded, seeing sense in this. "Speaking of blanks to be filled in, are we revealing our little secret yet?"

She recoiled from him. "Of course we aren't!"

"Ever?"

"No—I mean yes. I mean, we're going to have to say something, eventually." She chewed her lower lip. "Just not now."

"Okeydoke." (I'll go out on a limb and assume he gave his beard a glimpse in the mirror here.) "It's all good. No reason to steal Ditters' thunder at the dinner."

"Yes," said Ate dully. "Ditters' dinner."

Hutton squinted at her. "What's the matter now? Don't you like Ditters' dinner?"

"I don't like anyone's dinner. When you have a name spelled like mine, no matter how it's pronounced, people tend to be—" She arched an eyebrow. "Irritating."

Hutton agreed people were frequently that. "Still, when your host's name is Dittersdorf, how much do you have to be concerned about, really?" He paused, smiling. "Little Ditters Dittersdorf," he said, shaking his head. "Seems like only yesterday—"

At this point I am almost certain Ate Fleet rolled her eyes.

Continuing my out-of-body narrative—if I was going to be murdered in a couple days, I might as well enjoy a few perks—I take you to a charming upstate bistro owned by Walter and Betty Dittersdorf.

The happy pair was in a tiny alcove off the kitchen. It was a sort of office/closet/place for paperwork to come to die. Betty, pleasingly plump and as apple-cheeked as the day Ditters met her, hung up the phone—a landline, so she had no need for any freezing balconies.

"How nice. That was your friend John Hathaway."

Ditters, his own apple cheeks flushed in concentration, looked up. "Hath? Brilliant! What did he have to say?"

"Not very much. He seemed in a rush about something. He wanted to apologize for taking so long getting back to us—he and his wife only got home from their honeymoon today. They wanted to say that they would be delighted to come Saturday."

Ditters was thrilled. "I'm glad everyone will be there. Good old Hath and Hutton. I wonder if they've kept in touch?"

"I suppose they must have."

"I wonder," said Ditters. "You know, I always felt awkward about that back in school."

"Awkward about what, darling?"

"I don't like to brag—"

"No, no."

"But I always thought they seemed tighter with me than they were with each other."

"Oh, I see."

"I tried to give them equal portions of my time, of course."

"Of course."

"I hate playing favorites—you know that. But—well, you know. You can't push people together, can you? It causes a strain."

Betty nodded in agreement. She gazed lovingly past her husband to the mishmash of paper and ledgers at his elbow. "What are you working on?"

He slid a stack of bills off to the side. He was a conscientious young man and hated bothering his wife unnecessarily. "Oh, this and that. This and that." He peered down at their guest list. "We've got quite a party coming, don't we? Friends, family, celebrities. Who invites all these people?"

Betty nodded once more, misinterpreting his question as a figure of speech.

Ditters was reading the list again. One name jumped out at him. It also puzzled him. "*Enescu* Fleet," he said, struggling with the foreign pronunciation. "That's a funny one, isn't it?"

If I had been there, I would have given him an icy stare. As Hutton had indicated, someone named Dittersdorf should always take the high road.

"Now who is that?" he wondered. "I know I know it."

"I believe he's a famous detective or something."

"Oh right. I think Hutton is seeing his daughter. Yes, of course. That makes sense."

But it didn't. It didn't make any sense at all.

It's amazing. If only Ditters had delved into the matter, or Betty had delved into it, or some passing kitchen helper, eavesdropping on their conversation, had delved, it might have saved everyone a lot of trouble.

Not to mention a corpse or two.

3 — Amuse-bouche

Two days later, Lesley and I pulled up outside my friend Ditters' restaurant, the much ballyhooed *Le Vrai Cornichon.* (My French isn't wonderful, but I had a pretty decent bead on that one.)

It was the only structure for miles, situated at the peak of a long, tree-dominated hill. No doubt this isolation saved Ditters a bundle on the monthly lease, but I couldn't help wondering what it would do for business. From the look of the surroundings, even the local hermit would have found it desolate.

Nevertheless, it seemed a pleasant establishment, in the farmhouse style, with tons of Tudor charm. There were thatched roofs, timber frames and other things Tudor builders enjoyed. It looked like the country seat of a retired Shakespearean actor.

The remnants of the last few snowfalls still clung to the roof, the framing and the gables, contributing to the delicate country-inn flavor.

"Dinky," said Lesley, as we got out of the car, and she meant it as a compliment.

A gentle mist had begun to fall as we approached the entrance. This contributed to my wife's not-so-delicate sense of self-righteousness when it came to winter precipitation.

"I told you it was going to storm," she stated for the umpteenth time. "*Ice.*"

I held the heavy wooden door for her—I always strive for chivalry—and said *yes, yes.* I didn't share her endless fascination with weather prediction. And besides, it wasn't ice. It was rain, a drizzle. A light, refreshing, wintery Maine drizzle. I followed her in.

We were greeted by an empty lobby. It was dark and dank and smelt of vinegar and dill—much as I remembered my old friend, the proprietor, smelling. A lot of wood went into the interior construction: the walls, the floors, even the ceiling. We might as well have stepped inside an ancient puzzle box.

"Is that John Hathaway?" said a voice. And, with that, the Pickle King was in our presence. Ditters Dittersdorf, in person.

He gave us both a hug, lifting Lesley out of her sensible snow boots with his embrace, and then tackling my midriff. He always had been a demonstrative little fellow.

The facial hair surprised me. Unlike Hutton, whose growth evoked the spirit of the thing rather than anything substantive, the double-D foliage had completely taken hold of Ditters' face. It encircled his cherub countenance like a mandibular version of a Friar Tuck hairdo.

For some reason, I was immediately put in mind of stage make-up: a touch of theatrics applied before treading the boards in a fourth-grade production of *The Cherry Orchard.* It both confounded and fascinated my sensibilities. Deciding there was no reason why Ditters would opt to host a restaurant gala in false whiskers, I had no choice but to accept it for what it was.

"I was beginning to think you weren't coming," continued the young hedgehog, having cracked two of my ribs. "Thought you had gotten too busy for your old buddy. You and your fancy lifestyle, doing your—your—what is it you're doing these days, Hath?"

"Oh, you know," I replied.

"A little of this and a little of that?"

"More *that* than *this*," I explained.

Ditters understood, which was more than I could say for Lesley. Poor woman didn't speak a word of our language.

"Still doing the freelance couriering?" he asked, frowning at the mouthfeel of the verb. "The *courier-ing*...the process of *courieriering*... Are you still a courier?" he wondered.

I shook my head. "Not really. I've been doing some private-eyeing lately." I stated this modestly—like you do. Lesley sniffed.

"Have you?" Ditters gaped. "Ever hear of Eskimo Fleet?"

I assured him that I had. His friends called him Enescu.

"He's coming here, you know?" said Ditters.

I assured him that I knew that too.

"You seem to know everything. I guess that's your investigator's muscle flexing?"

Lesley sniffed again.

A flash of auburn in the distance drew Ditters' attention. "Is that you, Betty? Come and say hello to our friends."

Betty came and said hello. She was the same short and curvaceous young woman I had met all those summers ago at Roger Banbury's mansion (another Maine backwood).

Whereas her husband had grown older and hairier, she only seemed gigglier. "It's such a pleasure to see you both again!" she declared, brushing back her Titian curls. She didn't wear her hair very long in the back, but the foreground was plenty well represented. "You both look wonderful!"

I never know what to do when I encounter the wives and significant others of old friends. Hug? Peck on the cheek? It's very awkward. If only a hearty handshake would meet the case. With hearty handshakes I knew where I was.

Lesley took up the slack for me, wife engaging wife. She hugged and pecked, then Betty hugged and pecked, and then they both giggled. (I never would have thought of that.) "You have a wonderful place here," Lesley told her.

I backed her up on this. "Yes, wonderful. First-rate."

"So picturesque and out-of-the-way!" Lesley proceeded.

"Thank you so much!" said Betty.

"It's so cozy and dinky."

"Do you really think so?"

"Oh yes. Yes, I do. Ever so dinky."

"Dinky's good, right?"

"Dinky's very good," said Lesley. "I'd give a packet to be this dinky," she added. I was reasonably certain she was still speaking English.

"I'm so happy you like it," said Betty. "I could listen to your accent all day long. It's like Walter's, only completely different. Walter has got me watching PBS so I can learn all your wonderful figures of speech, but I can never seem to keep track of them all."

Lesley agreed that the Brits had lashings of expressions, alright.

Betty's eyes widened. "Are lashings a lot?"

Lesley agreed that lashings were loads.

They took a break here. I was glad—I could do with a breather myself. "So what's on the menu?" I asked them.

Betty looked mildly startled, and Lesley glared. I didn't get it. Why was that a rude question? It was a restaurant.

Ditters bobbed to the surface again. Good egg, Ditters—you could always depend on him when a man was outnumbered. "You're in for a treat, Hath."

"Oh yes?" I knew all about his treats.

"Our menu is very eclectic."

"Eclectic how?"

He looked to Betty, who smiled at him. The smile said, *Go ahead, you explain it better.* "It's sort of fusion cuisine. French Deli."

"Like Indian?" Lesley asked.

"No, not that Delhi. Deli. As in delicatessen."

We both said ah. Sounded delicious.

"That's what the name is all about. *Le Vrai Cornichon.* Get it, Hath?"

I told him I got it.

"It means *The Real Pickle,*" he explained. "Actually, it could also be *The True Pickle,* but that's because I couldn't find a word for *real* in French. Stupid Frogs. Anyway, I doubt anyone has ever heard of combining traditional French cooking with the taste of the delicatessen."

I had to agree with him there. I hadn't. And there might be a reason for that. "What does it entail exactly?" I inquired. "This *Deli Français?*"

"It's hard to explain. You have to taste it to believe it."

This time only I said ah. Lesley smiled. Weakly.

In the last few years, my English wife had come to love southern American barbecue, non-batter-fried fish and (evidently) conch cooked in lime juice—but this might be asking too much of her.

"I do hope the weather holds up," she tossed out vaguely. Kind of random, I thought, but it struck the right chord.

"Oh, I do too," Betty replied.

"Have you looked at the forecast?"

"I was studying it with our hostess Evelynn. An hour ago it looked like it could go either way, but now I just don't know."

"That's what I was thinking," said Lesley. "It could be ice mixed with snow or snow mixed with ice or possibly it might rain. Of course, yesterday they were calling for partly cloudy with patches of sunshine. I do find the forecasting so helpful, though, don't you?"

"Oh, I do," said Betty. "Even when it's not precise, it's nice to know what you know and what you don't know, if you know what I mean?"

"Exactly," said her fellow weather junkie. Now I was certain they weren't speaking English.

I think they might have wrapped it up here, were it not for a new arrival to the panel.

"We talking weather?" asked a boisterous woman, clomping into the foyer.

She was an attractive addition—in a galumphing sort of way: tall and well-endowed, with a single platinum bang across her forehead. If it weren't for a pair of overly heavy feet and a voice that could strip paint, she would have been pretty hot.

"I checked the radar again," she said, "and they're calling for a real doozy now. Or it might pass us by completely—they're not certain."

"Oh really?" asked Lesley.

"My, my," whispered Betty.

"I know, right!" said the weather herald. And now there were three of them. I wasn't up on your more technical meteorological terms, but doozy sounded like a lot.

"This is Evelynn," said Betty. "Our new hostess."

Evelynn said hiya.

The ladies went on discussing the approaching storm. Evelynn asked what apps the girls used. Lesley said *Weather Brainiac* was her choice, while Betty preferred the simpler *Whether Weather.* Evelynn leaned toward *Weather Monkey* herself but had heard good things about *Weather Whackadoodle 5000.* They continued for some time on the theme of rain, freezing rain, sleet, hail and ice, before Lesley incorporated me back into the conversation.

"I've been saying to Johnny all day that we should expect some weather."

I grunted. You can always expect some weather. All weather is some weather.

She pointed up at the transom. "Look and see. It's a real wintery mix out there."

I grunted again. "Just a little rain," I said.

"And?" she prompted.

"Snow and ice," I said, grunting for a third time. Lesley said ha.

"Well, anyway," spoke up Ditters, once more rallying to the side of his beleaguered crony. "At least most of the guests are already here. And, speaking of which, what are we doing standing on the doorstep? Come in and meet the rest of the party!"

The rest of the party was in one of the *Cornichon's* smaller dining rooms. It was a lovely little room, possibly even dinky, with more wood paneling and a tin ceiling—silver, with a floral pattern. The tin made for a welcome break in the textural styling. I looked up at it for a total of five seconds before crossing the threshold. Ever since a certain adventure with Enescu Fleet six months ago, I've learned to check the ceiling any time I enter a room.

I recognized the music playing inside: Boccherini's Minuet.

I'm sure you all know the Minuet. In classic cinema, it's the piece you hear playing in the background at some refined reception or other, moments before Rodney Dangerfield careens through the garden hedge on waterskis.

"Come meet the celebs," Ditters beckoned to us.

He wasn't exaggerating: these *were* celebs—TV celebs. Well, TV *food* celebs, at any rate. Fleet might have some competition for the limelight tonight.

Ditters made the introductions. First up, there was Vivian Birch, host of *Vive la Vivian*, an eclectic cooking show for the urban professional. She was a large and brassy sort with mischievous eyes. These she fixed on Lesley and myself throughout the formalities. She had either taken an instant dislike to us or wanted to know if we would like an autograph.

Later, when we were alone, Lesley said how much she adored Vivian's skin and how it reminded her of a silky scoop of cappuccino ice cream. I didn't see it myself, but I seldom think of people's skins in terms of confectionary.

Beside her was Elsie Farmer, host of *Farmer to Table*. She was a real stunner, Elsie: a tasty red-haired cinnamon stick, all bright teeth and candy-apple lipstick. She smiled her welcome, and this smile was a beacon of warmth. Then she switched it off, and it was as if a beautiful Greek siren had slapped you in the face with a fillet of halibut. She continued her conversation with the third food celebrity in attendance, Cesar Bloom.

Cesar, I was vaguely aware, had been host to a number of shows—*Great Cesar's Roast*, *Blooming Cesar Bloom* and *Little Cesar's Little Italy*. Currently, he was a man without a vehicle. No food analogies suggested themselves with him. He was a stocky man with a shaved head and a thoughtful brow. I suppose he looked a little like an unshelled pistachio around the forehead and jaw.

All three celebrities had participated in dozens of food competition shows on TV. They had judged amateurs, judged chefs and cheffed with judges. They were the king and queens of culinary judgment.

They were also finished with us now. We could go.

As we shifted quietly out of their orbit, I could hear Cesar stating that he enjoyed the savory profiterole, but what was up with the lime dill sauce? Vivian dug the lime dill but had a real problem with the grade of hickory used in the smoked salmon tapenade. Elsie thought the plastic toothpicks used on the brie wedges with pimento-edged gold leaf were tacky and dated.

Lesley and the girls had already re-picked up the threads on their new ice-age discussion, so Ditters drew me over to the back of the room, just us guys. It was warmer here than in the foyer, though not as warm as by the fireplace. The beautiful people were hogging that space.

He asked if I wanted a drink. Since there were no beverages in the immediate vicinity, and no one on hand to fetch one, I told him I was fine.

I thought he seemed nervous while introducing Elsie. Hesitant. Slightly awkward. (I guess I couldn't help flexing my detective's muscles, after all—even if the thews and sinews weren't quite as chiseled as I made them out to be.)

"I'm impressed," I said. "I more or less recognize these people, Ditters. How did you manage to get them here?"

"Oh that? That was Nancy."

"Nancy?"

"Our PR lady. She arranged it all. She's a dynamo."

"She must be. Not one, but *three* slightly known personalities. Nicely done."

"She's a wonder," he agreed. He seemed distracted still. "I know the three of them live in the Boston area now—and so does Nancy—so that might have had something to do with it. They like to support local business."

I was still amazed: the backwoods of Maine was hardly local. "This Nancy is worth what you're paying her. TV hosts can only add clout."

"Daytime TV hosts," he corrected. "That's why they're still fairly down-to-earth. Not that any one of them wouldn't poison their grandmothers for a prime-time spot."

I nodded. I could definitely see Elsie Farmer doing that. There's something about these striking beauties with the undercurrent of ice in their veins that gives a man the heebie-jeebies. I could see her poisoning a granny in a heartbeat to further her career. Not sure how it would, of course, but she might be willing to try.

"Have you two met before?" I wondered.

Ditters jumped. "What? Why? Who?"

"The Farmer chick."

"Why would you ask that!"

I didn't know why I asked it. If I knew why I asked more things, I probably wouldn't have to ask them.

"No—I mean, we don't—oh look, there's Zoe," he said.

I couldn't figure what Zoe had to do with it. And while we were on the subject, who the hell was Zoe?

Zoe Norris, it turned out, was Ditters' sole waitress for the evening. She was a timid-looking thing—what I would refer to as mousy and Lesley would call a rabbit. I guess, in England, rabbits have less dominating personalities than mice. She wore white-rimmed glasses and her black hair pulled back in a bun.

Despite her lack of impact, I suspected she had spunk: perhaps even a smattering of hidden rage. When Ditters leapt to her side and jerked the hors d'oeuvre tray from her fingertips, I thought for a moment the rabbit was going to tear out his throat.

She didn't, though. She held herself down, watching with ill-concealed fury as her employer dashed from point to point, pressing pâté-stuffed dill pickles on people.

He never offered me any, so I couldn't say how well this combination worked.

Normally, I wouldn't have minded getting left out of the taste test, but I was hungry, and even *Pickle de Provence* sounded pretty good right about then.

Once the tray had been emptied—again, not with my help—he tossed it to Zoe, the brash knight handing off his shield to his faithful squirette.

"Come and see the kitchen, Hath," he said to me, so I came and saw the kitchen. Perhaps I could get some food in there.

We didn't go immediately to the kitchen. That would have been too easy. Instead, we headed up a narrow flight of stairs to the second floor. There, Ditters showed me a restroom, several more private dining rooms (for those guests who couldn't abide the hurly-burly of the first floor), another room he and Betty were planning on offering to business types for luncheon meetings (owing to the long, thin design and lack of windows—business types don't need windows), and finally a well-appointed room that looked more like an old-fashioned drawing room than a dining room. I mentioned this to Ditters, and he admitted that it did seem like the ideal place to reveal a murderer's identity on a snowbound evening. Not that he had ever revealed any murderers himself, snowbound or in balmier months.

"This might be your chance," I said, indicating the storm in the window—damn that Lesley. Ditters said yes, it was getting rather sloppy out, wasn't it? We were as bad as our womenfolk.

Originally, the idea had been to have the party up here, with its old-world feel and view of the mountainside, but he had to eighty-six that in deference to Ms. Farmer.

This surprised me. What could Elsie Farmer have against a drawing room? This one was snazzy. It had wood paneling, a bookshelf complete with volumes on the art of pickle making, its own cache of liquor (helpful for washing down all those pickle books) and a picturesque view through six dazzling, antique-paned windows. Lug up a few TV trays and a handful of folding chairs, and you were good to go.

"The woman hate mountain vistas or something?"

Ditters shook his head. "It's the tight staircase. It's not generally known, but she suffers from claustrophobia. She can't handle confined spaces," he clarified.

"I know what claustrophobia is," I said.

I frowned. Something didn't fit, and I didn't mean the claustrophobe on the staircase.

"So how'd *you* know, then?" I asked.

"It's a fairly common mental disorder, Hath, written up in all the textbooks—"

"How'd you know Elsie suffered from it? If it's not generally known?"

He went pale beneath the pelage. "Never mind how I know!"

I might have told him that I did mind—I always minded when people held back on me, whether information or food. I decided not to press him, though. It didn't befit the dignity of an honored guest to constantly pry and question my host. Besides, he had already flounced from the spot and was halfway down the stairs by now. I doubted he could have heard my prying and questioning even if it did befit my dignity.

"Cool rug," I said, leaving the room.

"Alpaca wool," he called up through the banisters. "Handwoven."

Evidently, he could hear pretty well, after all.

4 — Fresh Confidences

From the foyer, we headed around a dimly lit corner and outside onto a covered terrace. Even with the overhead protection, it was freezing. I had to object to this ponderous route. I mean, where was he taking me? Not the kitchen. If we had been a couple of gangsters, I would have thought he was escorting me somewhere to get whacked.

"I want to show you my greenhouse," he hollered back to me. I shivered and picked up my feet in pursuit.

He showed me his greenhouse. It looked a lot like a greenhouse.

Apparently, it wasn't only beards that my host cultivated; the place had a little of everything. There were cucumbers (of course), tomatoes (Ditters said *tomotoes*), lettuce of all sorts and sizes, baby lettuce of all sorts and sizes, kale, curly kale, baby kale, haricot vert (which looked a lot like string beans), sprouts, carrots and cauliflower. He even had a whole section of barley.

"Why do you have a whole section of barley?" I asked him.

"That? I was thinking of making my own whisky."

I nodded my approval. I could go for a good malt. I peered back at the golden strands. He was going to need a lot more barley.

Overhead, the panes of the greenhouse were getting plinked more heavily now. I guess you would call it sleet. Unless it was hail. I can never keep those two straight. Call it a kind of sleety hail.

"You expecting anyone else tonight, Ditters?"

He came out of his reverie. He had fallen into one shortly after pointing out an abnormally shaped butternut squash on our way in. "What? No. Just your friend Escalator."

"Enescu."

"Yes, him as well." He truly did seem out of it. "Oh, and my father-in-law," he added absently.

I remembered Ditters' father-in-law well: Sheriff Adwick, also known as the law in the tiny town of Baccup, Maine—about thirty minutes north of here. We had encountered each other the weekend Lesley and I met. The sheriff portion of the weekend hadn't been all that pleasant for us. (Just a slight misunderstanding on a bit of burglary and attempted murder, no reason to rehash it all now.)

I wasn't too pleased to learn that he was coming here tonight. Still, what's past is past. As long as he refrained from arresting me or my wife, I would consider it a real stride in what had been, up until that point, a fairly one dimensional relationship

I must have dipped into a reverie myself, because Ditters had to poke my ribs several times before I came out of the fog. "Stop that," I said, and he stopped.

"Can I ask you something, Hath?"

"If you must."

"How are you and your pop-in-law getting along these days?"

"Lesley's dad? Fair to middling. He couldn't stand me at first, but he came around eventually."

"How'd you manage that?"

I made a vague gesture. "Just my natural charm and winning personality, I suppose."

"No, seriously." He really wanted to know.

I glanced around before speaking. This was strictly between him, me and the haricots. "I learned something about him that he wouldn't want known. Ever since then he has been much more sympathetic to his daughter's mate."

Ditters' eyebrows shot up. You didn't tend to notice these—not in proportion to the band of fur on his face—but they were abnormally large for eyebrows, and probably required some effort to raise. "What did you learn?"

"It's not important."

"Seriously—what was it?"

I lowered my voice further. Only a select few of us knew the Darlington family secret. "In his youth he had been a notorious art thief." (Another long story, details of which abound in a previous volume.)

My confidant drew away. Like Elsie Farmer, he needed more space.

"Not really!"

"Really."

"Does Lesley know?"

"No. And it needs to stay that way."

"Of course."

He paused, grappling with his astonishment. At least, I thought that was what he was grappling with. "You wouldn't mind if—no, forget it."

"What?"

"No. You would never go for it."

"Just say it, Ditters."

"Alright. Would you mind terribly—I mean, would it be a terrible imposition, if I—" He peered around again—"if I were to turn over your father-in-law to my father-in-law?"

He beamed up at me eagerly, awaiting an answer.

I drew away. "Yes, Ditters, it would be an imposition if you turned in my father-in-law."

"Just to my father-in-law," he said.

"Nevertheless."

He frowned. I don't think he cared for my tone. "It was just a thought, Hath. It would go a long way to ingratiating myself with the man. He's not sheriffing anymore—he retired a while back—but he still dabbles. This would tickle him. Give him something to do in an official capacity again."

I understood. And Mr. Adwick could go on dabbling without sending up my wife's father.

Ditters could see there would be no budging me on this. It was just as well, he said. Lesley's dad lived in England, and airline tickets cost money. An old scoundrel like Mr. Darlington would probably insist on first class.

I put my arm around him and guided him away from the barley. It kept twinkling at me in the lights, and in another couple minutes I might have been tempted to reach in and sample some raw. I was starving.

"All this time, and you still haven't ingratiated yourself with him?" I asked.

"Not a bit. If anything, our gratiation is more on the outs than ever."

"That's not a word."

"No," said Ditters, shuffling his feet sadly. He didn't suppose it was.

"You just need to find something in common," I told him—"like you did with your previous fiancée's father. You remember, you both liked collecting old junk? It was something you and he could see eye to eye on. And shortly before you ditched his daughter and ran off with Betty, it was something that brought you together. What's something that could bring you and Adwick together?"

We pondered in silence. It wasn't as easy as it sounded, discovering this link between the generations. Something occurred to me. Adwick's name sounded British. Ditters, despite the sound of his name, was a Brit. Anything there? I asked him.

Ditters didn't think so. Adwick was ridiculously American. I wasn't sure what he meant by the word *ridiculously*, but let it pass.

"Besides, I think my ancestors were German," he said.

"Close enough," I remarked. "And you can't go by names. Enescu Fleet's name comes from Romania, and he's about as Romanian as Swiss cheese."

Ditters still wouldn't go for it. "Even if Betty's dad and I did share an English ancestry, it would probably turn out that my ancestors had once stiffed his ancestors on a round of grog at the village pub, leading to many decades of clan feuding. It's no hope."

I was out of suggestions. "Why do you need to be ingratiated with your wife's father anyway? You don't see him that much, do you? Just give him a haughty look when he arrives, mutter that he'll never prove it was your family's turn on the grog, and let the evening flow past. What's wrong with that?"

"It's complicated. Especially with the—never mind," he grumbled.

This was the second helping of never mind he had dished out in the last ten minutes. I was determined not to choke it down this time.

"What's going on with you, Ditters? You didn't give me the grand tour and bring me all the way out here just to show me a butternut squash and wait for our gonads to freeze. You wanted privacy. Well, out with it."

He peered down at his trousers. He struck me as someone suddenly and poignantly aware of his gonads and their low temperature. He peered up again. "What's wrong with my butternut squash?" he asked.

"Nothing at all."

"It's a lovely squash. I was thinking of pickling it."

"I wouldn't," I said.

"No?"

"No. It's better that you don't," I assured him. "But that doesn't answer my question. What's up with you? I know we haven't seen each other in a while, but I can still recognize when you've got something on your mind."

He nodded. "You do know me, Hath, and you're a good detective. There *are* things on my mind."

"Well?"

"It's Elspeth."

"Elspeth?"

"Elsie. Elsie Farmer. And it's not really her. It's Betty."

"Betty?"

"My wife. Although she's not really involved. That's up to Elspeth."

"So it is Elsie, then?"

"It's both. I don't want Betty to find out about Elsie."

"Find out what?"

"A while back, I knew her."

I gave him a look. "How while aback? And how well knew?" I asked him. I didn't like the sound of this.

"A *long* while back. Give me some credit, would you? It was long before I met Betty. I hadn't even met Adrienne Banbury yet."

"So what happened?"

"Nothing much. It was just one of those things. Elsie wasn't famous then. It was before the explosion of food celebrities and home-decorating celebrities and all the other celebrities who become famous doing things most people would find boring in their own lives. I was in France for something or other. Elsie was in France too, and, well—"

"That's all it took," I said.

I rolled my eyes. The number of women who had scooped Ditters up with a ladle over the years was baffling to me. This Adrienne Banbury he mentioned, the one whose father collected useless crap, was a perfect case in point. In looks and personality, she came off like an equal mix of supermodel and up-and-comer for Empress of the World. And yet, she had fallen for him. And not one of those passing fancies—she showed a willing desire to become Mrs. Ditters Dittersdorf. And there had been others before her. It was nothing against my friend, but I wasn't sure where the fascination lay. The addition of the luscious Elsie Farmer to the list—well, that just made my mind boggle.

"Even still," I said, "I'm not sure I see the problem."

"Why 'even still'?" he frowned.

"Nothing. Just something I was thinking to myself. Why is some past fling an issue?"

"It's complicated."

"You told me that already."

"Well, it is. I don't want to cause tension for Betty. She can be very jealous."

I stared at him. "Betty? Your wife? Looks like a Mouseketeer, only purer? *She* can be very jealous?"

"Incredibly. And it's not even her."

I was getting a little tired of things not being people. "Then who is it, damn you!"

"Her father."

I didn't get it. What could a small-time ex-sheriff living thirty miles away have to do with Ditters' matrimonial bliss at the *Happy Pickle*?

"He wants a grandson, and we haven't been able to give him one."

I nodded. Babies. I knew how that could be.

"Betty wants a baby too, and—"

"Let me deduce," I said. "You haven't been able to give her one?"

"No. And there's something else…"

I waited patiently for him to elaborate. But no elaboration came.

"It's not important," he said. "I've bored you long enough." And with these words, he went mute.

He turned off the lights. "You might as well come in and meet the rest of the staff," he sighed. "We only got a skeleton crew on tonight. The real number is a cast of thousands. How I'm going to afford them all…" he muttered.

I followed him out into the cold. I sensed that he had more on his mind than babies, old flames and butternut squash. I was determined to get to the core of it.

5 — Storm Brewing

At long last we arrived at the kitchen. Its expansiveness surprised me. The *Cornichon* wasn't exactly small, but the plethora of tiny rooms deceived you into thinking it wasn't all that large either.

The kitchen altered that perception. It spread out in every direction, with alcoves, islands and pantries peppering the horizon as far north as Canada. Baffled by this design choice, I wondered if the original architect had gotten a few pages stuck together on ye olde construction manifest. I could see him prying open a crate, slapping his forehead and saying, *Egad, they sent us the Vanderbilt order by mistake.*

Lesley hastened to my side. Apparently, while Ditters and I were off having our frank, manly discussion in private—the way real men do: in greenhouses, with gourds and veggies all around—she and the ladies had moved their Algonquin Weather Club in here.

Their insights no longer seemed to grip her. She slipped a hand in mine and shot me a reproachful look.

I've gotten pretty good at interpreting these. This one said, *Where the hell were you?* That, and so much more. I could appreciate her look's point of view. Fun is fun, but after a while you run out of stories about freezing rain and need your spouse's support meeting and assimilating new faces. This was especially true when those faces included the sour mug of Ditters Dittersdorf's chef, Sven.

"This is Sven," said Ditters, as we drifted toward him.

I remarked, "Hi, Sven."

He wasn't much for greetings. He peered sullenly across the butcher-block counter and went back to slaying parsnips. There was a lot of white-blond about the *Cornichon* cook: a white blond slick of hair; a large, white-blond horseshoe mustache, full and imposing in its blondness—even his skin looked oddly blond (probably from consuming too many parsnips). He had a cylindrically shaped head, a square jaw and an endomorphic build. Don't run away with the idea that this made him cuddly, however. He had a raw and wild-eyed look about him. Not the sort of guy you'd want to bump into at a deserted frying station in the middle of the night.

I'll say this, he and Ditters made an amusing pair standing next to each other. The height difference, for one. Sven was about nine feet taller than Ditters—the ideal physical dichotomy for any comedy duo. But their facial growths also contrasted nicely. Ditters', as I've said, was all cheeks, the finest face ruff you will ever see. Sven, in contradistinction, had concentrated all his efforts on the mustache. Looking them over, I realized that—together—they had the ingredients to construct a really fine, multicolored beard.

"This is Nancy Mortimer," said Ditters, having departed the chef's domain.

The PR dynamo strode into view. Before I could remark, "Hi, Nancy," the woman was all over me. She squeaked out a greeting, shook my hand with vigor, and smacked my shoulder, also with vigor.

I would estimate she ran about four-four. Some would have called her hair dark blonde. Others would call it light brown—and they'd be wrong. It was dark blonde. She had on smart business attire in muted vermillion, heels (good move) and wore the aforementioned hair in a windswept style: all in all, the perfect imitation of a garden sprite about to meet with corporate. She had no visible upper lip—I'm sure she had one; it just wasn't showing itself—an absence which stood out all the more in someone who smiled so much.

I don't know who would have won out in a cheeriness competition—Nancy or the hostess with the mostess, Evelynn—but the savvy wager was on Nancy. Pound for pound, she had no equal.

"You've met our hostess," said Ditters, moving down the line. Evelynn said hiya (again). "And Zoe, our waitress." Zoe nodded dully. (I felt like I was inspecting the troops.) "And this is our French baker—

Madeleine Abrams," he concluded, indicating a troop that wasn't there. He realized his omission and gawked accordingly. "Where's Madeleine?" he asked his wife.

His co-commander bounded to attention. She had been present throughout the ceremonies, beaming amiably. "Madeleine's lying down, darling. She was up until four a.m. baking, remember?"

Ditters, who didn't remember anything of the sort, said oh right. "That would tucker her out, wouldn't it? I guess we should let her rest."

His comment brought a sniff of derision from Sven. "That woman rests more than her dough!" he snorted.

He guffawed at his own witticism. You can't beat the comedy of Oslo. And a cooking metaphor to boot.

I expected him to have a heavier accent. I've noticed that about some Scandinavians: they can be comparatively mild in their drawl. They end up sounding like they're from Minnesota or somewhere.

"Well, I guess that's all of them for now," said Ditters.

I don't think he cared much for Sven's gibe. He turned his attention to a stray lemon someone had left lying out on the counter. Picking this up and examining its rind, he spun around and accosted his chef with a fire lit in his apple cheeks.

"What's this?" he demanded.

Sven might have been tempted to remark *a lemon*, but he had already used his one quip for the evening, and Norwegians are not known for excess.

Ditters carried on, "What did I tell you about citrus zest? Can't stand the stuff! Makes everything taste like furniture polish. Lemon is the worst!"

Sven, who had many qualities of a lemon—except for the zest—remained silent. Still without speaking, he brought his cleaver down hard on the cutting board. A kumquat narrowly escaped with its life.

Ditters' bluster was harsh but not long lasting. Turning away again, he peered at a distorted reflection of himself in the stainless steel refrigerator. He dragged a hand through his hair, sending the strands spronging out at the sides.

"Well, never mind, then. We should be getting back to our other guests, I suppose." He jumped at this sudden reminder. "Oh Lord!

We're all in here. They're all in there. Alone! Three semifamous television stars—"

Betty was a good wife. "I'll go, sweetheart."

"Yes," he agreed, his hand tousling what remained of the afternoon's combing. "You go. It would be better if you went. I'll be in straightaway."

In all the years I'd known him, I'd never seen my friend looking less self-possessed.

For Sven, Ditters' discomfiture suggested a strategic advantage. "Shall we be serving *all the pickles* this evening, *sir*?" he asked with a jeer.

I can't quite describe the emphasis he placed on the word *pickles*. (He used it with the *sir* as well, to even stronger effect.) He somehow pronounced the words without actually forming them on his lips.

It was pretty clear that he didn't appreciate Ditters' art form. Which was funny. I had always thought that these Nordic types got a kick out of pickling things.

Ditters twirled around once more. (Mark my words, he was going to knock over a tray at some point this evening.)

"What?" he snapped. His face twitched with rage. "Yes. Of course! We discussed this. It's our name, isn't it?"

"Very well, sir. Perhaps you would care to select the appropriate *jars*."

There it was again. Ventriloquists could have taken lessons from him.

Ditters opened his mouth to retort. What he nearly said, I couldn't say—but to employ Evelynn's excellent expression, I would bet it was a doozy. Fortunately, cooler heads prevailed.

Ditters said he would select them, yes. Sven said very well. Ditters said that it was well, wasn't it, and then Hutton arrived.

He came in the employee entrance because, well, Hutton was Hutton.

"Hello all. What's this, the kitchen?" He shook snow from his lanky frame like a bespectacled greyhound back from the hunt.

Ate stepped in after him. She wore an air of apology (also, a charming black dress and an adorable purple beret. But mostly an air of apology). "I hope it's okay to come in this way."

Hutton explained that the front door seemed a touch too *on the nose* to them. "Also, you're getting quite a sheet of ice mounting on the steps. Someone's going to slip and crack their skull open, and that's bad for business. Can't have your entranceway piled up with frozen corpses, now can we?"

Ditters waved off these explanations, if you could call Hutton's remarks an explanation. The wave suggested none of it mattered to him anyway. What difference could a few corpses make? He had a Norwegian chef and a hateful in-law on the way. His life sucked.

Despite all that, he applied a couple hearty bear hugs to his guests, old and new alike. There was perhaps slightly less of the grizzly about the embraces this time. More like a ferocious koala. You have to make allowances, though. When Lesley and I arrived, he hadn't had most of his verve sapped rassling with men named Sven.

Ditters' gaze went immediately to Hutton's face. I sensed a battle of beards gearing up. "What made you sprout the wheat field?" he asked.

Hutton replied, "Oh, I don't know. Seemed the thing to do." A cryptic answer for a cryptic fellow.

"Well, keep at it," Ditters encouraged him, fondling his own dense forest. "You'll make something of it eventually."

I could be mistaken, but I could have sworn I saw Hutton wince. I think the comment wounded his feelings (I wasn't sure I had seen that before—who knew that Hutton had any?). What Ditters didn't seem to understand was, when it came to Hutton's bristles, this was as good as they got.

"Did you say something about ice?" the former proceeded, having insulted one guest and detached his face from the torso of the other. This was the first time he and Ate had met in person, and the little ladykiller had a lot of time to make up for.

Hutton gave a nod. "I was saying that you have made a fine rink of it on your porch. Is that the effect you were going for?"

"No, not really."

If Ditters had a fault, it was that he could be a tad too literal. Hutton, on the other hand, had hardly spoken an unfacetious word in his life.

"The porch, you say," said our host. "I guess I should do something about that." He stood musing on porches and what one might do about them. "I am the proprietor, after all." He gazed idly around the room. He wasn't going to do anything about it. "Have you met everyone yet?" he wondered.

Hutton said not that you would notice, no.

Ditters ran through the introductions again. When it came time for the guests to identify themselves, it was Nancy who struck the jarring note—with Ate. *"Ah-tay?"* she said. "What an unusual name. How's that spelled?"

Ate gave her a look. Removing her beret and squaring her supple shoulders, she spelled it. That done, she glared from one side of the kitchen to the other. She was asking if anyone wanted to make anything of it.

Nancy evidently did. Through a toothy, lipless grin, she laughed, "You must have gotten a lot of ribbing as a kid. Ah-tay *ate* it. Ha-ha! Here's one you probably haven't heard—"

"I've heard them all," replied Ate. "And it's *Ah-tee*, not—"

Nancy wasn't listening. "Oh! I just thought of another one—"

The hostess Evelynn, showing remarkably good sense, interrupted here. She wasn't just a shapely clodhopper with a pretty face and an interest in Doppler radar. The giantess had people skills as well.

"You know, I think everyone hates their name on some level. I mean, look at what I got handed at birth. Evelynn *Brine*. Now there's a name you don't enjoy growing up with. Although, sometimes I wonder if it's the reason why Mr. Dittersdorf hired me. The Brine girl for the pickle man! Ha!"

Ditters peered up in confusion. Brine? Pickle? Oh yes. He got it. What were they talking about?

Evelynn pressed on, "Of course, you must know what it's like, people making fun of your name?" She let the question hang cheerfully in the air a moment for her employer to scoop up and run with.

Ditters wasn't much of a runner these days. "Like what?" he asked. "What's wrong with the name Dittersdorf?"

"Nothing," said his hostess quickly. "Nothing at all." And with that, the jolly atmosphere she had attempted to infuse fizzled.

Luckily, she wasn't the only *Cornichon* employee with a sense of humor. Suddenly, the girl Zoe sprang to life. I told you she had spunk. (Also three pints of chardonnay, apparently. I had seen her sneaking samples off the counter throughout the exchanges.)

"You know what's really funny," she said. "You're *Brine*, which is something cooks do—but you're a *hostess*. Meanwhile, cook is named Sven *Hosten*. Ha-ha!"

We all had a good laugh about that one. Everyone except Evelynn, Ditters, Lesley, Ate, Hutton, Sven and myself. The chef glowered more coldly than he had over the citrus zest.

"I am not 'cook,' young lady, as you so crassly put it. I am chef de cuisine!"

Zoe replied, "Whatever! You old grump!" She tittered into her mousy hand. She was completely out of her shell now. Personally, I wouldn't have minded helping her back inside it.

"You know what I've always wondered," said Ditters, resuming the mantle of a charming host, "what Hutton's real name is. What about it, Hut?"

I had forgotten that Ditters didn't know Hutton's actual name. I had learned it myself a while back (after twenty-some years), but, you know, Hutton and I were pretty tight.

Ditters put it to him plainly. "So what is it?"

"Never mind," said Hutton and Ate in unison.

Already familiar with the expression, Ditters nodded agreeably. He could take it as well as dole it out.

Now that the ice had been broken, or as broken as it would ever be, Nancy picked up a tray of hors d'oeuvres and held it out to the room. "Cheese puff, Ah-tay?"

Ate shook off the offer with a polite smile. Lesley and Hutton snagged a couple of choice specimens, as did Evelynn and Zoe. I managed to land a single puff before Nancy snarfed the last three.

What I tasted was surprisingly good. Delicate, with a subtle flaky texture, and not a suggestion of pickle juice. I later learned that they were not so much puffs as smoked Edam beignets, but Nancy's homespun manner naturally gravitated to the simpler term.

"Love these things," she chewed. "That Madeleine is a genius."

"We should probably go easy on them," Evelynn recommended. "They're about a thousand calories each."

"Oh, I don't mind," said the dynamo. "I've always been able to eat anything I want."

I saw Ate mouth to Hutton, *"I-hate-her."* He nodded knowingly.

Ditters looked up at the clock. "I'm surprised everyone else isn't here yet. Were the roads very messy?"

Hutton answered that one at length. He could tell us all sorts of things about the roads: their condition, their treatment, the use of salt, sand, plowing apparati. But none of it was as bad as last year, he said. Last year, he went on to explain—and I tuned out here. I never would have thunk it, but all this time my friend was a closet weather fanatic.

"And so," he wrapped up, "in reply to your question…"

"They were messy," said Ate.

"Yes," Hutton stated. "A real slop-fest. That's why we're late. Of course, the traffic lights didn't help. Don't get me started on traffic lights!"

Ate nodded vehemently. "Yes, please don't get him started," she said.

"Did I ever share with you my theory on traffic signals?" Hutton asked me. "My theory on traffic signals," he continued, not waiting for my reply, "is that your government, in an attempt to grapple with overpopulation, has timed these lights in such a way as to increase everyone's blood pressure. This leads to hypertension and, eventually, less population. It's cunning when you think about it."

I preferred not to think about it. "How many lights did you have?"

"Thousands."

"Four," said Ate.

"Yes, four," conceded Hutton, speaking the number with a certain grandeur. "And we missed every one of them."

And here I was thinking that Ditters had problems balancing an unruly kitchen staff and maintaining harmony within his extended family. He had it easy.

"Shall we adjourn to the dining room?" he asked us.

"Yes, adjourn," Sven snarled from the pantry.

I was going to miss him.

We proceeded en masse down the corridor. Ditters led the way ahead of Lesley, Ate and Hutton. Nancy and the rest of the staff would join us later.

While we walked, I became increasingly aware of the sounds of a hubbub drifting down the hall in our direction. Sort of a hoo-ha. Almost a hullabaloo. One might even refer to it as the makings of a hootenanny.

As nothing had suggested the slightest indication of any hoots before then, and certainly not any nannies, I increased my speed and reached the doorway alongside Ditters, my curiosity piqued.

My curiosity was satisfied.

Despite how it sounded, the food celebrities had not gotten into the tawny port. There was a simpler explanation.

Enescu Fleet, ex-private detective and current man of the world, was in the building.

6 — Over Flame(s)

I identified this fact at once. Even before spotting the man.

My method of deduction? Well, we PIs don't like to share too many industry secrets—it dilutes the investigator mystique—but I think I can fill you in on this one without receiving any nasty looks from the ethics board.

A small Maltese, shaggy of hair and with the frenzied gait of an animal called something like…oh, I don't know…*Pixie,* had just streaked past my feet.

And there you had it. Wherever the beloved pooch of Fleet's late wife went, so too must follow Enescu Fleet.

Deduction complete.

It appeared that his "plus-one" was wasting no time in airing herself out after the long car ride. Her tiny paws, failing to grip the hardwood, skidded a touch here and there, but she made up for it with a can-do attitude.

Her owner was chatting up Betty Dittersdorf. From the unsuppressed mirth illuminating the latter's face—far beyond her usual giggle—I could surmise he was in good form tonight. Enescu Fleet's charm was like the yolk of a properly made poached egg. It didn't take much of a poke to get it flowing.

We came over and said hello. He returned our hellos with relish. Having kissed Lesley on both cheeks, he grasped my hand warmly.

No offense to my little buddy, but I would take a handshake from Fleet over one of Ditters' bear hugs any day. (Sorry, man.) There was something about the simple benevolence of his greetings that always made me feel like one of the family. I'm not certain Ate would agree with that last part, but you know how metaphorical siblings can be. As for Pixie, she hardly bothered to lick my knuckle in passing anymore. Far too busy.

I was glad Fleet was different. He looked well—he always did. Robust and hearty, with a twinkle in his eye. His beard was as a beard should be: well cropped but not too cropped, fully formed—neck, mustache and jaw—but not so full that it lent any dimension to his profile. It was mostly gray, but a few flecks of color still remained, showing there was life in the old dog yet.

"Johnny and Lesley Hathaway!" he said. "My goodness. Did you airdrop in today?"

"Almost," Lesley smiled. "We got back Thursday."

"Wonderful. And where did you end up honeymooning?"

"It's funny you should ask that," I replied. "We—"

At this juncture, Ditters interrupted to say hello and welcome to his new guest. He also wanted to point out that his new guest's dog had just taken off like a shot down the hall. This was shortly after consuming three hickory-turkey crudos and a cocktail napkin.

"She'll be back," Fleet assured him, as a woman's scream echoed in the distance. It sounded like Zoe Norris. "You were saying, Johnny?"

"What? Oh yes—we ended up—"

Our waitress reappeared before I could finish. She was panting slightly and holding Pixie out from her uniform like a furry rump roast. She presented the prize to Ditters and strode off. She was going to require more chardonnay.

"Remarkable," said her employer, staring down at the writhing hellhound.

I didn't know what was so remarkable about it. Bizarre, maybe. Off-putting, perhaps. But remarkable?

"Hold on a second," he said, handing off the pup to me. (Fleet was otherwise engaged recounting an amusing anecdote to Vivian Birch about a case he once had involving a Chilean assassin and a well-timed avocado pit to the base of the skull.)

I gazed down at the detective's bundle of joy, her claws tearing into my new charcoal-gray cardigan. (It was a really cool cardigan, not the nerdy kind.) I wondered what Ditters' other guests thought about the canine angle. A dog before dining didn't exactly represent the height of haute cuisine.

The regular gang was fairly laid-back about it. I know I personally had grown used to the mutt's nonsense. Lesley liked dogs—her sister was a vet. Ate was practically related, and Hutton never minded anything likely to cause a stir.

I might have been used to it, but that didn't mean I had to like it. In fact, I was a little annoyed. I knew how much Ditters had riding on this. I'm not sure Fleet did. Clearly, he never bothered to ask himself if two new restaurateurs, opening their doors for the first time, wanted a rambunctious hairball as a complement to the evening's festivities. He naturally assumed that they did.

Ditters rejoined us during these reflections. I had to blink twice. In his arms was a fluffy doppelgänger: a near-perfect image of the half-pint I held squirming against my chest. I couldn't figure it. My buddy had somehow discovered how to clone Maltese.

Upon closer inspection, the clone wasn't all that precise. Ditters' version was beefier, the eyes not quite so beady and raisin-like as Pixie's. It was a kinder, mellower clone.

"This is Phillip," said Ditters. That made sense too. Another dog. (Didn't anyone follow a health code anymore?)

Betty came over and tousled Phillip's puffy head. "He belongs to our baker. Don't you, cutie. You're her li'l man, aren't you! Yeah, you are! Yeah, you are!"

Phillip made no reply to this, except for a long, dry yawn.

Ditters gestured toward Pixie, who was now attempting to tunnel out through my abdomen. "I thought it might calm her down to meet Phil."

Only Ditters Dittersdorf would think that.

I don't think I have to give you the upshot. Pixie sprang from my grip. Phillip, feeling that no chick was going to show him up in his house, slithered free and landed atop Ditters' mukluks. They met in the middle.

Just before they butted heads, I peered over at the beautiful people (and Cesar Bloom).

They appeared strangely good-natured. Maybe celebrities *were* just like you and me.

Other than a hushed "Good God, there's two of them now!", Cesar seemed pretty cool about the livestock. Dogs must have been a regular feature on the mean streets where he had learned to cook. Vivian was positively tickled by it all (perhaps her sister was a vet too).

Elsie was another story. Elsie hadn't liked the intrusion of Pixie, and she liked Ditters' Malta-multiplication even less. She tried to conceal it, but I saw her scowl, once for Pixie and once for Phillip.

It was the exact look of scorn I had seen TV critics like herself exhibit when tasting dishes overseasoned with truffle oil. Throw in Phillip, and she might as well have been handed a plate that not only wafted of too much truffle, but also the pig that found it. I guess you truly can have too much of a good thing.

With that said, I had to admit I was wrong about Phillip. When the dogs hit the mat, I figured Ditters and Betty would be picking Maltese fluff out of the walls for weeks. No such concern here. I won't say Ditters was anything but a fathead for bringing him in. He was. But it had calmed Pixie down. I was amazed.

Fleet wasn't the only male in the room with a magnetic personality. For a scrappy little guy who resembled a 1930s hobo in canine form, Phillip was the goods. He immediately transfixed Pixie with his mellow aura. It wasn't more than a few seconds before they were lying together on the floor, their bellies upturned and their tiny brains thinking whatever thoughts Maltese think.

I must have been pretty transfixed myself, for it was at least half a minute before I registered a new person standing in the doorway. She smiled graciously toward the gathering, prompting Ditters to snap back into his introductions.

"This is—"

"Madeleine," said Enescu Fleet.

So it was, Ditters confirmed. Madeleine Abrams, the baker. I guess she had finished with her lie-down.

I was confused. I hadn't spotted any clues that would have led Fleet to his conclusion. Even if he had identified some imperceptible measure of dog fur on the newcomer's capri pants, I was certain Betty hadn't used her name when speaking of Phillip. She had simply said *our baker*. So what I wanted to know was—what gave?

Obviously, Fleet's methods of deduction were well beyond mine. I was going to require some elucidation on this, and the board of ethics could go screw themselves.

Fleet moved closer, careful not to squash any furry bellies as he stepped. He took her hand in his. "How long has it been?"

"Years," gasped his fellow Maltese owner.

"It seems like only yesterday," he replied.

I was beginning to get a fix on this. It wasn't as complicated as I had originally thought. They knew each other—Fleet and this Madeleine woman.

"You must be Ate," she said. She pronounced the name perfectly.

Ate nodded. I hadn't observed Fleet's daughter nonplussed on many occasions, but she was nonplussed now. "Y-yes—" she replied. "I'm Ate." She threw together a smile. Not one of her best.

"I'm so glad to see you again, Ate. You've become a beautiful young woman."

Ate thanked her. She turned to Hutton. "This is my boy—" She hesitated. "This is Hutton," she remarked.

Hutton said yo. He had been studying American colloquialisms as of late. Apparently, he had been putting in a lot of coursework in 1970s Philly.

Most people wouldn't have picked up on the hitch in Ate's speech, the one-eighty on the term "boyfriend." It only made her sound more street. "This is my *boy* Hutton"—or so sez *Ahtay*, the gumshoe princess. I picked up on it, however, and I bet Hutton did too.

Fleet was too busy gazing at the ghost from the past to pick up on much of anything. She was an attractive woman, for a ghost. She had medium-length, fluffy brown hair, very light (not dark blonde), skin the color of a nectarine custard, and a drowsy yet kindly expression. This shined out from a pair of Mediterranean-blue eyes, some of the brightest I had seen in some time. Picture a well-preserved Miss Côte d'Azur after an especially rigorous portion of the pageant's talent competition, and that was Ms. Madeleine Abrams. She had on an oversized rugby shirt, navy and red striped, cut low to the chest. It suited her.

"So you two know each other, then?" asked Ditters. I was glad I wasn't the slowest one on the uptake in the room.

"I should have recognized your photography," said Fleet, still speaking to Madeleine.

I peered around. He was right. There was photography on the walls. Mostly local studies of ships and things. They were good.

"You must be slipping," said the baker-photographer-dog-owner-ex-lady-friend. I kept expecting an accent from these people, but nothing doing. Too bad—a saucy French articulation would have completed the package.

Fleet accepted the dig with a smile. "Wine, Maddy?"

"None right now. But I'll have some time alone with you, Nessie."

Fleet (aka "Nessie"—Nessie!) bowed. Taking her hand in his once again, he escorted her across their dogs and over toward the fireplace.

Ate and Hutton split from the pack at this point as well, as did Lesley and Betty. That left Ditters and yours truly on our own once more. Somehow, the divvying up didn't go quite as I would have planned. Not that I had anything against conversing with my old buddy Ditters. Again. And again, and again.

Having exhausted our reminiscences earlier, I struggled for a new topic of conversation. I glanced at his wife. She was stooping over Pixie and Phillip, rubbing their stomachs. Cesar Bloom and Vivian Birch looked on pleasantly; Elsie scowled. It was definitely not a good look on her.

Ditters broke in on my survey. I hadn't heard a word he said.

I turned and stared at him. There was no excusing my bad manners. Where I had failed miserably to find a topic to amuse, he had succeeded—and, from the sounds of it, succeeded for some time now. "Sorry," I said, "what were you saying?"

"I was *saying*," he said, "that I don't know what's keeping my father-in-law. I guess it's too much to hope that he skidded off the road in the storm and froze to death."

I gazed at him. "Don't take this the wrong way, Ditters, but I think I've spotted where your lack of harmony stems."

"It's not me," he protested. "I'm delightful. It's him. Nothing I do is good enough for his little girl. He thinks I'm nothing more than an irritating little picklemonger."

"So how did you come to invite Fleet?" I asked, changing the subject.

I was good at that at parties. I might not know any bawdy jokes, and I might not have the ability to imitate any foreign accents—except for my own strange verbal concoction, honed from splitting my youth in England and the United States—but I am an expert at sidestepping awkward topics.

"So how do you know Fleet?" I said again. Apparently, it was Ditters' turn to ignore me.

"Huh?"

"Enescu Fleet. What made you invite him?"

"I didn't."

An odd reply, but that was Ditters. "Another of the dynamo's doings?" I hazarded.

"I don't think so. Nancy thought he was a Romanian count when she saw his name on the list. It must have been Betty."

It was a specious explanation. But how would Betty Dittersdorf have met a famous private eye? Through her father? Not likely. Fleet knew nearly everyone, but there were limits.

I was determined to get to the bottom of this.

"Do—?" I began, to which Ditters replied to hell with Escargot Fleet, there was lemon zest burning in the kitchen. He left.

"Howdy, stranger," said my wife, poking me in the base of the spine. "Fun party, huh?"

I said indeed.

"Who knew that Fleet had a 'past,' huh?" She meant the term in the romantic sense. We all knew that Fleet had plenty of pasts in other areas. "That woman has taken him right out of himself. Look."

I looked. He seemed somewhat out of himself, yes.

"At least the lady he came with doesn't look too jealous about it." She pointed to Pixie, who was playing "Who's got the meatball?" with Cesar and Phillip. Lesley shook her head. "It's crazy. You or I bring a dog to a soiree and we'd be cut by the county for years—not that there's much county around here to do any cutting. Fleet brings one and he's the party's popular pet. Or his pet is, anyway."

I agreed that such was the world of Enescu Fleet. You could only embrace it.

I did take issue with her on one point, however: "He and Pixie are not popular pets with everybody."

Lesley understood. She didn't even have to follow my stare to Elsie. "She is something of a copper-haired cow, isn't she?" (I never tired of the British gift for understatement.) "Gorgeous, though."

"Is she?" I squinted across the room. "Yes, I suppose she is. Fair to middling gorgeous." I passed quickly from this inadequate reply—Lesley wasn't buying it. "Oh, remind me to tell you something about her later. It's pretty juicy."

"Is it that Ditters and Elsie were once entwined?"

I gaped at her. Was *everyone* a better detective than I was? "Wait, who told you? Not Ditters?"

"No."

"Not Betty? She doesn't know."

"It was Hutton and Ate."

I gaped again. "How the hell did they know?"

"Ditters told Hutton, and Hutton told Ate. Then they told me."

I would have gaped a third time, if not for the arrival of Evelynn Brine, handing out more appetizers with a flourish. Something about her lighthearted manner suggested she might toss a stuffed artichoke into my open maw if the opportunity presented itself, and I didn't feel like getting Heimliched this evening

"I'm astonished," I said. "Shocked and astonished. Ditters acted like he was sharing some precious secret. See if I join him in any greenhouses in the future. The next time he wants someone to brood over his butternut, he can ask Hutton!"

Lesley looked confused and vaguely perturbed by my mutterings. Shrugging them off as slang for some new form of male camaraderie, she said, "I was shocked too. He doesn't seem like the Don Juan type, does he?"

"No, he does not."

"I hope it doesn't cause any friction. I like Betty."

I agreed that Betty was a peach.

"You know her father's coming tonight?" Lesley asked me. (I said I knew. I did know some things.) "Not our favorite person, right? And if he finds out about Elsie, he's likely to cut up rough on behalf of Betty. Not that he has any right to—it's not like there was any extra-marital jiggery-pokery going on. Elsie came along long before Betty, or that's what I was told. Of course, she and Ditters did get in touch for a while just before the wedding, but there was nothing going on, according to Hutton. Just asking her advice on some food matters. Still, I'd hate for her father to pull his investment simply because he thought his son-in-law was getting off with somebody else. Or trying to get off, as it were."

I wasn't overly pleased to hear that Ditters and Elsie had been in touch after he met Betty. It was the sort of thing he would do (innocently), but I wished he had resisted the impulse.

"Investment?" I asked. Oddly enough, it was the one word in Lesley's speech that had tripped me up.

"Didn't you know? Mr. Adwick is heavily invested in the restaurant. If he gets the wind up for any reason, he could pull his funds, and then where would they be?"

Where indeed? I asked myself. I was beginning to see how the situation was complicated.

I could see it playing out a number of ways, and none of them good for Ditters. They all ended the same way. Betty throws a jealous fit because he never told her about his old girlfriend. Adwick, on hand and looking for any excuse to break up the marriage, pulls the doubloons out of Dittersdorf Amalgamated. Before Betty has had a chance to cool off, her father is introducing her to a stream of pickpockets and embezzlers he knew when he was sheriff. Charming fellows. Good earning potentials. All this, while filling her head with the wonders of modern divorce. It could happen.

"Hutton told you about this?"

"Ate."

"As informed by Hutton?"

"As informed by Ditters—yes."

I nodded. Everyone was nicely informed. All except me—or I wouldn't have been, if not for Lesley and her gossiping. I knew I had married her for a reason.

I tried to look on the bright side again. "Hopefully, Fleet's air of quiet dignity will keep these uglier emotions in check."

I turned and watched him lean into Madeleine Abrams. They both laughed uncontrollably.

"That is, assuming he doesn't get distracted by his own brand of piggery-pokery," I remarked, "or whatever you called it before. Normally, he's pretty good at getting people to get along."

"Yes. It was smart of Ditters to invite him."

"He didn't," I replied—and tossed in a Ha! for good measure. Finally something I knew that she didn't. "Betty did."

"But she didn't," Lesley stated calmly. "I was asking her something about it, and she said she assumed that her husband had."

Now I truly was baffled. "You mean she really didn't invite him?"

"No."

"And Ditters didn't?"

"That's what you just said."

"And you didn't, and I didn't, and Ate and Hutton didn't. And Ditters said Nancy didn't."

"I don't think Ate likes Nancy," said Lesley.

I dismissed this slice of human drama. I had more interesting things on my mind than who Ate Fleet liked and disliked. Besides, if she disliked anyone, it was Madeleine Abrams. The ex-lover. The replacement. *The woman*. It was classic daddy-daughter stuff.

But back to more important topics: "If no one invited Fleet, then how come he received an invitation?"

Lesley had no answer to this. We stared at each other in confusion. There was something unsettling about it. I couldn't put my finger on what.

While we struggled for a solution—or I struggled, and Lesley stirred her drink—I could hear the invitee's voice drifting out from the crowd. It was dry and engaging, as always.

"I suspect we might be stuck here awhile," he said.

He and Madeleine were no longer alone at the fireplace. The television stars had formed a triad around them—a triad of fascination. Three mildly celebrated flies drawn to his fame.

Evelynn Brine was also there. "These storms just roll in out of the clear blue sky, don't they! You're lucky you got here when you did."

Fleet agreed with her. "There was only one other car on the road when I came up the hill. It was slipping and sliding, fighting the slush—and the slush was winning. I offered to help, but the man said he was a retired officer of the law and didn't require any civilian assistance, thank you very much. Not a very gracious sort."

"Dad!" exclaimed Betty, and dashed from the room.

Ditters, who had only now returned, followed her out again, shaking his head. I could read his mind. Whenever search parties were assembled and dispersed, the man in the new mukluks was the first to go.

"So we're stranded, then?" grinned Elsie Farmer. It was a remarkably warm grin for someone so quick to the scowl. She always knew when the camera was on her. "Lucky I always travel with a toothbrush!" she laughed, showing off her pearly whites again.

"Slumber party, y'all!" uttered Vivian Birch.

Cesar Bloom smiled but made no contribution to his companions' frivolity. His was a more thoughtful manner. "Tonight's beginning to shape up like one of your cases, isn't it, Mr. Fleet? A remote inn, cut off from the world so even the authorities can't reach it. A dozen mysterious characters, all with their dark and secret pasts. We're only missing the dead body."

Fleet confessed that it did sound like the setting for a good parlor mystery. "Regarding my previous cases, however, I think you may have me confused with someone else. Hercule Poirot perhaps. Or Dorothy L. Sayers."

"You mean you haven't been in this situation before?" asked Elsie.

"Not as such. But I was only a private investigator for several decades. On the whole, you'd be surprised how few of us get snowed in with corpses."

"Still—it's a hoot, isn't it?" said Vivian Birch.

My God, they were good sports.

Fleet agreed that it did have some aspects of a hoot, yes. He paused, musing on the setting the way a connoisseur sips at an intriguing Beaujolais. "Yes, almost perfect," he said.

"Almost?" wondered Cesar Bloom.

Fleet gave a mellow nod. "Almost. As you pointed out, we lack a body, but that can be remedied. Outside that, I believe the flavor here falls down in one significant area."

"Too lemon zesty?" I asked.

"Too inviting," he answered. "On a cold, blustery evening such as this, stranded in an out-of-the-way hostelry, what you really need is a dimly lit room with sinister candles flickering on the mantelpiece. It's far too bright and welcoming in here. Due in no small part," he added gallantly, "to the present charming company. With this sort of lustrous backdrop, what hope does an aspiring murderer have?" And on that note, the power went out, followed shortly by another scream from Zoe Norris.

He'd gotten his wish. Atmosphere. How? He's "Eskimo" *Effing* Fleet. That's how.

7 — Tossed Together

"Well done!" cried Vivian Birch. A sleuth who knew how to bring it! She loved it!

She applauded vigorously less than an inch from my head. I wasn't clear what *it* was, and whether the *it* he brought was also the *it* she loved, but whatever they were, she was a fan.

Cesar Bloom concurred. In part. He admired the timing of the power outage, but he didn't like the screaming (either time). Too jarring. Elsie Farmer, sadly, didn't care for the outage or the screams. She was going to be a tough one to please tonight.

We stood a moment in silence. From his corner of the darkness, Fleet assured us that he had nothing to do with this.

"You had me fooled!" bellowed Vivian again, also an inch from my ear. "I thought you had your mojo on. A wave of the hand, a little Jedi-Sherlock trickery and presto—ambiance!"

"Too much ambiance for my tastes," said Elsie, speaking softly but no less bitchily.

We stood a moment longer in silence. It was very dark.

I don't know why I expected Ditters to have a backup generator. From the looks of his porch steps, he didn't even own a snow shovel.

Eventually, several of us took out our phones and fired up the screens. A moody, modern lambency enveloped the room. Not quite the flickering candles on the mantelpiece Fleet had been dreaming of, but one had to move with the times.

Betty Dittersdorf came bustling across the threshold. Our collective screen-shine in her direction caused her to focus a large LED flashlight toward us. In response to our growls, she lowered the high beams, and we all blinked a lot.

"The ice must have knocked out the power lines. Walter is going downstairs to check the fuse box, just to be sure."

(Sound of Ditters Dittersdorf banging about in darkness, swearing.)

"Is there anything we can do in the meantime?" I heard Hutton ask.

"You can take your foot off my toe for starters," proposed Ate.

(Sound of Hutton removing foot from toe.)

"Is everyone else okay?" Betty wondered. She inched her miniature photon cannon upward once more. "No one is injured, are they?"

I don't know why she was asking us. She would have done better to ask her husband. I fancied I could hear him bouncing down the basement steps as we spoke.

(Far-off sound of Ditters bouncing.)

"I thought someone screamed," she explained.

"That was just the Norris wench again," said Hutton, raising his palm to deflect Betty's limelight. He looked like an aristocrat fending off paparazzi flashbulbs outside a Parisian brothel.

"Zoe?" she repeated.

"Yes?" answered the Norris wench, apparently among us.

We focused our efforts on her. Dappled in light, with her head held up to avoid the glare, she had the effect, for a split-second, of a runway model pausing under the strobe lights—a mousy runway model in glasses, who screamed a lot.

I hadn't realized she was there. She hadn't been when she screamed. Thank goodness for that. For such an unprepossessing chick, she had a lot of resonance. She must have scurried in after the lights went out. I wondered how many more were in here with us.

Betty continued to highlight the face of her waitress, long after the rest of us had grown bored and moved on to better things. "Was that you screaming, Zoe?"

"Yes. I mean, I did before. And then I screamed again."

"Why did you scream, Zoe?"

"I don't know. The power going out gave me a fright, didn't it?"

I happened to catch Betty's rosy features on one of my passes with my phone, and she didn't look pleased with this response. Not pleased at all. "Don't scream so much, Zoe."

"No?"

"No. It gives me a headache."

So concluded Zoe Norris' employee evaluation.

On the heels of their chat, Sven stormed in, followed by Nancy. Sven looked practically translucent in the phone lights; Nancy more sprite-like.

Their comments varied according to character. Nancy said: "Well, this is fun." Sven said: "What the hell?"

I could hear a door open and close. "Anybody else hear a door open and close?" I asked.

Someone—Evelynn Brine—said she heard a hinge *creak*. Was that what I meant?

I said yes. Opening. Closing. *Creaking*. They were all from one basic food group, weren't they? "Any idea where it came from?" I whispered to Lesley. If people were leaving, I wanted to be among them.

"I can't see anything," she said.

"Was that someone's shoulder?" asked Cesar Bloom.

Elsie Farmer said it was not. And if he went for it again, she was going to need a marriage proposal, or at least an endorsement deal.

Ate spoke up over the clamor. "You know," she said drily, "most of our phones have flashlights built right into them. The flashlights are much brighter."

She demonstrated this. She was right. Much brighter than the screens. The brighter light enabled me to see her face, and it looked pretty pleased with itself. I guess she had earned that. Of course, before inspiration struck and she had this allegory-of-the-cave moment, she had stood there straining at the shadows along with the rest of us. A truly brainy innovator would have proposed the flashlight maneuver the instant the power went out.

"Where's Dad and Mrs. Abrams?" she asked.

The light brigade swept the room once more, beginning with Cesar, Viv, Nancy and Sven. They all looked fabulous.

It spotlighted Hutton and Ate next, then Evelynn and Elsie Farmer (Evelynn waved). It moved on to Pixie and Phillip after that (their heads raised in anticipation, the way shoppers do when a supermarket clerk calls their number for cold cuts)—before wrapping up with Betty, Zoe, Lesley, myself and a thick-browed man whom I couldn't place at first.

He wore a heavy cardigan (not the cool kind) and a fedora hat, or possibly it was a trilby. I couldn't be certain, but it looked an awful lot like a trilby hat I had misplaced years ago during my trip to Roger Banbury's upstate mansion.

He stepped more fully into the light. His sour and pinched expression put you in mind, on first glance, of a human fireplug with a touch of the gout.

"Who the hell is that?" asked Ate. She was startled, and I couldn't blame her.

I was startled too—that is, until the years rolled back and I was once more the young man-about-town of a half decade before, standing face-to-face with the sheriff of Baccup, Maine. With his limited height, it was more like face-to-sternum, but that was neither here nor there.

"Sheriff Adwick," I announced.

"Mr. Hathaway," he retorted.

It occurred to me that we hadn't seen each other since that fateful evening five years ago, when he accused Lesley and myself of stealing an artifact from a prominent British eccentric.

There was nothing in it, of course. I was the one who had brought the thing to Sir Roger in the first place (Sir Roger Banbury was the prominent eccentric). As for Lesley, why would she steal priceless trinkets? It made no sense.

I mean, yes, it would later turn out that her father had dabbled in more than his share of art and trinket thefts in his day, but Adwick didn't know that. He couldn't have. Lesley wasn't even traveling under her own name at the time.

If that didn't prove her innocence, I didn't know what would.

He looked as accusatory as ever. Whether the years were rolling back for him too, making him the slightly-less-ancient sheriff-about-town of the past, I couldn't say, but he had clearly not forgotten our time together. I fully expected him to clamp a hand on my shoulder and start demanding to know where I was when the power went out. A good job for Mr. Hathaway, he seemed to be saying with his cold, dead expression. Check your pockets, everyone; Mr. Hathaway is up to his old tricks.

I don't know why his look was so hard on me. During that weekend at Sir Roger Banbury's place, Ditters had not only broken the sheriff's arm but also knocked him out cold with a tuba to the back of the head. Two separate incidents—arm and tuba. That took some effort, getting both activities in. It wasn't even a three-day weekend.

"Nice to see you again, Sheriff," I said. Not that I could see very much of him at the moment. Nor was it very nice.

I remembered too late that he liked people to call him *chief.* He wasn't a chief—the town of Baccup didn't have enough population for a post office, let alone a chief of police—but who was I to deny him these simple amusements?

"Come in, Chief, and have a drink or two," I remarked. He was retired now, so I knew he couldn't say he was on duty.

"Mr. Hathaway," was his only reply. Turning on his heel, he faded into the darkness.

I followed him with my light and saw his daughter explaining the situation: the weather, the power, Ditters' heroic battle with the fuse box.

The ex-lawman grunted at intervals and then replied, "I'm fully aware of the weather conditions, Betty. We just spent the last half hour trudging through the sleet and snow."

"I know, I know. Are your feet very cold?"

"I'm fine."

"Do you want something to drink? They say people get twice as dehydrated in the cold than the heat, which I always thought was very odd. I mean, heat is so hot. Get you a coffee? Or maybe that should be an iced coffee. I forget what's better when you're dehydrated."

"I'm fine."

"Would you like something to eat? Sven and Madeleine have outdone themselves."

"I'm fine," he replied—it was either that or "Mr. Hathaway," his favorite go-to phrases. "I assume you've made preparations for canceling tonight?" he asked.

"Canceling? I—well—"

She was plainly flustered by her father's question. I shined my light on her and checked. Yup, flustered.

"I—we—the thing is—"

"Certainly you don't propose to proceed?"

"Well—"

"The weather report was so encouraging this morning!" piped up Evelynn, the faithful hostess and weather devotee.

I couldn't make out Adwick's expression in the dark—you try shining a light in the man's face and see how he likes it—but I assumed this rationalization was met with a sullen sneer.

"My dear people, we can't eat dinner in the dark!"

And with this pronouncement, the lights came back on. The Enescu Fleet maneuver, in reverse. Apparently, it worked both ways.

Shortly after the illumination came Fleet in person. With him was Madeleine.

They smiled sheepishly, if you can picture Enescu Fleet as sheepish. (I admit, it's difficult for me to do, and I was there.)

"Madeleine was showing me a trick with the fuse box," he said.

Lesley whispered, "Jiggery-pokery," and she meant it in the ribald sense.

I suppressed a slight shiver. This was no reflection on Madeleine's looks. She was a hot older lady, as we have already established; the perfect combination of nurturer and saucy temptress. If she had ever been a home economics teacher, I'm sure she would have driven the boys mad, causing them to forget the exact time it takes to hard-boil an egg, or some other vital kernel of information for the semester final. It was also no reflection on Fleet. He was a handsome old duffer, the perfect combination of rogue and whatever else women look for in duffers. It was the image Lesley had conjured up. It was like picturing your parents.

Forgetting her own parent for once, Betty said, "But Walter was attending to the fuse box. He's been down in the basement for the last twenty minutes."

"Yes," answered Fleet. "There in lay the trick Madeleine showed me."

"What trick?"

"The fuse box is in the garage."

On that cue, her husband returned.

"I can't locate the fuse box anywhere, Betty. I did find that slipper we were looking for, though." He held up an old and raggedy moccasin you couldn't have paid me to slip my foot in.

Having produced this exhibit, he stared blankly at his surroundings. He looked from the slipper to the lights, then from the lights back to the slipper, struggling for a connection.

During this intellectual exertion, I peered over at Hutton, who was frowning thoughtfully.

I figured I knew why. Once you had eliminated the weather as the culprit behind the outage—and leaving aside Ditters' electric-slipper theory, which would likely require many more years of development—there seemed to be no explanation for the fuses getting tripped. Not across the board. It's not like it was a thunderstorm. It seemed like a pretty enormous coincidence, having the power go out during an ice storm when it wasn't the ice storm that did it. It was suspicious—but suspicious how? That's what I kept asking myself.

I had no answer, and evidently neither did Hutton. If he had theories, he'd have shared them with us.

I've often wondered whether the events of that night would have gone any differently if he had. Probably not. Sometimes things just have to develop for themselves. Now, if Fleet hadn't been so distracted...but there is no point in speculating.

"Dad's here," said Betty, bringing her husband up with a start.

Ditters smiled. He waved the footwear toward his father-in-law, who responded, "Dittersdorf."

It was interesting that I merited a *Mr.*, while Ditters had to have his name addressed nude. Poor guy. I thought I had drawn a doozy with Lesley's father. Not even close.

Cesar broke in on the awkward silence. "If we're going to be stuck here for the foreseeable future, and the power continues to cooperate, we might as well eat."

Fleet seconded this, followed by Hutton, Ate, Nancy and several other people—the order of which I can't recall.

I liked the baldy Cesar's practical good sense, especially when that practical good sense ended with something to gnaw on.

This could become a whole new vehicle for him: *Cesar Bloom tackles the country's most awkward family get-togethers.* They could call it "Cesar, Adjust Us."

There were a few dissenting looks, most notably Sheriff Adwick's. I suspect he wasn't accustomed to people ignoring his authority.

He turned to me, an unlikely ally, and blinked up into my sympathetic face. Had we been a friendlier retired law official/one-time suspected criminal, he might have asked, "What just happened?"

I slapped him on the back anyway. "Sorry, Chief, looks like we're gonna have to ask you not to leave town for a while—or through dinner at any rate."

I followed the gang into the dining room, smiling pleasantly to myself.

If only things had remained that pleasant throughout the meal.

8 — Chilled Entrée

Just when you thought we couldn't cram any more raw pleasure into the evening, we had another addition to the dinner table. I don't mean Mayhem—that perennial gatecrasher would make an appearance at some point, I was sure; the Enescu Fleet track record demanded it. I wouldn't be surprised if the two didn't check each other's schedules before RSVPing to an event.

The addition I'm referring to was spectacularly mundane: a long, lean man of fifty-some years of age, with sad eyes and a clipped mustache. He reminded me of a thinner, bonier, more mustached Sir Sidney Poitier, though about twenty times more solemn. Sidney Poitier was rollicking compared with this guy. He came in and took a seat, introducing himself as Dom Jacobs, Sheriff Adwick's plus-one.

The identification brought a look of surprise from Betty. Up until then, the quintessential Betty-beam had been in full swing, twinkling prettily and indicating the more the merrier to this new guest, whoever he might be. Now she stutter-stepped, much as her husband had when presented with his arriving in-law.

"How nice. A friend of Dad's. Did you two work together?"

Dom Jacobs said, "Something like that, yes."

"But you're not the new sheriff." The successor to her father (I've been told), was a heavyset, perpetually grinning young man of Asian descent, who never reminded anyone of Sir Sidney Poitier.

"No, I am not the sheriff," he replied simply.

"Well, you don't look like a deputy!" Betty quipped.

I had to agree. CEO of a boutique financial firm perhaps, or ambassador to Japan, but not a deputy. Then again, he didn't look very much like Chief Adwick's plus-one—so who knew what anyone looked like?

He apologized for any delay he may have caused. He had been trying to get a signal outside on his cell phone. He assumed their landlines were in working order?

Betty waved aside the landlines. The landlines were not the issue here. "Do you two—? Oh, hell, here are the salads," she said with a smile, and conversation shifted to other topics.

I would describe the salads as bizarre. They had nice, fresh ingredients, well prepared, but they were also, well, bizarre. On a bed of grilled frisée and mixed turnip greens lay a mound of smoked duck—I'm not big on duck—together with pickled carrot, pickled radish, pickled horseradish and pickled pickle. There were also pastrami-encrusted croutons made of rye, and then, as a final salute to the French delicatessen, a spicy brown mustard vinaigrette with caraway seeds and a touch of duck fat.

I would take a nibble and like it okay, and then about ten seconds later I would wish I could spit it out into my napkin.

I ended up eating most of the frisée—I enjoy frisée—and then having picked out the pastrami croutons, hid the rest under Lesley's charger plate.

I peered around the dining room. No one saw.

The seating arrangement was as odd as the salad. I would call it *restrained cozy*. Three tables had been scooted close together to form a triple diamond shape. My table had Lesley, Hutton and Ate. Next came the nibs: Elsie Farmer, Vivian Birch, Cesar Bloom and, of course, Enescu Fleet. At the head table sat Ditters, Betty, Betty's father and the mysterious Mr. Jacobs.

Zoe and Evelynn brought in each course. Zoe cleared. Sven cooked. (I don't know who washed up.) The remainder of the *Cornichon* staff—Nancy and Madeleine—did not join us. It wouldn't have looked right. Even Phillip had taken his leave for now. Evidently, he was a dog of traditional ideals and held strong with social convention.

Hobnobbing tended to contain itself to a single table unit. Made sense, given our stations. You can't have too much intermixing between guests and "super-guests." The logistics of the seating also helped—half the room had their backs to the other half. Occasionally, some crossover would branch out. At one point, Fleet engaged his host in a pleasant talk, mainly on the subject of his name and how it was not Escargot or even Eskimo.

"So you're saying it's Enescu," the latter concluded, somewhat skeptically.

"I am and it is," replied Fleet.

"Funny sort of name," said Ditters Dittersdorf. "Romanian did you say?"

"Romanian indeed."

"But you're not Romanian?"

"Not at all."

"No," Ditters conceded. It would have been weird if he were. "My name is German, but I'm not German." He was gazing at Elsie gazing at Cesar gazing at his dinner roll. Ditters' gaze was anxious, Elsie's supercilious, Cesar's warm and kindly. I wasn't surprised. They were good dinner rolls.

"Austrian," said Betty, contributing her part to the discussion.

"Huh?" said Ditters. He was so intent on Elsie and whether she was going to let something out of the bag about their past relationship that he had been ignoring the woman he wished to protect. "Who's Australian?"

"Austrian, dear. And we are. Or our name is anyway." She put special emphasis on the *our*, making it clear to her father that his little girl was a Dittersdorf, a fact that was here to stay.

The looks now shifted from Ditters looking at Elsie to Ditters looking at Betty looking at her father looking at his son-in-law. The last was not warm or kindly.

"It's funny you should bring up names," said Fleet. He spoke mostly to Betty, but an observation from Enescu Fleet is fun for the whole family. "I was wondering if your husband might be descended from Carl Ditters von Dittersdorf."

"Uh?" asked Walter Ditters von Distracted.

"I was speaking of the name Dittersdorf. I believe it gives us something in common."

Ditters blinked at him. "Well, we both have beards—"

"Our names each come from a composer," agreed the detective. "Yours, I believe, comes from the man I mentioned, the well-known Austrian composer and silviculturist Carl Ditters von Dittersdorf; mine from George Enescu."

"Enescu?" The name was new to Ditters.

"The well-known Romanian composer."

But not silviculturist, Ditters observed. "He was Romanian?"

"Very."

Ditters said ah. He figured someone was. "So you think I'm one of those Dittersdorf?"

"It's very possible. How many Dittersdorf do you know?"

The chief snorted, implying that he personally knew one too many.

"Well, I've never heard of the dude," Ditters confessed.

"He was a good chap," Fleet assured him. "Used to hang out with Wolfgang Mozart."

Ditters liked Mozart. "What's a silviculturist again?"

"Sort of a highfalutin tree lover."

Ditters said neat. "I like plants. As for music, I did own a kazoo once." The reference reminded him that he had been remiss in not putting something playing in the dining room (hopefully not kazoo music). He got up and attended to it.

In his absence, the room delved further into the topic of names—"how ya got 'em," and "what to do with 'em once you had 'em."

Cesar Bloom kicked things off, stating that his mother had obviously thought very highly of his prospects as a newborn, thus the Caesar designation. (She had originally included the extra "a," but he dropped it when he went into cooking. No sense overdoing it.) Though they had never been wealthy, they were a proud family. There had been Blooms on the *Mayflower*, he said.

While I thought this was a hilarious way to put it, no one else even cracked a smile. Again, I guess you had to be there. Apparently I was, and nobody else.

I chuckled to myself, until Lesley nudged me in the ribs and asked me to knock it off. I went back to my soup, which was delicious, except for the pickled caviar garnish on top. Lesley had some kind of chilled cucumber purée topped with crème fraîche and pickled melon. I was beginning to detect a theme.

I reached for my water with a sliver of gherkin floating in it. (I guess it was too much to expect a lemon from Ditters.)

The discussion went on. Elsie Farmer said she had always found her name a giant bore. She had considered changing it to "Farmiga" or something lovely like that, but by then they had already produced the promo ads for *Farmer to Table*, and she had to live with it.

Vivian Birch admitted that Birch wasn't her real name, and that her real one was too ridiculous for words. Lesley said try going through school with Darlington!

Dom Jacobs, breaking a ten-minute silence, said he had sometimes found his given name somewhat trying as a child, at which point I weighed in to say that I liked my names, both of them, a comment that resulted in another nudge from Lesley. This time I almost choked on a pickled quail egg someone had left on my crostini.

"Don't stick on side about things," she muttered. "It's not like your name is so great."

"Well, you're *stuck* with it, aren't you?" I smiled, quick as a shot. She had no reply. Point Johnny.

Ditters rejoined us here, having put on his musical accompaniment (not Dittersdorf, from the sound of it, but thankfully not kazoo either). It was also not Mozart. It was one of those pieces that started out sounding like light jazz, then said *only foolin'* and poured it on with saccharin pop vocals. I missed the Boccherini something fierce.

"I'm still waiting for an answer on what Hutton's true label is," said Ditters, resuming his seat and correctly inferring that we were still playing the name game.

Hutton looked up. He was unusually quiet tonight. Both he and the girlfriend. I wondered if they were having trouble. "Come on, out with it," demanded our host playfully.

Hutton shook his head. "Not on, old friend."

I was secretly pleased that I knew the answer myself. I so seldom do, you see.

Ditters went on: "Well, you can at least tell us what you've been doing with yourself. You're so damned secretive when we talk. So what's your bag these days?"

Hutton replied that his bag was private investigator. His bag had always been private investigator, for years and years. He made no secret of it.

It was still news to Ditters. "You're a shamus too?" He peered around. "How about that! You, Hath, Enesco there. All God's children are private investigators. How do you like that!"

Hutton said he liked it fine. Realizing Ditters' observation had been merely rhetorical, he returned his attention to his lox au gratin.

Vivian commended him on the secrecy about his name. She wouldn't reveal hers if you stuck lit bamboo shoots under her (bright purple) fingernails.

Elsie said it couldn't be any worse than Farmer, and her colleague grimaced. It was. Much worse.

Lesley waded into the conversation here. I was wondering how long it would be before she returned to her favorite subject. "Of course, you can't always control your last name, but you can still pick a good first name for your baby."

Ate's face jerked up. The black-pepper brisket in aspic dribbled off her fork and hit her plate with a splat. "Why did you say that? Who was talking about babies?"

I was surprised at her. Usually the detective's daughter was more observant than that. The answer to the question *Who's talking about babies?* was Lesley Hathaway, always. She had talked about babies over cocktails, stating that the only problem with getting pregnant is you have to lay off these things. She had talked about babies when Phillip had nuzzled Pixie, stating that didn't the pair make a dinky little couple, and how adorable and dinky would their doggy babies be! And then she had talked about babies two and a half minutes ago, when Zoe Norris had brought around a palate cleanser of roasted *baby* pattypan squash on (*baby*-sized) blueberry bagel chips. The woman saw babies everywhere.

She looked flummoxed by her friend's admonishment. I was flummoxed myself—it wasn't like Ate at all—but that didn't prevent me from taking the opportunity to get a little of my own back from the little mother wannabe.

Leaning in, I whispered: "Told you not to be so baby crazy."

Lesley glared. "I am NOT *baby crazy*, Johnny!" Spotting a straggler on my plate, she said, "Oo, *baby* carrot!" She gobbled this up, before commenting, slightly less enthusiastically, "Ugh, *pickled* baby carrot."

"Are you pregnant?" cried out Betty. She clasped her hands together in glee.

Lesley shook her head. It occurred to me that, had she been pregnant, she probably would have enjoyed the pickles a lot more. "Not yet," she said, glaring my way again. I had no response to this. Did she expect me to do something about it now?

"We've been trying too," said Betty, to the burbles of good wishes from the various women in the room. If you listened closely, you could hear Evelynn, Nancy and Madeleine imparting their positive female energy from as far away as the kitchen.

The men looked down at their plates and pushed around their food.

I noticed Ate didn't speak. She didn't burble, she didn't push, she didn't do anything. She was a mystery to both sexes.

"Well, best of luck to you all," said Elsie Farmer, a little late for the other well-wishers. "I don't see having children myself—they seem such a bore—but some people must like it." She turned to Ditters. "You'll make a good father. You've always loved children. I could never understand why." She stated this suddenly and with a distinct clarity of purpose.

The collective voices in the room slowed to a halt. Betty looked at Elsie. Elsie looked at Betty. Ditters looked at his father-in-law, while Adwick and Dom Jacobs both looked at Ditters. Nobody looked at Dom (except for me, I guess, and that was only for a moment).

No one knew quite what to say. Elsie's remarks seemed to strike everyone as peculiar and overly personal for a comparative stranger.

Cesar opened his mouth, but for once the culinary Solomon had no wise words to impart. He closed his lips around the last of his dinner roll instead.

I hadn't formed a complete opinion of Elsie Farmer before then. Before that comment, she had seemed slightly insincere, slightly aloof, and very hot. I had my opinion now. The evil curve to her mouth told you everything you needed to know.

Betty recovered nicely. If the comment disturbed her, she appeared no more frazzled by it than her normal level of frazzle. "Yes, well, while Zoe clears away the dishes from the last course, we have a little surprise for everyone. In honor of Mr. Fleet,"—she indicated the man, for those who may have forgotten—"we have devised a game to pass the time before the risotto arrives. If you lift your charger, you will see an individually selected mystery puzzle. Mr. Fleet and my father are excluded, for obvious reasons—they used to do this sort of thing for a living. But let's see how many of you can track down the clues yourselves. You might have to poke around a little."

"So it's a kind of treasure hunt," said Elsie. "How delightful."

"They're not as fun as you might think," replied my wife. She and I knew all about treasure hunts.

I didn't lift up my charger right away. Something was off again, not quite right. I could feel it in my gut. Unless that was the duck fat.

Everyone else examined their riddles. There were polite smiles all around, a few attempts at solving. Ate said hers was pretty crazy; Cesar said it would take the wisdom of a real emperor to solve his; Hutton said he didn't know why *he* wasn't excluded—he solved mysteries for a living too; and Lesley said something about a pile of goo someone had hidden under hers.

After a prolonged pause, I picked up my plate and read the attached paper:

> *Poor Johnny lies dead in the middle of the farmer's market, his foolish head split asunder with a meat cleaver. In his hand sits another foolish head, made of romaine lettuce. Not a very discerning selection, Johnny, we must say! But, alas, could our intrepid victim have an agenda? Could this ingenuous/ingenious device unlock the identity of a killer? Johnny lies dead. But where does the key lie?*

I had to say, I didn't much care for the tone of this plate puzzler. Seemed in bad taste. And it was confusing. How should I know where the key lay? What key? Lay in what way?

Vivian Birch said, "How clever of you, darlings. Dinner theater under your dinner!"

"I can't take the credit," replied Betty, smiling at her husband. He looked blank.

"You're really going all out for the murder-mystery vibe, aren't you?" continued Vivian.

"At least we don't have Thirteen at Dinner," said Cesar Bloom. He was referring to the quaint English superstition, as well as the mystery novel of the same name. He had spent many an enjoyable afternoon in his youth reading a tattered Agatha Christie from the local library.

Vivian counted around the room: "Ten, eleven, twelve. Phew!"

Fleet said ahem. He pointed to the floor, where a nonplussed Pixie was staring up at us from a bowl of salmon pumpernickel moose. "Thirteen, I believe."

Glaring in jest, Vivian replied, "Oh! You've done it now, Enescu!"

Fleet spread his hands in apology, surreptitiously slipping his dog a treat from his jacket pocket.

Elsie Farmer replaced her plate on the table. She had a quizzical look on her face, not unlike the evil grin she had exhibited a moment before but with a smidgeon more whimsy. "Excuse me a minute, won't you? I think I need to freshen up."

"I'll show you the way," said Betty. Ditters' head shot up in alarm.

An element of tension seemed to depart the room as they left. I wonder why!

Everyone loosened up. Several people wheedled Fleet for a hint to their puzzle, but he only replied, "You heard the lady. I'm the expert here. Wouldn't be right."

I heard Hutton grumble something under his breath. Ate asked if he had solved his yet, and he grumbled something else.

I had no clue what the answer to mine was. I was too busy feeling chagrined by its subject matter and the overly playful description of my foolish, split-open head. If I had been less distracted—by my gut feelings, by the inexplicable things people said and did, by the notion that Enescu Fleet could go by the nickname "Nessie"—I might have been able to devote more brainpower to it.

Several more guests excused themselves. It seemed like a good time for a break.

As Betty was coming back, Vivian and Cesar went out to avail themselves of the little chef's room. Dom Jacobs mentioned that he would like to try his cell outside again and, barring that, perhaps use the landline. There was someone he was meant to call tonight. Adwick told him he'd show him where the office was, and they went out together. Fleet followed, mentioning something about paying

Madeleine a visit. She would probably be getting lonely in the kitchen by now. Not likely, I thought, with Evelynn and Nancy yammering at her.

He left regardless, and then there were six (Pixie had skipped out a few minutes before, most likely to catch up with Phillip).

It was just the old gang now. Dit and Bet. Hut and Ate. Les and the Hath man.

I would have preferred a setting a little less intimate. After Elsie's ill-bred comment, I was expecting Betty to start asking some awkward questions of her husband. She had the perfect opportunity now.

I saw her turn to him, but before she could say anything guests began drifting back in. Fleet and Pixie arrived first, followed by Adwick and Dom Jacobs. Vivian and Cesar returned after them. Elsie Farmer was still AWOL.

Zoe came through and refreshed drinks, cleared dishes, and looked mousy. Evelynn followed, tidying up where Zoe had missed and occasionally talking weather. Apparently, the conditions outside had gone from bad to worse. Or so said her *Weather Monkey* app.

"Anyone seen Ms. Farmer?" asked Betty, after several minutes had elapsed. No one had. "She wasn't in the restroom?"

Vivian said not that she noticed, no.

"Maybe she went to make a call," Hutton suggested.

"Not on her cell," Dom Jacobs replied. "There's still no signal." He also hadn't seen her in the vicinity of the office phone.

"Well, I'm sure she'll return eventually," said Ditters. He spoke jovially. His brow, however, betrayed other emotions. He had clearly had enough of Elsie Farmer for one night.

The room continued to talk amongst itself. A few grinders kept at their riddles; most everyone else spoke about the food, TV network policies, the inequity of traffic lights and whether it's best to give birth to a baby girl or a baby boy first.

After about ten more minutes, Sven and Madeleine were brought in to see how everyone had liked everything so far. Madeleine looked modest and pleased with the praise she received for her baked goods, Sven puffy and annoyed with the smattering of applause he got for his "preparations."

After they left, Vivian burst out, "I think I have it! My plate puzzle. The killer is the lobster trapper." She peered over at Betty. "Am I right? What do I win?"

Betty smiled. "It sounds good. But I'm not the final word on the solutions. Walter?"

Ditters looked blank for a second time. "How should I know?" he asked.

His wife's smile struggled mightily. "But, Walter darling, you're the one who came up with all this."

She glanced around the room and laughed. She continued to bolster her smile with whatever twigs of good nature she could lay her hands on.

Ditters smiled back at her. "I really don't know what you mean," he replied from between clenched teeth.

Betty leaned closer. "Didn't you devise these riddles and leave them out for us in the office?"

Ditters said of course he didn't. He couldn't devise a riddle to please a saint.

Betty slumped back. "Then if you didn't, and I didn't—" She let the question dangle.

The voices in the room had taken on a different flavor now. I recognized the key ingredients. Concern, bewilderment, a dash of fretfulness. Now they knew how my gut felt. I knew it wasn't the duck fat. I also knew what had bugged me before. If Betty hadn't invited Fleet, and her husband hadn't invited him, then what was with all that *guest of honor* rigmarole? Whose hospitality was this?

Fleet rose to his feet. I thought for a moment he was going to abandon his reserve on assisting us with the riddles.

Not so much. His address was of a more dire nature.

"Ladies and gentlemen," he said, "we need to locate Miss Farmer—immediately."

No one asked any questions—which was good, because I doubt anyone had any answers.

We spread out and searched. Lesley and I started with the room where the cocktails had been served. Hutton, Ate, Dom and Adwick took the outside. Ditters and his wife inspected the second level, while the remaining food celebs, Fleet and Pixie scoured the kitchen and surrounding areas.

The majority of the indoor crew reconvened in the foyer five minutes later, in time to see Ate motioning to us from the kitchen. We followed, and after some difficulty navigating the passageway in a clump, proceeded out one of the back exits and around the corner.

Phillip was there, staring up at us from the frozen earth beneath our feet. "You can't pin this on me," he appeared to be saying.

I didn't notice Fleet among the gathering. I pushed my way through the crowd and saw him kneeling over the body of Elsie Farmer. She was laid out on the snow/ice/sleet/hail. She wasn't moving.

He shook his head.

Even in death, there was an icy-hot beauty to the woman. But that could have just been all the ice.

9 — Spoiled Supper

Nobody knew how to react. Cesar, Vivian, the *Cornichon* staff—they all struggled for speech. Not in an emotional way, more like a long, pronounced lull in a conversation no one expected to have. If I had to describe it in a word, I would have called it awkward.

Even among us old regulars to crime, there was no immediate spring to action. Every murder affects you differently, and you can't anticipate how you'll react until you're staring it in the face. Before then, you can have a feeling in your gut; you can keep yourself on your toes and remain on the lookout for danger, but until you are confronted with an actual body deprived of actual life, you're never fully vested in it. As soon as you are, everything slows to a crawl, and nothing feels quite real for a couple minutes.

Around that time—roughly ninety seconds in, tonight—the shock begins to wear off, and someone feels the need to break the silence. The human mind demands an answer to every question, and when it can't pinpoint one right off, it goes with the next best thing. We got *the next to the next to the next best* thing. If that.

"This is a crime scene," said Adwick importantly. Was my gut deceiving me again, or was he enjoying himself?

"Why is it a crime scene?" Vivian Birch came back at him fiercely. She punctuated each syllable with a look of righteous hauteur. "Maybe she slipped on the ice or something—you don't know!"

It was lucky for the ex-chief that he had an ex-PI to back him up. Adwick was from the school of public relations that looked puff-faced and stoic in response to every inquiry, especially when he had no clue what was going on. Vivian would eat that type alive.

"This was no accident," said the smoother ex. "Your colleague was murdered."

Vivian made a little gasp—little for her, which sounded like a five-pound corn kernel popping. She said it was horrible. Cesar said it was a shock, certainly, to which Vivian added that it was a horrible shock. *Murder*, she muttered to herself in disbelief. A really horrible *murder*, Cesar whispered by way of helpful amendment.

Fleet's revelation only led to more questions from Vivian, Cesar, Zoe, Evelynn, Betty and Madeleine. *How did she die? Who did it? What was she doing out here? Who found her? Was she already dead? Did anyone see the killer?*

I noticed no one bothered to ask Fleet how he could be so sure or why anyone would want to do such a thing to poor Elsie. The answers to both these questions were taken as givens.

Adwick wrangled the inquisitive crowd the best he could. "That's enough for now. Everyone inside, please."

He succeeded in disbanding the horde eventually.

Observing Fleet lingering, I broke away to join him. He welcomed me with a nod, somewhat distracted and appropriately solemn. He appeared to be studying the "crime scene."

Normally, Fleet isn't much of a whale on the physical details of a murder. He also doesn't roll much with psychology and profiling—too many variables and bad assumptions. And don't get him started on forensics. I've never actually figured out what his method is, to be absolutely honest. He seems to come about his conclusions by divine intervention. Whatever he does, it works, so why question it?

Feeling there was a first time for everything, I knelt beside him to study the evidence of the dead woman. Feeling squeamish and creeped out by this, I got up, moved about five feet away, and knelt again. "Her shoe is missing. Her right shoe."

Fleet said, "Good. What else?"

"Her foot is a little bloody."

"She may have cut it kicking on the shed door. That's also, no doubt, how she lost the shoe." He held this up and showed it to me.

I was confused. "Was she inside a shed?"

"Most definitely."

"How do you know?"

"When I opened the door, she toppled out of it."

I nodded. That would certainly support his assertion.

I returned to my examination. "She's got a run in her stocking."

"Done, no doubt, when I dragged her out of the shed."

I acknowledged this. If I had gone to the stocking first, I probably could have inferred the whole Elsie-in-the-shed thing. Maybe even deduced her killer. Too late now, of course.

I stood up. The snow was freezing my knees. "How did she die?"

I expected Fleet to suggest, insufferably, that I look to the clues again, possibly revisit a tiny oblong scratch on the bottom of her other heel. He didn't.

"Have a look at this," he said, walking me over to the shed.

Thanks to an awning that ran along this side of the building, not too much accumulation had fallen here. He showed me a hose trailing out from the bottom of the doorway. It was shoved down tight into the snow. The door would have barely shut above it.

"Where does it lead?"

He showed me that too. Around the side of the restaurant was some wooden lattice enclosing a platform. On the platform was a backup generator. Evidently, Ditters did own one. It was still warm to the touch.

I could do this: hose, generator, gas-powered. "Someone trapped her inside the shed and poisoned her with the fumes?" I paused, pondering my own words. "Seems like a pretty rotten thing to do."

"Murder usually is," Fleet agreed.

And complicated, I pointed out—especially if she put up a fight.

I had another inspiration. "Is that where the blood came from? Did someone kick her in the foot, then drag her out here and put her in the shed?"

This time, the look I received was less encouraging. "You're overlooking an obvious feature."

I was good at that. I peered back at the body and shook my head. "What?"

"She's dressed up in her winter woolies—hat, gloves, scarf."

"I think they call that a *stole* actually," I corrected him. Lesley had one. I had no idea why—she never wore it.

"Stole, then. In either event, she met her killer willingly."

It was possible, I thought. It was also possible that she had thrown on her winter woolies to make a break for it. It was either that or face Ditters' variation on a dessert pickle.

Fleet rubbed his hands together. I joined him. Neither of us had on gloves—or a stole. "I suppose," he said, "that we should do the same."

I stared at him, befuddled. I was almost as good at befuddled staring as I was at overlooking obvious features.

"Elsie met her killer willingly," he explained. He gazed toward the kitchen door, on the other side of which twelve or so suspects awaited us. "We should do the same," he said.

I got it. Elsie had met with one of them before she died, and it was the last meeting she would ever take. We should do the same. Meet her killer.

I did wonder if Fleet meant meet *her* murderer, meaning Elsie's, or meet our own personal murderer. I would have greatly preferred the former.

As it turned out, it was a trick question. Hate those.

10 — Sitting Ducks

We returned to the toasty confines of the *Cornichon*'s kitchen, only to discover Adwick throwing his weight around again. The man was definitely enjoying himself.

He was asking the party to remain calm and answer a few questions. First and foremost, he was trying to ascertain everyone's whereabouts at the time of Elsie's death. His methods, poking and prodding all and sundry, did little to facilitate this request.

"Well, you were there," said Vivian Birch, during a pause in the free-for-all, "why don't *you* tell me where I was!"

Betty was doing her best to temper the stress of the moment. "Maybe if we all had a nice cup of tea—" she offered. Married to an Englishman, she would naturally assume that tea was a cure-all for all the world's ills.

As a whole, the Adwicks weren't having much success tonight, father and daughter alike. Too coarse or too gentle, they just couldn't seem to get it right.

When we came in, Fleet had gone straight to Madeleine, taking her aside and speaking words of comfort (I guess his daughter could supply her own words). As he departed my sphere, Lesley stepped into it. She was wearing one of her looks again. It was very much the kind of look she had worn earlier when I had come in from Ditters' greenhouse. It was a look of frustrated abandonment.

With everyone pairing off—even Pixie and Phillip were back together again—I glanced over to see how Ate was bearing up with Hutton.

He wasn't there. He was over by the stovetop, poking and prodding Sven's cooking. Half a dozen pots and pans were burbling away atop the burners. Apparently, a violent death did not provide sufficient cause for the cook to quit cooking. There would be risotto, whether people died or not.

Actually, to be precise, there would not be risotto. Betty had promised us some before the murder, but evidently that was merely one of those cruel lies restaurateurs tell their patrons in order to assert their authority over them.

Hutton broke the scandal first. "Risotto off?" he asked Sven.

The chef glowered. "It went bad while I was outside with everyone."

Hutton understood, and he sympathized. "A risotto has to be stirred constantly. Once you start it, you can't quit on it. Otherwise, it gums up." He dug the chef, and he felt his pain. "Still, it's a brilliant-looking pilaf you got there." He slapped the man on the back and ambled away under the latter's hot glare.

Adwick continued his interrogations after a brief pause. (They never used to discuss risotto at crime scenes in his day.) He cleared his throat. "Someone here had a motive for wanting that young woman out of the way, and I'm determined to find out who. Let's start with those who knew her the longest."

Ditters flipped a tray of dishes onto the floor.

"We can go one by one—" said the ex-sheriff, scowling at the racket.

Vivian held up a hand. She had been patient up until now and held her temper, but the moment had come to speak. "Does anyone want to catch us up? You all seem to know how Elsie died, and why she died, and why we should be suspected of having a hand in her death. I don't know this. Do you know this?" she asked Cesar. Cesar didn't know this, no. "Well, what the hell is going on, then?" she demanded.

Fleet took the floor. He explained what we had observed outside.

Ditters stared blankly while he spoke. Having managed to pick up the majority of the stemware he had dropped, he flipped the tray over again. "Our Power Buddy 1000 killed her?"

No one bothered to look his way this time. Dom Jacobs replaced Fleet in the center of the room. He was about to make one of his rare statements. "I would like everyone to be aware that we have no outside communication available to us at the present moment. As I have pointed out on several occasions, cell phone coverage in this mountain range appears to be nonexistent. As for the landline in the office, there is no signal. Whether this is the result of the storm, or the hand that brought about Ms. Farmer's demise, I am not in a position to say. But I thought everyone should know what we are up against."

I had previously described the staff and guests as good sports. Whether waiting out bad weather, or enduring the Dittersdorf-Hosten battle for menu supremacy, they had maintained a stiff upper lip. All except Nancy, whose upper lip wouldn't have shown in any event.

But now the saturation point had been reached. As far as the *Cornichon* gang was concerned, this was a brioche too far.

Vivian and Cesar led the exodus. One of their own had been murdered, and they were supposed to sit around and wait? Vivian didn't think so! Did Cesar? Cesar didn't either.

Their dash to the hallway quickly descended into a great scramble for the exit. Beautiful people, not-so-beautiful people—they all wanted out. It wasn't pretty.

We definitely had to work on these mass movements of ours. The *Cornichon* kitchen might be expansive, but the rest of the place simply wasn't built for it. People scattered about, grabbing winter woolies, many of which weren't even their own. They pushed forward toward the door without regard for safety or building-code violations. Several toes got smushed, and I distinctly saw Dom Jacobs snatch up Lesley's mittens in error. It was utter chaos.

Only Hutton proved intrepid enough to block their egress. I wouldn't have been surprised if, in Lesley's book o' names, "Hutton" meant "brave defender."

"Just a minute, folks," he said, holding them in place with an icy stare. "The inspector has a point."

"I am not an inspector," corrected the retired officer. I thought it ironic that he did. He wasn't a chief, and that never seemed to bug him.

"Acting inspector, then," said Hutton. "What he said in the kitchen made sense, people."

I didn't get this approach. It was all well and good to use humor to break the ice, but this was crazy talk. Chief Adwick with a point *and* talking sense? Not possible.

The mob appeared to agree. They mumbled angrily and shifted forward.

Fortunately, morbid curiosity got the better of them, and they delayed trampling him for the time being and let him speak.

"There is nothing gained by panicking," Hutton said. "And even if there was, I doubt any of your vehicles could handle the roads. I say let someone with a little hazardous-driving experience go for help. That person should be me. I have a Jeep. Well, in all modesty, I have *the* Jeep. A Jeep for the ages."

I sensed an ironic twitch at my side.

Ate's head had dipped ever so slightly in response to her boyfriend's nobility. "Wait for it," she whispered.

Hutton was busy regaling us with the various attributes of his souped-up Wrangler. This wasn't the sort of soup they knew and loved, he clarified—it was a soup of power. A mechanical chowder of four-wheel-drive excellence: oversized tires, raised suspension, a winch. If he couldn't get through, no one could.

Ate looked at her watch. She shook her head. Trainers in the fifty-yard dash often looked this way when their athletes tripped and stumbled on a pebble during their practice laps.

"In conclusion," said Hutton, wrapping up why he, and he alone, was the arctic-expedition candidate they could feel good about endorsing, "I think you will agree that I—oh bollocks!" he remarked. "We didn't take the Jeep today." It was back in the shop—getting more souped up. "Never mind," he smiled.

The crowd blinked in confusion.

"We took my car," Ate explained.

They all turned to her. "And what do you drive?" Cesar asked.

"Just a plain-Jane SUV."

"Oh good."

"But it's two-wheel drive."

"Oh crap."

Ditters stepped forward to offer his views. "With the roads a mess and the phones wonky, it looks like we're going to be trapped here for a while. We might as well make the best of it. Easy there, Vivian. I know jujitsu, and I'm not afraid to use it."

I joined them at the embankment. If I got crushed to death in the push, at least I would have died shoulder to shoulder with my two mates. (Well, one mate and a guy I saw once and a while, every five years or so.)

I brightened suddenly. I had just remembered. "What about your old army Jeep, Ditters? That antique you used to drive? It was pretty rugged." It also had no top and no seats, but it wasn't like I would be the one driving it.

He frowned. "I don't think it would go in the ice as well as you think, Hath."

"No?"

"Not really. Also, I sold it two years ago."

The great race movement shoved past us. They would not be endorsing Hutton as their arctic-expedition candidate. As for Ditters and his restaurant parties—their psychiatrists owed him a huge debt for the next decade of therapy.

We burst back out into the open air. I hadn't grabbed my jacket, but it wasn't important. Somehow, I knew we wouldn't be outside long.

The leaders of the pack crept out onto the porch. The going had worsened considerably since last seen. I stepped out behind them, nearly slipping twice. I hadn't been on roller skates for almost thirty years now, but if I had—well, that wouldn't have changed the ice any.

Inspired by Hutton's valiant stand inside, Adwick marched through the wavering figures. He stated bluntly, "No one is going anywhere, ladies and gentlemen. I may not be officially embodied to keep you here, but as long as there is life in these old bones—"

There was probably more, but as he spoke these inspirational words, he skated past us, and the crux of his argument was lost to the ages.

I would never have called the chief graceful, but there was something you couldn't help admiring in the stately pose he adopted as his feet no longer held any sway in his momentum. His face remained stern; his stubby arms never ceased gesticulating. He just kept on keeping on, whooshing over the top of the steps and disappearing from view.

Betty squeaked in distress. Using the rail to support herself—it's nice when the younger generation learns from its predecessor's mistakes—she hastened to his side.

"I'm fine," he told her. I knew he was going to say that.

She called for more salt for the porch, prompting Zoe to mince forward with a plastic bucket. Betty and Ditters carried her father inside, while their waitress sprinkled crystals in their wake like an Inuit flower girl. Back in the foyer, people stripped off their woolies again, grumbling about the weather and how, if they died here, their agents were going to hear about it.

We all stared at Adwick, sitting crumpled in a side chair by the door.

Undampened by his experience outside, though still somewhat damp, he bounced up and immediately began running the show once more. "As Mr. Hathaway so astutely pointed out," he said, "we are all trapped here for the foreseeable future."

Ditters muttered that it was not Hath but he who had made that point.

His father-in-law ignored him. "I would like to take everyone one by one for questions. Maybe then we can make some headway before the backup arrives and very possibly prevent the killer among us from claiming another innocent victim."

I think he expected these words to carry a certain impact, but hardly anyone stirred. We were beaten down and tired, and the killer among us could go to hell.

"I guess we can begin," he proceeded, somewhat disappointed. He was like a man expecting a large laugh during a wedding toast and receiving a sullen silence instead. "Yes, we should probably get started," he said. He was startled to discover Enescu Fleet at his side. "Perhaps Mr. Fleet, having slightly more experience in this area, would be so good as to assist?"

Fleet replied that he would be delighted.

"It's all arranged, then," said Adwick. "We will use the front room, I think."

Fleet agreed that the front room would be smashing. I swear he picked up these terms from Hutton. "Just one request of my own," he tacked on.

"Yes?"

"I would like Johnny to be present. He has an open and ingenuous insight that I think you might find helpful." Now he was picking up terms from my plate.

Adwick's lip curled, and he shivered violently. After a trek through the snow and a tumble on the ice, it took a single Hathaway to get that reaction.

He grunted his reluctant approval. "Mr. Hathaway," he said, extending a hand in the direction of the interview room.

It could have been my open and ingenuous insight, but I knew he was going to say that too.

11 — Flummery

The chief asked Dom Jacobs to be present. If Fleet had his personal liaison, then Adwick would have his.

I could play that way too. I insisted Lesley join us. Actually, Lesley insisted Lesley join us. Fleet embraced the idea, and I knew better than to argue. If she got bored, she could always talk to Dom.

I was really beginning to wonder about this Jacobs guy. He and Adwick didn't seem like friends. They didn't seem like colleagues either, despite what the man had said over dinner. So who was he?

If I didn't know better, I would have said he was Sheriff Adwick's bodyguard—they do give ex-elected officials one sometimes—but Dom didn't look like a bodyguard. Do they give ex-elected officials Certified Financial Planners?

These questions and more ran through my open and ingenuous mind as we got down to it.

We started with Vivian Birch and Cesar Bloom. Adwick had asked to see each guest on their own, but Vivian had already proven herself a nonconformist on most things.

Adwick accepted her defiance without comment. A short talk with Dom a minute before had mellowed him considerably. (Perhaps he had made a killing in his portfolio last quarter.)

"I know this must seem somewhat unorthodox," began the chief, taking a seat by the fire. "Nevertheless, the more information we can glean from this tragedy while we wait for the authorities to arrive, the better off we will be in the long run. We appreciate any assistance you can give us."

Cesar nodded intelligently, and Vivian sniffed. Adwick went on:

"And have no concern about the man—or woman—who perpetrated this crime. You will be fine as long as you stay close. We can protect you."

Cesar frowned skeptically, and Vivian scoffed.

Adwick said good, well pleased with this attitude of cooperation. "Let us begin, then. How long had you known the victim?"

"Nine years," answered Cesar.

Vivian nodded. Nine years. For a time, they had all run bistros in Boston, and before that, they worked as critics for the paper and local TV network.

"You got along well?"

"Excellent," said Cesar. Vivian nodded. They couldn't have been happier.

"No professional jealously?"

"No, nothing," said Cesar. Vivian scowled. Where exactly was Adwick going with this?

The investigating officer paused. "No good-natured competition between rivals?" he wondered.

"We weren't rivals," insisted Vivian. Cesar seconded her insistence. What was the sheriff implying?

The chief smiled. "I know emotions run high for people in your walk of life. Hollywood can be a dog-eat-dog business."

I peered around to locate Pixie, but she must have been off visiting Phillip again. She usually had much to say about these crass canine idioms.

"We don't work in Hollywood," stated Vivian haughtily—they weren't actors.

Cesar Bloom concurred. Although, to be absolutely accurate, he had once prepared crêpes Suzette onstage in a little theater in Brooklyn. Sold-out show, one night only.

Adwick leaned in for the kill. "When did you first realize that you hated your friend?"

"What?" gaped Cesar.

"Of all the—" Vivian started to say.

A gentle "ahem" from the direction of Dom Jacobs, sitting in the corner, curbed Adwick's killer instinct. He leaned back. "So you're saying you didn't dislike Elsie Farmer?"

"She was my girl," argued Vivian. She was thrilled for her success, absolutely thrilled. She was sad, very sad that she had to die—now of all times.

Cesar said he liked Elsie fine. They seemed decidedly out of sync now.

Lesley whispered in my ear that she was pretty sure that Cesar had done it.

Enescu Fleet wondered if he could pose a question. Adwick gladly turned over the interview to the other semiretiree.

"You haven't visited here before?" he asked Cesar.

"Maine?"

"This part of Maine. Specifically, this location."

It was not what either celeb expected. "You mean *Le Vrai Cornichon*?"

Fleet waited patiently until the man answered his own question.

"No. Why would I?"

Vivian nodded. Why would they?

"Good, good," Fleet told them. He spoke almost playfully. "That's a relief."

I had no idea what had brought about this sudden whimsy, but there was definitely a theatrical edge to his voice now. The way he said "good," and "that's a relief," and "good" a second time. Very actorly. Perhaps he, too, had once fried pancakes off-Broadway.

He answered our questioning gaze. "The murderer definitely possessed a working knowledge of the layout of this property. You agree, Sheriff?"

Adwick said oh yes. Yes, of course. You can't skirt a working knowledge in these cases.

"That's why I'm pleased that you say you have never visited here before," he explained. "It's so easy to check up on a person's whereabouts, especially someone as celebrated as you, Cesar. It's wonderful that you can spare us the trouble."

Cesar Bloom looked to Vivian Birch, Vivian Birch to Cesar Bloom. Cesar's look said *I'm going to tell them*; Vivian's said *Don't you do it*; Cesar's

I'm doing it. (Apparently, Lesley's looks weren't the only ones I could read.)

"Ohhhh—" he said, drawing the word out like the point of a perfectly whipped meringue. "Have I ever visited *here* before? This locale, you mean? Yes, I have. About a week ago. I was scouting locations for a new restaurant in the area and dropped in for a moment to see this place. Since we were coming here later in the month, I thought I would. The owners weren't around. I talked to the hostess girl a minute and left. Evelynn, I think her name is."

Vivian Birch nodded. Her name was Evelynn.

Lesley whispered that she thought that Vivian had probably done it.

Fleet leaned forward. He looked at Vivian. "So you joined him on this junket?"

"Who, me? No. Why would I?"

"He must have told you about it, then?"

She blinked at him. "Why would he?"

Fleet had no wish to be indelicate. "You two are, shall we say—together?"

Vivian glanced at Cesar, Cesar at Vivian. Vivian's glance said *I guess we should come clean about that too;* Cesar's said *Fine, come clean—this weekend sucks.*

"Yeah, we're together," she admitted. "It's no big deal. I'm divorced."

"And I'm getting divorced," said Cesar.

"But you're not divorced yet," Fleet replied.

For some reason, his simple restatement of fact sounded more profound than it might have done from someone else—me, for instance. "I can understand why you would want to keep your relationship a secret. These celebrity divorces can get very ugly."

"And expensive!" said Vivian. Cesar glared at her.

Fleet acknowledged this with a nod. "It must have been very awkward when Elsie Farmer learned your secret."

If they hadn't expected the previous questions, this totally floored them.

"How did—?" Cesar saw no reason to fight it. "Yes, it was awkward," he said.

Fleet ran his hand over the salt-and-pepper in his beard. I won't say that he leaned in for the kill, because the Fleets don't kill unless provoked, but he did lean in for the schmooze.

"Now that we have cleared away the preliminary nonsense, how about the three of us jump right into the main course. What can you tell us about Elspeth Farmer? *Honestly* tell us about her."

The celebrities didn't know what to say. They knew fine food and how to critique it. Here, they were out of their depth.

"What do you want to know?" asked Cesar.

"We'd like to know about the true woman. Not the things you read about her in cooking magazines or see when you watch her on TV. The real Elsie."

Cesar took a breath. He looked like a man who could tell you gobs about the real Elsie. "Elsie Farmer was a talented, steely eyed bitch. She enjoyed watching people squirm. For all her moralizing when she found out about us, she had more affairs than you could count. She never minded screwing someone over if it advanced her career; she had a taste for younger men; she hated animals; she was vindictive; and when she was in one of her moods, a review from her could close down a restaurant."

I mused on these points, particularly the part about animals. I thought I had sensed that. I whispered in Lesley's ear that I bet Pixie had done it.

"You would say, then," concluded Fleet, "that plenty of people wished her ill."

The celebs agreed that there was no danger of supplies running low.

"And how many of the people who might have done her harm also knew that she suffered from claustrophobia?"

I was surprised he knew this. Well, not surprised—but I marveled at how well informed he was. He always was.

Cesar replied, "Quite a few of them. She got locked in a bathroom once at the network, and it got around how she flew into a rage. Why?"

Fleet did not respond.

"Now we're getting somewhere," Adwick simpered after they had gone. He clasped his hands together in glee. I thought his *we* was a little out of place, and apparently Dom Jacobs agreed with me. He went "ahem" again, and Adwick cooled it.

Despite his tendency to hog the limelight, the chief could give credit where it was due. "Genius how you slipped that part in about the claustrophobia," he said. He paused. "*Did* Ms. Farmer suffer from claustrophobia?"

Fleet replied that she had. At least, she had according to something their host mentioned.

Ha, I thought. Ditters told him. One mystery solved.

Adwick went on, "You established one thing for certain. Whoever killed Elsie Farmer likely knew she was a claustrophobic. Cruel touch, that. It's one thing to kill the woman. But jamming her in a shed to boot? Nasty."

Fleet responded with a gentle nod of the head. "Yes. And that's just what bothers me about it."

Ignoring this comment, for it had no place in his simplified mind, Adwick called in Zoe Norris.

His wishes were completely subverted this time. Not only did we get Zoe but Madeleine Abrams and Evelynn Brine.

They took their seats, and Adwick started in again: *Had they met Ms. Farmer before tonight? At any point in the evening had she seemed concerned about her own safety? Were they aware—or could they ascertain—whether the chef put cumin in his fruit salad?* It was the standard array of questions.

The trio answered *No*, *No* and *Yes*. Sven did use cumin, just a dash for a savory punch.

Adwick bobbed his head complacently to these questions, especially the last one. "How long have you three worked here?" he asked.

It was a pretty pointless question, since the restaurant had only opened tonight.

Zoe answered *three weeks*—that's how long it took her to train. Madeleine answered *three weeks*. Evelynn, after a moment's hesitation, answered *three weeks*.

Something about her hesitation prodded my unconscious mind. Without knowing I was going to speak, I spoke. "So who did you take over for?" I wondered.

The room turned to stare.

"What do you mean?" asked Evelynn.

I had to think a second. "When Betty introduced you, she said our 'new' hostess. I assumed by that someone had come before you."

I could be wrong, but I believe Adwick was favorably impressed by my technique. My wife certainly was, and Fleet smiled knowingly. He knew I would confirm his faith eventually.

Evelynn said, "No, you're right. Originally, Mrs. Dittersdorf was going to be the hostess and front-of-house manager all in one. But she must have changed her mind."

Zoe Norris backed her up on this. "It was around the time that Nancy arranged for the celebrity big shots to visit. Once the last of them had confirmed, Betty realized that she would have her hands full and hired Evelynn."

"And who was the last to confirm their invitation?" Fleet wanted to know.

"That red-haired hussy," said Zoe. "You know, the deceased."

I shook my head. Someone had gotten into the Chablis again.

Adwick seemed satisfied with this explanation. "Mr. Fleet?"

The elder investigator was lost in a daydream. "Pardon? No, that's all, thank you." He held up a hand. "I'm sorry, just one last question. You're sure you had never run into Elsie before?" he asked Zoe. "Overseas perhaps?"

Zoe said no. She had never been abroad. Fleet thanked her, and the three of them left.

Sheriff Adwick might have been satisfied with their progress, but Fleet was far from it. He shook his head slowly, as something didn't appear to agree with his mental digestion.

"Shall we take a short break?" the chief asked. Now that he knew there was cumin in the fruit salad, he wouldn't mind having another go at it.

Lesley needed a moment to freshen up, so I returned to the dining room and found Hutton brooding in the dark.

He was lying on the table. Actually, with his height, he took up all three—one giant platter of PI, there for your enjoyment.

"You're lying on the table," I told him.

He was aware of that. "I think better lying down."

"On a table?"

"Not always a table," he replied.

Rolling my eyes, I poured myself out a swig of wine from the decanter and took a seat at his elbow. I tried to resist the urge to use his head as a coaster. "Where is everybody?"

"Ditters is in the basement again, trying to figure out what went wrong with the landline."

I nodded. Perhaps he could locate the other slipper this time.

"Ate's in the kitchen having a nosh. Sven is at his stove again, cooking and muttering in Norwegian. Nancy Mortimer is trying to solicit volunteers to head out for the nearest precinct. She hasn't received much support for this idea—no doubt owing to the fact that the nearest precinct resides somewhere near Bar Harbor."

I nodded again. "Who's she trying to railroad into that junket?" I asked. Fleet had used the word during the interviews, and I liked it.

"No one specific. Although, I believe your name was bandied about at one point."

I said of course it was. I made a mental note to ask my good friend Sven to slip some rat poison into Nancy's next helping of canapés.

I sat and drank in silence, and then, having stood up and refreshed my glass, sat and drank some more. I was in an unusually reflective mood all of a sudden. "Ate doesn't seem herself today."

"Whose self does she seem like?" asked Hutton.

I didn't know. Just not hers. "You guys doing okay?"

"We're fabulous."

I wasn't satisfied with this answer. I knew how Enescu Fleet felt—receiving unsatisfactory answers. Not the beloved and respected-by-all part.

A remnant of pickle stared up at me from a plate. It inspired a strange and fanciful train of thought. Crankiness, strange eating patterns, a tendency to startle at the merest mention of bonnets and rattles. "Hutton," I began cautiously, "Ate isn't—?"

Betty Dittersdorf swept into the room before I could finish. "This is NOT how we wanted our opening night to come off," she declared.

I offered my support with a sympathetic bow. I could see how a dead body in the utility shed would rank low on their keys to success.

Throw in the ice and the snow, and the marooning everyone in the storm, and it was like the culinary gods weren't even trying.

"Still, you're charming hosts," I said, saluting her and Ditters with my goblet. "And a lovely couple. Elsie was right. You'll make wonderful parents."

As soon as I said it, I wished I hadn't. Not just because it was inappropriate in the context, and demonstrated that I, like Zoe, could stand to lay off the vintages for a while—but because it brought the conversation back around to the very topic I had hoped to avoid. I had been dreading Betty asking about Elsie and her unusual comments, and here I was giving the woman a perfect opening.

She definitely had something on her mind. She was poised to get it off her chest too. (Evidently, I could read chests as well as people's looks.)

Ditters, Lesley and Ate had only just rejoined us when she blurted out the question that had been rankling since dinner: "Does anyone else think that Dom Jacobs is my father's boyfriend?"

Ate dropped her nosh plate (I had been trying to see if it was pickle and ice cream). Lesley let fly a hairbrush that she had been returning to her purse, while I sprang up and doused the tablecloth with cabernet. Hutton flicked a portion of this off his knuckles.

Only Ditters reacted positively. An impish smile had creased his whiskered cheeks, and he nodded his head.

He didn't know where his wife was going with this, but he liked it.

"It's just," she elaborated, "they're obviously friends of some sort, and I was wondering if they might be 'special friends.' "

We continued to stare at her.

"You see, when my mom left him, he never said much. Then she remarried, and he totally clammed up about it. Maybe they couldn't get along because, well—you know."

Ditters took her hand. His voice was soft and encouraging. "Betty, you have to put this in perspective. We've had a murder. We're trapped here with the killer, and who knows when the authorities might arrive. And beyond it all, what exactly are you worried about? You want your father to be happy, don't you? Rather than condemning him for his life's choice and holding him up to ridicule—the important thing to consider is, he can't possibly have any problem with me now. I mean, if the tough ex-copper man is dating a bloke, and one who looks like Mr. Death on downers, he's no one to talk about *your* choice of life partner." He nodded thoughtfully to himself at these words, feeling he had said a mouthful.

Betty looked less than consoled by his morsel of wisdom. She wriggled her fingers through her hair and emitted a sad giggle.

No one else knew how to respond. Ditters had said it all. It didn't matter anyway, because the subject under consideration came bounding into the room now, cardigan flapping in the breeze.

He was obviously agitated. Dom strolled in behind him, observing each of our reactions. He was always observing, that guy.

"The body has disappeared!" the chief exclaimed.

I didn't look up. I was too busy dabbing wine from my own cardigan—the not-gay kind.

I wasn't surprised by the sheriff's pronouncement, or by much of anything anymore.

Of course the body had disappeared. Why wouldn't it?

12 — Half-Baked

I had experienced this sort of thing before. Several times, actually. It can totally throw off your inventory.

Following the sheriff's lead, we paraded down the hall, through the kitchen and out the back exit. As usual, we picked up participants as we went. Anytime anyone went anywhere in this place, it felt like the big cast scene at the end of a rollicking stage musical.

(Not that I've seen many of these myself. Adwick maybe. Not me.)

We arrived outside, which was still freezing, and discovered that his senses had not deceived him. Elsie Farmer's body was, indeed, missing.

Betty opened the door of the shed and peered inside, remarking that it wasn't in there either. I'm not sure why she thought it would be. Once you accepted the notion that a body could get up and move of its own accord, why set your sights so low? A really motivated corpse could have been halfway to Massachusetts by now.

"What the hell is going on?" asked Vivian.

"I'm really beginning to get creeped out here," said Zoe.

"Could the body be covered in snow?" Nancy shivered.

Ate pointed out that not enough precipitation had fallen in the last hour to cover any bodies. This wasn't totally true. There wasn't sufficient snow to cover *most* bodies. The drifts, however, had already risen well above Pixie and Phillip. The two dogs woofed from the covered porch, lamenting over this species discrimination.

"The killer moved it," said Madeleine. She also shivered, but not from the cold.

"I have something to say," announced Ditters, and proceeded to say nothing.

We wheeled around and focused our attention on him.

Somehow, we had managed to form a ring around him in the snow—a ring of scrutiny—and this did nothing to loosen his reserve.

Drawing upon his pickle-maker's resolve, the type of fortitude that had once given him the courage to combine garlic, scallion and essence of fig in one amazing jar, he hesitated no longer. "I moved her," he said.

That was his first mistake, using the personal pronoun. He should have said "it." *It*, the body. It might seem cold, but sometimes coldness is the way to go. It also fit the weather.

"You moved the body?" Adwick asked him. He had thought his son-in-law a dolt, but he never considered him a dolt who obstructed the authorities in their (semiretired) duties. "Why would you move the body? Where did you move the body? When did you move the body?" he asked, running the gamut of inquiry.

"How did you move it?" wondered Nancy, capping things off for him.

I had already figured out the *how* myself. The lanes in the snow told the story. Ditters had spirited away the body via sled. It was the old Rosebud maneuver. When you absolutely, positively needed a body moved over snow or ice, a sled was your best option.

"I shifted her to the greenhouse," he responded with dignity. "On a sleigh."

I called it a sled, he called it a sleigh—I still nailed it.

"But why would you do that?" gaped Betty. Her father had already asked that question, but it was okay—we could go over it again. We had plenty of time. No need to go inside and warm up or anything. It was fine.

Ditters continued nobly, a tad too nobly if he knew what was good for him. "She wouldn't have liked it," he answered. "Elsie wouldn't. Lying out in the garden like that. She might have been a cruel woman in a lot of ways, but she didn't deserve that. No one does."

There it was again. *She.* Three *she's*, in fact. I realized he couldn't very well have said *it* this time, but what was wrong with saying nothing? Or just, *I don't know, just thought I would.*

Betty was staring at him. So was everyone, but it was Betty's stare I was most concerned about. "Walter—you're talking as if—as if—"

"Oh, they were lovers, for goodness sake!" spouted Zoe Norris.

I have attributed a lot of the lady's behavior these last few hours to the consumption of demon rum, or demon Chablis in her case, but somehow I felt this went deeper than burgundy. She must have gotten into the fortified stuff.

"Love—" began Betty.

"—vers," finished the waitress, rubbing it in. "Don't worry, it was before he knew you."

Betty looked to Ditters. "Is this true?"

Ditters hesitated again. This time I didn't blame him. "Well—a long time ago, she and I, which is to say, I and she—we—" He turned on his employee bitterly. "What the hell is wrong with you!" I'd never seen Ditters shout, really shout, at someone. It was weird. "I told you that in confidence!"

I could only shake my head—again. I was going to get a crick in my neck by the end of the evening. If Ditters had another fault, it was that he told far too many people far too many things he should have told no one.

Zoe was looking like some hidden hand had spiked her rabbit food. "You—I thought it—I thought it best that she knew!"

"You thought it best she knew!"

"You said it yourself—you couldn't bear keeping things from her."

Ditters stared at her. "I liked it just fine!" he responded.

"We—you—" Words failed her. "I can't do anything right for you! All you ever worry about is your stupid wife!" And with these bizarre, blustering words, she fled back toward the building with tiny fists clenched in anger.

Both her employers were left speechless. Feeling she should really say something—anything—Betty called after her, "You still haven't cleared away the plates from dinner, Zoe!" Things might descend into chaos, emotions might swell up and burst into little fragments across the frozen courtyard, but you could still be a good influence on your staff.

"Well, well, well," said Adwick, speaking as the wrathful father-in-law now, not the wrathful police officer. "This is how you treat my daughter?"

With Zoe absent, the ring of scrutiny closed in tighter around Ditters.

"Well—" he said.

"Invite your floozies here—?"

"Well—"

"And lie about it to my daughter's face—?"

"Well—"

I felt we were making some progress here. Adwick had said "Well, well, well," and here was Ditters saying "Well, well, well," too—granted split over three pauses and more pathetically.

"I have a good mind—"

"Daddy, it's fine," said Betty. I wasn't expecting that.

Neither was Ditters. "Really? It's fine? You don't mind?"

"Of course I mind, Walter. You should have told me. But what's past is past. Marrying you, I knew you'd had previous romantic entanglements. I used to work for one, remember? I accepted it. A man like you is bound to have loads of ex-flames."

The ring of scrutiny furrowed its brow. A man like him? Really? We were still talking about Ditters Dittersdorf, right?

"You said it before, we need to put things in perspective. Our love is stronger than this. It's strong enough to bear any of these hiccups. I love you, Walter."

"I love you, Betty!"

Now things were only getting mawkish. The ring of scrutiny shifted its feet awkwardly.

Adwick alone remained unswayed.

Taking advantage of the lull in his fury, Ditters extended his variation of an olive branch. "Chief, I need to tell you something. When I moved the body, I noticed something peculiar. I knew you wouldn't want anyone disturbing it, so I left it alone. But it may have a bearing on your investigation."

He had found his talking point. The officer's eyes lit up. "A clue," he said. Some men like a cordial after dinner, others a cheese course. Ex-Sheriff Adwick enjoyed clues.

He rubbed his hands together in anticipation. His daughter's happiness was all well and good, but the case was the case. Besides, it seemed like the two young people had everything worked out anyway. The truth had been told, and all was forgiven. Stand-up guy, that Walter Dittersdorf, he had always thought so.

"We should have a look at it. Where did you say you shifted the woman?"

"My greenhouse. I slid her in between the haricot vert and the sprouts. I can show you."

The chief said excellent. He had always liked sprouts.

Personally, I wasn't so sure I did anymore. I made a mental note to avoid the fresh veggies for the remainder of our stay.

"Mind if I come?" Hutton asked them.

He seemed slightly out of breath. Reflecting back, I hadn't noticed him among our circle of judgment before then. He must have just arrived.

Ditters gestured him along, and I looked to Fleet. "Don't you want in on this?" Surely, Adwick and Hutton weren't the only investigators with a taste for fresh developments.

Fleet shook his head. If he missed a clue, then more power to the new guard. He would gladly learn all about it at the go-getters' earliest convenience. Right now, he needed some time alone inside.

It was all agreed, then. Just before departing with the guys, Hutton turned and produced a sheaf of paper from beneath his fisherman's sweater. In a muffled voice, he quickly explained that he had liberated it from Ditters and Betty's office whilst everyone else was out here mucking about. I guess you might call that go-getting too.

Pressing it into my hand, he whispered to Ate, "Keep a watch on Nancy and Sluggo. There's more to those two than meets the eye."

She gave a determined nod.

I wasn't quite so well collected. New developments. Secret papers. People named Sluggo. It was probably half an hour before I realized that *Sluggo* meant *Sven*.

I don't know why everyone always has to talk in code.

I took the sheaf to the dining room to examine. I asked Lesley to join me.

The paperwork all seemed to relate to the financials of *Le Vrai Cornichon*. I couldn't make sense of most of it—my financial expertise runs more toward pressing the Apple Pay button on my watch and calling it a day—but one thing stood out among the paraphernalia.

"Sven is part owner of the restaurant," said Lesley. "He's one of the investors, along with Mr. Adwick and Nancy Mortimer. Isn't that interesting."

I agreed it was. Very interesting. "Not only part owner. Sven seems to have financed it from day one. Adwick and Nancy stuck some money into it, but Sven is the big cheese at the *Happy Pickle*. According to this, he not only funded a good deal of it, he continues to oversee the finances. His signature is everywhere. What do you think this clause here means?"

Lesley wasn't sure. "Maybe we should ask Dom Jacobs?"

"Why Dom Jacobs?"

"I don't know. He looks like a money minder, doesn't he?"

I agreed that he did look like a money minder, yes. I had been thinking that very thing. "A very solemn money minder."

"He is solemn, isn't he?" She paused, brooding on his solemnness. "I seem to think I've met him somewhere before."

That ruled him out as a financial expert. She couldn't have met him in the context of our vast wealth, because we didn't have any. Just ask Apple Pay.

I was looking over the wording of the contract. "It seems as though, if the bistro fails—"

Betty interrupted us again. I couldn't tell if she was doing this on purpose, but her consistency was amazing. "Are the men back yet?"

I shook my head, hastily concealing the paperwork from view. I didn't think she would appreciate her guests poring through her personal files.

She sat down across from us and sighed. Then she got up and sighed again. As she started in on a third one, Fleet appeared.

I nodded his way. He was a man—she could talk to him.

For once, he seemed to be in no mood for schmoozing. He went around the tables and picked up one plate after another, reading each puzzle in turn. It seemed a little weird, playing now, but if he really wanted to try—

He set Elsie's charger back on the table and shook his head. "I've been underestimating everyone," was all he said.

Just then, "the men" returned from the hunt. Ditters and Adwick led the way, with Hutton walking slowly behind them. He appeared even more dour than before—and this was one of his dour weekends.

"Did you see the famous 'clue'?" I asked him.

He nodded.

"So what was it?"

"A cookie," said Adwick. The buttinsky. I wasn't asking him.

I looked to Hutton, who said it was a cookie.

"A cookie?" said Lesley. "What do you mean a cookie?"

Hutton said he meant a cookie.

The buttinsky Adwick elaborated, "The victim had a cookie squeezed inside her fist. We probably didn't notice it before because the snow and ice had mixed in with the cookie crumbs. We might have missed it altogether if Dittersdorf here hadn't thought to move the body." He slapped his son-in-law proudly on the back. So that was all it took. Disturbing the physical evidence of a crime scene. Interesting.

That was plausible, Lesley supposed—the snow and ice concealing the clue, not the brilliance of Ditters' icky sled journey. That still seemed mental to her.

The identification of the clue only prompted more questions from her and Betty, such as: *Why would the dead woman have a cookie in her hand?* And: *What kind of cookie was it?*

Hutton sat down beside us. He also sighed. "It's a soft, cake-like cookie very popular in French bakeries."

"Oh yes?" said Lesley. "Well, good for it. I hope it's the princess of the cookie-dough ball."

"It's called a *madeleine*," he added.

Dourly.

13 — A Question of Hospitality

I wasn't surprised that Maddy Abrams entered the room at this instant. I would have expected nothing less at this boîte of bedlam. It was how the *Delightful Pickle* rolled.

She was joined by Nancy and the two living food celebrities. This was also not surprising. Nobody ever traveled alone in this joint. (Except for Elsie, and you saw how she wound up.)

The baker seemed to sense something was amiss. "What?" she asked. "Why is everyone staring at me?"

Several faces lowered, including Ditters'. But not Adwick's. His pinched expression shone with a cat-like smugness. He was practically purring. I was surprised Pixie and Phillip didn't start chivvying him around the dining room.

Hutton took the initiative. "A certain guest, who shall remain nameless—mostly because I can't remember his name—thinks you may have been involved in our little murder."

"What! Why?"

"There was a baked good pressed in the victim's hand."

"So?"

"So—it was a cookie. A madeleine cookie."

Madeleine, not the cookie, had no response to this. Unaccustomed to the nature of our cases, she wouldn't have. "A madeleine?"

"It's your name," whispered Ditters helpfully, leaning in during another lull. He lowered his head again. These employee evaluations were getting awkwarder and awkwarder.

"So what if it is?"

"Some folks here find it suggestive," said Hutton

Maddy retorted, "Do they really. And do you?" she asked Fleet. "Do your investigations normally hinge on such things?"

"More often than you might think," he replied solemnly. Very solemnly. Dom Jacobs could have received pointers from him. "Not always cookies, of course. But yes."

"It's ridiculous," she said. "First of all, a madeleine is not a cookie. It's a cake. What's more, I haven't baked any, so I highly doubt you found one. Lastly—" I thought she might descend into her native French, but she held it together. "Lastly, please explain, why would I kill this Elspeth Farmer? A woman I hardly knew?"

Before anyone could answer, Dom Jacobs appeared. He went to Adwick, drooping over him like an stringy witness for the prosecution: "I confirmed in Ms. Abrams' employee file that she was employed by Ms. Farmer three years ago."

The room gasped. I would like to say I didn't, but I can't. I gasped like gangbusters.

Madeleine's gasp came stiffer and more ferociously than the rest. "You looked in my file?"

Dom Jacobs nodded. "I found your employment history among the paperwork in Mr. and Mrs. Dittersdorf's office."

Ditters was shaking his head. The gesture mirrored Fleet's, whose head was also oscillating. Ditters' came a little slower—no doubt due to the aerodynamics of their beards.

He ceased waggling. "Wait, you looked in our files?"

Dom Jacobs nodded.

"You might have asked!"

Dom Jacobs blinked.

"I had completely forgotten about her employment history," said Betty. "I guess no one can remember everything. So much to do," she sighed, referring to running a restaurant.

No one cared.

"Well, I never knew it," said Ditters. He looked to Dom again. "Can't believe you went through our files."

I surreptitiously slid the paperwork Hutton had liberated further out of view.

Adwick, the guest who would no longer remain nameless, stepped up. “Ms. Abrams,” he said, addressing her in that pompous manner that made you want to kick him in the groin, “I think it would be best—”

“Just a moment, Sheriff,” interrupted Fleet.

“Ah, now he speaks!” said Madeleine. The French can be so sarcastic. I was pretty sure she was French. Maybe she was Belgian.

“I believe you are on the verge of making a grave error,” said the PI, still running solemn.

Adwick gazed at him crossly. He was getting a little tired, I think, of everyone undermining his authority. He had forgiven his son-in-law’s transgressions, but enough already. “I don’t believe I am. She lied about her relationship to the deceased—”

“She omitted to mention that she had once worked for the victim, but that is not a crime. It is technically not even a lie. She was Elsie Farmer’s baking consultant on *Farmer to Table*. She was summarily dismissed when the latter decided to go gluten-free and reformatted the entire show.”

Maddy jerked her hand up in exasperation. This anti-gluten cooking. It was not French!

“But wait,” she gasped, not so ferocious this time. “You knew?”

“That you once worked with Elsie? Yes, I knew. I have followed your career rather closely over the years.”

She continued to soften. “Then you must have thought you were protecting me.”

“I’m not sure I’ve done such a great job of that,” he replied. He gazed into her eyes. I would have done the same. They were pretty mesmerizing.

Adwick, meanwhile, wasn’t so entranced. “Ms. Abrams’ dismissal gives her a motive,” he stated proudly. “And then there’s the clue.”

“Yes, the clue,” said Fleet. “A clue that was clearly planted.”

The room gasped again (not I this time, I kept my cool).

Fleet’s spirits had lightened. He was definitely from the school of master detective who enjoyed stringing along with a theory just so he could dash it to earth. “I’m afraid I don’t buy that Elsie grasped the telling madeleine cookie—”

"It is not a cookie," said Maddy doggedly.

"—just before she succumbed to the murderous fumes of the backup generator. Where would she have procured such a dying clue? In the utility shed? Why would she procure it?"

"She clearly snapped it up on her way through the kitchen," replied Adwick, fighting in the last ditch. "Just to have handy if she needed it."

"I see. And then having armed herself with this valuable confectionary evidence, she steps inside a utility shed and allows herself to be poisoned, secure in the knowledge that her killer might eventually be brought to justice? No, not even on one of our cases. She was obviously gripping the cookie, but it wasn't to identify her murderer."

"You tell him, Nessie," Madeleine applauded. "And it is not a cookie," she said again.

Adwick was still trying to absorb the finer points of Fleet's tirade. He must have thought the latter was such a nice semiretired PI before then. "Maybe she was shoved inside while holding the clue."

"My dear man, Elsie suffered from claustrophobia. Do you really think she would wantonly wander anywhere near a tiny space like that?"

"She was carried inside it, then."

"All the while holding the informative dessert? Ridiculous!"

"Fine. What's your take on it?"

"She was called to that spot by someone she knew—I'll explain how in a moment. But she didn't go to the spot you think she went. It was on a slightly higher plane."

Adwick looked squiggly eyed at his mental superior. He didn't come here to talk philosophy. "Are we speaking of planes of existence?" he asked.

"Not in this instance, Sheriff; although it never hurts to remain spiritually minded." He paused for effect. "Perhaps you would care to examine the second-story patio now. Although it's more of a deck than a patio, I suppose. It's around the corner from the kitchen, just before you reach the utility shed. We'll wait. You might want your mittens; it's cold out there."

Adwick left—*sans* mittens—and returned five minutes later, gaping. "There's a hole in the floor of the deck!"

Fleet agreed with him. A hole in the floor of the deck becoming a hole in the ceiling of the utility shed. The latter was nothing more than an enclosure under the structure. "I'm surprised no one else noticed that."

I kicked myself. It was like I said earlier, you should always look at the ceiling.

"So she fell through the balcony hole!" said Ditters, once again lending a hand.

Fleet nodded.

Ditters looked pleased, more pleased than he ought to have. "I get it now. After we bought the place, we noticed a section of decking had rotted away. We were planning on having it fixed this spring. I didn't realize that it went through to the shed. We had a tarp to cover it up. And some duct tape."

Fleet agreed that the tarp had worked admirably. "All the snow that blew under the awning the last few weeks had formed a perfect layer of deception for the trap."

Ditters had gone pale. "But, but—we had the deck closed off. There were signs, and ropes, cordoning it off."

"There weren't any ropes when I went out there," said Adwick.

"And there were no signs," added Fleet. "You see now that anyone familiar with the layout of this restaurant could have led Elsie Farmer to her death."

"The fall wouldn't have killed her," argued Ditters. "It was only about ten feet down."

"Would have made a mess of her, though," Vivian remarked. "Ten feet is farther than you think. She probably snapped both her ankles."

"Actually, she didn't," Fleet replied. "The length of the tarp, combined with the breadth of the hole, would have likely lowered her gently into the shed. It would have been a rapid descent, but I doubt it would have harmed her."

"There you have it," said Ditters proudly.

"That is why the killer saw to it that what followed the descent did kill her."

"Oh right." He had forgotten that part.

I sniffed thoughtfully. We had a case once, Fleet, Hutton, Ate, Lesley and I, where the victim appeared to have fallen to his death, when in fact he had been poisoned before the fall. And here was a case where the victim was poisoned after a fall. Funny how these things worked out.

"So you're saying someone who works at the restaurant did it?" asked Ditters.

Fleet shook his head. "Anyone could have taken advantage of the ready-made trap, provided they knew the lay of the land." He directed these words to certain food celebs who shall remain prime-time-vehicle-less.

"I'm confused," said Adwick. "How did the killer lead Ms. Farmer to her death? I'm not getting any of this."

"Of course you aren't," Fleet told him. I thought it was a good dig, until his next words followed more magnanimously: "No one could get it, because they don't have all the details I do. Allow me to enumerate them for you."

"Please."

"Over dinner," he enumerated, "Betty Dittersdorf introduced the mystery-puzzle game, a game, oddly enough, no one can remember arranging."

Adwick said he knew that. He was there.

"It was something to pass the time. Everyone lifted up their plate and read a puzzle personalized to themselves."

I remembered that part. Stupid plate puzzle.

"Elsie Farmer's plate held no such riddle, however. Hers contained a request to meet someone outside. It was addressed to Elspeth, so it was from someone who knew her well."

"There's nothing here," said Betty, tipping up the charger.

She showed us the underside. There was only an emblem of the plate manufacturer: an eagle sitting on the shoulder of a bear. Kind of a weird emblem. I guess if you can't have furtive messages, a weird-ass graphic was nearly as good.

Fleet was aware of this omission. Elsie had taken the paper with her. He, in turn, had retrieved it from a trash can in the restroom. She had stopped there before heading outside.

He read from the crumpled page: "*Elspeth, I can't stop thinking about you. Meet me outside on the second-story deck. No one will hear us there. I'll try to make it worth your while, I promise.*"

"What can we gather from this?" he asked.

"The killer was a man," stated Nancy firmly.

Fleet bowed to her expertise. "Of course, it could have easily been written by a woman trying to sound like a man."

"My money's on a man," said Nancy.

Fleet would tend to agree. "Especially if it was signed 'Cesar.' "

Cesar Bloom leapt to his feet. "Give me that!" he snarled, but the nimble-fingered detective had already returned the page to his pocket. "I know what you're thinking," Cesar told him, and then turned and told the room, "I didn't do this."

Fleet believed him. "No one is saying that you did. It takes a particular type of hardened man to kill his ex-lover. I don't think you're as hard as that—or as hard as you make yourself out to be."

I rolled my eyes for the millionth time. More old flames. We were going to have to start some kind of database just to keep track of them all.

"Your what?" Vivian asked.

Cesar scooted into the chair beside her. "It was a long time ago, baby—"

Vivian held up a hand. She didn't want to hear any *babies* from him. Betty Dittersdorf she was not. "You were with that—with that—" She held up the other hand.

Cesar was forced to speak out of self-preservation now. He could repair his love life some other time.

"I didn't kill the woman," he said to us. "I didn't lure her away from the table. Someone is trying to frame me."

"You misunderstood," replied Fleet. "I see your confusion. I said *if it was signed Cesar*. It was not. The note was not signed at all," he revealed, bringing out the most ridiculous goggling stare in the celebrity I had ever seen on a man of his rugged bearing.

"So, what do we know?" proceeded the PI, having thoroughly wreaked havoc on the Bloom-Birch romance. "The lady is called out to the balcony, ostensibly by Cesar Bloom—that much is certainly true. Someone was framing you through implication, if nothing else. The tone of the note was enough to lure her out into the cold. Once on the deck, she tumbles through the killer's booby trap into the shed, wherein she is locked far enough away from us that no one can hear her scream for help. The generator, with its exhaust hose pressed under the door, has already been switched on ahead of time. Even with the ventilation above, Elsie Farmer is dead within minutes."

"And the killer doesn't even have to be present for the murder," said Ditters. Very neat.

Adwick said yes, yes. They knew all this already. "But who killed the woman?" he wanted to know.

Fleet had no idea.

"What the f—" The lawman calmed his rage. There were women and small animals present. "If you didn't know, what was the point of all this?"

"There is always a point to examination. But you're still not asking the correct question."

"And what is the correct question?"

"On whose behalf was the killer working?"

Adwick glared at him. Since when was the killer working on anyone's behalf?

Fleet answered that question with another of his own. "Tell me something," he asked the room, "who invited me here?"

Ditters and Betty said, "Hutton." Hutton said, "Ditters and Betty." Ditters and Betty stared at Hutton, Hutton at Betty and Ditters.

"That's right," Fleet agreed. "No one invited me." I'd never seen a gatecrasher so proud of his accomplishment. "And I would wager that, if we delved into it further, the invitations to Elsie, Cesar and Vivian are equally obscured. I've spoken to everyone here, and it is entirely unclear who invited whom. Nancy Mortimer says the celebrity invitations were Betty's idea; Betty says they were her husband's. No one can own up to making the guest list, because it was not made in any kind of straightforward fashion. Suggestion and manipulation have brought us to this point."

"Then who?" begged Adwick. "Who suggested and manipulated it?"

Nancy, Betty and Ditters joined in on this query with nods of wonder, while the food celebs, forgetting their troubles for the moment, peered at each other in awe. They had never seen a dinner party quite like this, and they loved it. Except for the murder and mayhem—and a couple overly dressed salads.

Fleet held up Elsie's plate again. "Does this emblem mean anything to anyone?"

Everyone gawked uncomprehendingly at the eagle and bear.

All but one, that is. One person rose to the challenge.

"Arnold Bernard," I said quietly.
The room gasped.

14 — A Perfect Cornichon

Which made very little sense, considering that only a core few of us knew who Arnold Bernard was.

This seemed to dawn on the gaspers, as looks of shock and amazement faded into frowns of pique and confusion. I heard several people whisper, "Who's Arnold Bernard?" and one—Betty Dittersdorf—said, "I thought he said 'Harlan Peppard.' " In response, several other people whispered, "Who's Harlan Peppard?", to which Betty replied, "I thought you knew!"

Fleet laid it out for them. "Arnold Bernard," he said, "is a demented individual who, if not for the efforts of Johnny and Lesley, would have killed me a month ago. He's in prison now, but he is far from under wraps. It would seem that his confinement has not prevented him from lashing out from behind his steel cage."

I wasn't so sure about the steel cage. Someone with AB's gift for manipulation probably had a suite of rooms with his own personal attendant.

"You think this is all an elaborate setup to get at you?" asked Lesley.

"It is the only explanation that fits the facts. Arnold Bernard wants retribution. In fact, he made a promise to that effect when we last spoke. Since he cannot visit retribution upon me personally, he must have enlisted an accomplice—someone who can go where he no longer can."

We all peered around at each other, trying to detect the stench of collusion.

"Crazy," said Vivian, and Fleet and I both nodded. I think we had established that. "So how'd *you* recognize it was this Arnold What's-his-name's handiwork?" she asked me, somewhat nastily, I thought. She didn't have to lean so heavily on the *you*.

Lesley defended her husband. "Johnny recognizes loads of things," she shot back. Then, more softly in my direction, "So how'd you recognize it?"

"I recognized it," I told them, "through his calling card."

I picked up the plate.

"Eagle on grizzly," I said. "A 'special friendship' between bird and bear," I wondered, "or something more sinister? Thanks to my wife's insistence that we study all the baby names in her baby guide, I remembered immediately—or within half an hour anyway—that the name Arnold means 'brave as an eagle.' Whereupon Bernard means 'brave as a bear.' Pretty much everyone's name means brave *something*. And there you have it. Eagle Bear, *Arnold Bernard*."

I probably could have made the explanation a little shorter—but as it was, I received several hearty looks of admiration, and Betty said, "So there is no Harlan Peppard, then?" It was pretty gratifying.

Ditters picked up the charger. "This bastard has been stamping his crest on our crockery? I like his bloody nerve!"

Fleet appreciated his objection. "It goes to show how ensconced his presence is here."

"But one of the staff must have ordered these?"

"Possibly. Of course, these plates are brand new. Anyone could have had them shipped here, and they would have been unpacked and used without question."

We all peered around again.

Vivian couldn't understand it. "Someone really killed Elsie just to get at you?"

"It appears so. It wouldn't be the first time," he said.

Vivian said harrumph. His charm was wearing thin with Ms. Birch.

I felt it time that I defended the man. Yes, Elsie had died because of Fleet, but how many had he saved over the years? Plenty. Besides, from what Cesar had told us, a disgruntled wife or animal lover was likely to have offed her eventually anyway. "It's not Fleet's fault he incurred the ire of an obsessive madman. Detectives make enemies. Isn't that right, Hutton?"

I felt certain that Hutton would have endorsed this, for he made enemies easier than most, but Hutton wasn't there. He must have slipped out during my lecture on brave babies. He did have a pretty short attention span.

In his place, Evelynn galloped into the dining room. "Anyone seen Zoe around?" she asked. "I've been looking everywhere for her. She seemed pretty upset before."

I wasn't interested in hysterical waitresses. I was interested in mercurial best friends. "Have you seen Hutton?" I replied.

"No. Have you seen Zoe?"

"No. You sure you didn't see Hutton? He must have just left."

"No. And you definitely haven't seen Zoe?"

"No."

Apparently, we were at a deadlock. The hostess refused to swerve from her Zoe-centric perspective, and I wouldn't budge in my Hutton-mindedness.

Maybe I should have slipped her a sawbuck to loosen up. I've known it to work with maître d's.

As it happened, I was smart to save my money. Hutton would make his presence re-known without any effort from us. He loved dramatic entrances, and he enjoyed dramatic re-entrances even more.

Ate Fleet could have told us that.

And what of the detective's daughter? Where was she during all this?

I have since learned that while the rest of the restaurant plugged away at the meaning of life, cookies and balcony holes, Hutton's girl/deputy-detective was as good as her word, keeping an eye on Sid and Nancy—or whatever Hutton had called them.

This involved a lot of hanging about the kitchen, making small talk and resisting the impulse to bitch-slap the minuscule Ms. Mortimer every time she remarked how she could eat anything she wanted anytime she wanted.

When Nancy finally broke from her feeding frenzy and fell into conversation with Cesar and Vivian, Ate had a decision to make. Follow Nancy to the dining room, or stay planted watching Sven?

She stayed with Sven. Sid was the real wild card here; Nancy was harmless.

"So that's how you make a dill-and-vinegar-infused soufflé?" she yawned, some ten minutes after Nancy had left.

"That is how you make the soufflé," Sven agreed.

She nodded. If this was how PI work normally went, no wonder Hutton and her father constantly tried to glam it up with window dressing. "Crazy having a murder here, huh?" she asked casually.

"I take no interest in murder," said Sven, reducing some lingonberries. He shook the pan violently and placed it back on the burner.

"Some people say meat is murder," she continued conversationally, "but I like meat. Not this meat," she muttered to herself, sliding away a canapé of brie and brisket foam, "but, you know, actual meat."

She watched him reduce. "Did you know the victim? I only just met her."

"I have work to do," said Sven, and left for the pantry.

She walked over and turned down his reduction. Can't have people's lingonberries burning, she thought to herself. The number of Swedes who burst into a sheet of purple flame every year from lingonberry-related disasters was no doubt astounding. This one, at least, she could prevent.

She wondered about his carelessness. Had she struck a nerve? Perhaps this PI work wasn't so fruitless, after all.

She glanced out the window. It was totally dark out now. So dark that a light in the greenhouse attracted her attention. Was that a silhouette she saw moving around inside? She decided to investigate.

It couldn't be any worse than talking shop with Chef Frowns-a-lot.

"Hello?" she asked, peering inside the greenhouse door.

It occurred to her that this was just the sort of thing dumb chicks were always doing in slasher movies. A murderer on the loose, and the first thing she does is traipse outside alone. Why had she allowed Hutton to talk her out of bringing her gun tonight?

"No, you check the back," she said in a stagey drawl. It was an old maneuver she had learned from her father. When you haven't thought ahead to bring backup, fabricate some. "No, you take the Uzi. I'm good with this pickaxe."

Another drawl, not so stagey, greeted her: "I would have thought a truly gifted performer would have done all the voices." The gibe had come from the direction of the artichokes.

Ate's nerves calmed. "What the hell are you doing out here?"

"Come and see for yourself," said Hutton.

She stepped over. Her significant other was bent over a table, poking at some flour crumbs with a penknife. "Are you CSI-ing a cookie?"

He responded coldly that it was not a cookie. Madeleine Abrams would have been proud.

"Where did you find it?"

"In the victim's hand. It's the clue Ditters found."

Ate said uck. She stepped back and nearly stumbled over something strewn in the passageway. It was the victim's leg. It poked out from the rest of her body in a cozy spot where her ex-lover had lain her down to rest. "Is that—? For God's sake!"

"Talk to Ditters," said Hutton. "I would have put her in among the spuds."

Ate shivered and moved back toward the exit. "So I'll be going now," she started to say.

Hutton arrested her departure with a shout of joy. He twirled around, his eyes flashing bubbly brilliance from behind his specs. "That paperwork I showed you—" he asked.

"You showed me nothing."

"Right. That was Hath. There was some paperwork," he explained, "and it showed that our chef is quite the financial muckety-muck. And now—" He held up in his celebrations. "Didn't I tell you to keep an eye on Nancy and Sluggo?"

Ate snapped her fingers. It was *Sluggo*, not *Sid*.

It was driving her crazy, trying to remember.

"I *was* watching them. Then they split up, and I watched Sven for a while. Then I came out here."

Hutton waved aside the story of her life. “We have to act fast,” he told her.

“Act fast doing what?”

He didn’t answer her directly. “Time to talk to Norway Nick” was his only reply.

Ate followed him out of the greenhouse. Now it was “Norway Nick”? She had barely gotten used to “Sluggo.”

Back in the dining room, we were still bringing Evelynn up to speed. “So this Bernie—what did you say?”

“Arnold Bernard,” I said.

“You sure it isn’t Bernard Arnold? I’ve never known anyone with the last name Bernard.”

I told her I was sure.

“So this Arnold Bernard is behind the murder?”

“Not just the murder, young lady,” Fleet informed her. “The dinner party and everything you see here tonight.”

He hardly could have been behind the duck-fat gherkins, she argued. Only Mr. Dittersdorf and Sven could have dreamt those up. “So what do we do now?”

It was a good question, without a great answer. It seemed to me we should continue to do what we had been doing all along: eat, drink and try not to be murdered by Arnold Bernard’s agent. Perhaps Fleet had a better plan.

If he did, this was not the time for us to learn about it. From down the corridor, a great, piercing crash could be heard, rather like a pan of lingonberries igniting in their fury. This was followed by the screech of a large Scandinavian in the grip of rude justice.

We hurried down the hall again and found Hutton holding Sven pressed to the countertop.

Eventually freed at the insistence of Nancy Mortimer and Betty Dittersdorf, the cook pried himself up from a pool of splattered reduction.

“I give you Elsie Farmer’s killer,” said Hutton.

15 — Chef's Selection

"What is the meaning of this?" demanded Chief Adwick. If he didn't know better, he might think that this unofficial investigation, which he had officially spearheaded, was getting away from him.

"Sorry for the roughhousing," Hutton apologized, "but the prisoner proved unruly."

Ate, standing in the background, waved a noncommittal hand. You couldn't pin any of this on her.

"Prisoner?" asked Ditters. "What prisoner? Why prisoner? Prisoner how?" he said. It's not that he objected to Sven getting his face pressed down in the goo. He just needed context.

Pixie and Phillip woofed their support—Pixie because she always enjoyed a good brawl, Phillip (I suspect) over some past history involving Sven and a denial of kitchen scraps. The chef looked like the sort who would hoard roast trimmings.

Hutton stretched out his rotator cuff. Subduing angry Norwegians was strenuous work.

"I confronted good Prince Harald here after I discovered that we had misinterpreted Elsie's clue."

"You mean her *planted* clue?" Fleet asked him.

"But was it planted?" Hutton riposted. And if it was, maybe it was planted by someone who knew full well what they were planting.

"Explain," said the senior private eye.

Hutton stretched his other cuff. "In Ditters' office, you will discover a sheaf of paper outlining how Sven Hosten financed the Dittersdorf enterprise at the *Le Vrai Cornichon*. Or, that is, you would discover it, if I hadn't already removed it and given it to Hath."

"You went through our papers!" said Ditters, aghast. He swiveled around on me. "Has everyone been through our personal items?"

Hutton said yup. "You don't mind, do you?"

"You might have asked!" Ditters remarked. It was becoming his battle cry.

"Asked?"

"Never mind," said Ditters. He had grown weary of occupying the moral high ground. It didn't do any good. "What's this about a sheaf?"

"What's what about me?" asked Chief Adwick.

"Not *chief*, Chief," Hutton replied—"a *sheaf*. A sheaf of paper. In Ditters' office, there was a sheaf about the chef."

The chief said oh. A sheaf about the chef. "And where do I come in?"

"I'll start again," said Hutton. "I have recently learned, through my investigations, that Sven is the chief—is the *main* financing partner in this restaurant. He's quite the financial wizard. I saw a list of his credentials, and he used to work on the stock exchange before giving it up for the skillet and cheese grater. The man loves his numbers. Cash, numbers and too much lemon zest."

"Told ya," said Ditters.

"So what if I am the man of finance?" asked the chef. "What of it?"

In order to answer this, Hutton produced a handful of cookie crumbs from his pocket and slapped these down on the counter. "This is all that remains of Elsie Farmer's dying clue."

"The madeleine," said Nancy.

"Not a madeleine," he corrected. As Maddy had said, she never baked any madeleines. "This is a confection not unlike a madeleine, though. It is known as a *financier*. What do you have to say to that, King Kronor?"

King Kronor had nothing to say to it. He stammered and looked to Nancy.

"It means nothing!" she said.

"Or does it mean everything," argued Hutton.

He strolled around the kitchen island, smiling to himself. I wondered what it felt like, having the audience on tenterhooks, anxious to hear everything you had to say. Whenever I had the floor, I always seemed to come a cropper on some minor detail I hadn't thought through.

Hutton proceeded like he didn't know what a cropper was. "I first suspected Sven of this crime when I came upon the burnt risotto in the wastebasket. That was the smoking gun."

"Did he say the burned risotto was the smoking gun?" Adwick asked. Fleet nodded.

"You burned the risotto," Hutton went on, staring into Sven's bloated face, "which everyone knows has to be stirred constantly, during the discovery of Elsie Farmer's body."

Nancy puffed in exasperation. She'd have to be careful. Someone that small could blow out a lung doing that. "Of course he burned it! That only proves that he was as surprised as the rest of us when the body was found. He rushed outside and—"

"That's what I thought at first too," Hutton agreed. "But you misunderstood." He got that line from Fleet. "Sven didn't burn the risotto then, Nancy Drew. He burned the risotto before we ever found the body. If he hadn't, he never would have had time to put on a pan of thinly veiled rice pilaf in its place."

"Did he say thinly veiled pilaf?" asked Evelynn. Ate said shh. They were going to miss the best part.

"You see, ladies and gentlemen, the pilaf was too far along for Sven to have started it when we came back inside. And yet, he hardly would have been making both risotto and pilaf. Therefore, he made the pilaf to replace the risotto, which he had burned, by my estimate, ten minutes before. That gave him plenty of time to be monkeying around outside, finalizing the preparations for his shed of death."

Chef Sven had remained remarkably silent throughout all this. I guess when someone peppers you with phrases like "thinly veiled pilaf" and "shed of death" all you can do is sit and listen to them. He spoke up now. "I didn't do it. I demand for you to know that I didn't do it."

"You see," smiled Nancy. "He didn't do it."

"I did nothing wrong!" pleaded the chef. "It was a prank only."

"Shh," she frowned. "Shh, shh."

"We manufactured this—"

"Shh, shh, shh!"

"—as the comedy, not the tragedy."

I rather liked how he put that. The comedy not the tragedy. Neat.

"What are you talking about?" Fleet asked him.

Sven wiped a bead of sweat from his enormous brow. "I knew Elspeth Farmer years ago. We were at school together. Cooking school. She was not the sharpest toast point in the rack, but she had determination. She once replaced my sea salt with crushed rock sugar during exams. It cost a ribbon, that prank. Years later, when I had left the culinary arts to undertake a career in finance, we met up again, and she mocked my decision. She said that I could not take the heat of the kitchen. I told her that I took it very well, and from that point on I dedicated myself. I gave up my seat on the exchange and devoted myself to cooking. We had the unusual friendship, she and I."

I suspected that unusual was the only kind of friendship Sven had. "But were you 'special friends'?" I asked him. If Elsie could manage a Ditters and a Cesar, why not a Sven?

"What is this 'special'?"

"Any bedroom horseplay?" asked Lesley.

The chef shook his head. "I do not see women that way. I am married to my cuisine."

I said gotcha. A loveless marriage, then. "So when did you decide to kill her?" I wondered.

"I do not kill. It was a prank. I sent the note, yes, making it seem to have come from one of the men at the party. I knew she had the affairs with one or more of them. I knew she would fall through the hole and get stuck in the shed. With her phobia of the closets, I knew that would derange her. That was the whole of the prank."

"Hilarious," I said. "And the poisoning?"

"I had nothing to do with that. I insist that you believe me."

"But not demand it?" I replied.

"We knew nothing of the gas," insisted Sven—demandingly.

" 'We'?"

"Nancy and myself."

Nancy Mortimer gave another half-lipped grin and attempted to fade into the crowd. I didn't understand where her complicity came into it. I was sure the girl liked a prank as well as the next half-pint, but it seemed like a weird time to break out of her shell.

I would have insisted on some clarification, maybe even demanded it, but Fleet was in no mood for distractions. "Continue," he implored the chef.

Sven had little left to say.

"I saw her go outside. I hear the ruckus at first, the banging, then no ruckus at all. I pause, wondering if she is goading me into letting her out. After some time, I still hear nothing, and I become concerned. I rush outside, but it is too late. Already there are people running about and asking questions. I return quickly to the kitchen, though not quickly enough for my risotto."

Yes, the poor risotto. The true victim here.

"You expect us to believe all this?" asked Adwick.

"You must believe it."

"He demands and insists on it," I said.

"I can't see it myself. All this to get back at the woman over some rock salt?"

"Rock sugar, crushed up. And it was not the sugar on its own. Elspeth tormented many in her life, myself most of all. It was a retribution."

It was the second time we had heard that word in the last twenty minutes.

Fleet jumped on it. "You acted alone in this retribution?"

"Alone with some help." He peered up at Nancy Mortimer again, who looked like she might try to explain, then didn't.

"That is all? Just you and Nancy?"

"That is all."

"You would say the name Arnold Bernard means nothing to you, then?"

Sven appeared stunned. "What does—who is this Arnold Bernard?"

After a moment's hesitation, Fleet turned to Nancy. "And you?"

Nancy looked like a dying chipmunk. "I only knew Sven was trying a prank on someone. He didn't say who or what. He said it would lighten the mood at the party."

Sven was known for mood lightening, it was true.

"Why did he confide in you?"

"I don't know. He and I go back. I used to work with him on the exchange. When we came here, we came together. I guess I must have noticed he was acting strangely tonight, and he mentioned he was going to have some fun with one of the guests and I should just go with it. I had no idea it was something like that!"

I almost stuck in my two cents on this, but Hutton got in first. "It's all wrong," he said.

I encouraged him with a welcoming flourish of the hand, but he merely brought his down on the counter with a smack.

"It's all wrong," he repeated, wiping crumbs from his palm, "because they're telling the truth."

The audience, who had been missing cues left and right, gasped.

"It's the only thing that makes sense. It all comes back to the sheaf."

"Why me?" asked Adwick. He just couldn't seem to get the hang of that.

Hutton ignored him. "I'm no expert, but from what I can gather, looking over that paperwork, Sven owns the land this restaurant is on. Quite a few acres of it, in fact. If the *Cornichon* fails to hit certain financial goals by third quarter, their partnership is terminated, and Sven is free to lease the property to someone else. Isn't that correct?"

Sven didn't deny it.

"Pretty disadvantageous terms, if I do say so myself," said Hutton (himself). He gave Ditters a paternal look. "You should have consulted with someone like Dom before embarking on a deal like that."

"Why someone like me?" asked Dom Jacobs.

"Aren't you an attorney?"

"I am not."

"Ah," said Hutton. "You missed your calling, then. At any rate, that's what you wanted all along, isn't it, Sven? You had no intention of seriously harming Elsie—that would have done you no good at all. You just wanted her so enraged by what she had been through that she'd spare no effort closing this place down. You just wanted the land back. Why?"

There was another pregnant pause. Sven shifted in his seat and looked at Nancy again. Nancy looked at Sven and had another go at fading into the grain of the cabinetry—the wood sprite returning to her natural habitat.

Sven answered for the both of them. "It is the Golden Promise," he said impressively.

The audience—well, you know.

16 — Fleeting Promise

Now I knew how the rest of the audience felt when I unleashed my Arnold Bernard theory on them. Trying to appear hip, I repeated the phrase knowingly. I did more than repeat it. I rolled it over my cognitive taste buds and enjoyed the grandeur of it all. But, in truth, I had no idea what this *Promise* was, or why it was *Golden*. It sounded like something I should know, yet didn't.

I wasn't the only one out of my depth. "What's the Golden Promise?" asked Ate, Adwick and Madeleine.

The cat was out of the bag. We all nodded in unison with the question, even Pixie and Phillip (who enjoyed cats).

Fleet answered, "Golden Promise is a one-of-a-kind strain of English barley, historically used by the finest scotch distillers. It has been in rare supply the last few decades. The last I heard, it had all but disappeared off the earth."

"No longer," said Sven. "It has returned, here on my property in New England. It is a new variety of Promise. Heartier, with the same rich flavor. It also grows twice as fast. It is a grain touched by an angel."

I turned to Ditters, the closest thing to a grain angel I knew. "Did you do this?"

Hitching up his jaw, he said, "I might have done. I did tinker with the barley some. I could have infused a certain heartiness into its DNA. It's hard to say."

It grated on Sven to admit it, but his employer had, indeed, produced a miraculous grain.

"I was just mucking about," said the latter.

Sven sniffed. One man's muck was another man's ambrosia. "There are fields and fields here, on my land, in which to grow it. All that is needed is the Dittersdorf formula and the soil conditions he already used. I simply wanted—"

"—it all for yourself," Fleet filled in. "You and the other investors." He included Nancy in a less-than-paternal stare.

Adwick, their sometimes-silent partner, was spared the same scrutiny. "Well, I didn't know bupkis about any of this. I was all ready to pull my funds. Just looking for a way to break it to Betty and what's-his-name there."

"My husband Walter."

"Yeah, that guy. Never realized he was a barley savant."

Fleet nodded. It only went to show that you should never give into investor panic. He winked at Dom Jacobs, who replied that he was no more an expert on the commodity market than he was an attorney.

Fleet apologized. "And what is the value of this miracle grain in hard numbers?" he asked Sven.

The chef hedged on his reply. These cooking, financial wizards always do.

"We have buyers lined up. They will give us a substantial amount to lease the land and the building and license the formula. They were willing to purchase the grain from us alone, but they fell in love with the locale. They wish to turn the *Cornichon* into a distillery."

Ditters said brilliant. A Provence-inspired deli-distillery. The French and Scotch and Jewish peoples all living in harmony. He loved it.

Fleet was less sanguine. "It will be decades before these buyers realize any product."

Sven's investors were very patient about that. "They're Japanese," he explained. And therefore resolute, we were meant to infer.

"But you were not so patient," Fleet stated. "Not patient enough to wait for your other tenant to succeed or fail—or possibly discover what he had invented and horn in on your deal."

Once again, the chef did not deny it.

"You're a cruel and greedy little man, Sven Hosten," said Lesley, my wife.

Sven did not deny this either.

"And you—" Fleet frowned at Nancy and shook his head. He had nothing to say to the scheming sprite. "Unfortunately, you are also not murderers," he told them. (It was news to us as well.) "I understand now what Hutton was saying. Sven knew that, if Elsie was sufficiently incensed, the critic in her would awaken, and she would do everything in her power to bring this bistro down. As Hutton also said, however, killing her would have accomplished nothing. If anything, a murder would have made this locale a tourist trap for those ghoulishly inclined."

"So we're back to wondering whodunit?" asked Ate.

"We know who. Arnold Bernard *dunit*. The question is *whodunit* for him and why?"

I still didn't understand the dying clue. "Did Elsie finger the financier or not?"

Fleet said yes and no. He suspected that the dessert was left out on the railing as bait. He had found a piece of blue foil on the ground. This was probably used to make the bait stand out.

This was the first I had heard of any foil. If he was going to keep holding things back, how was I ever going to buff up my investigator's muscle?

"When Elsie stepped up on the deck, she must have picked up the confection. Before she knew it, she found herself plunging downward into the darkness. Once there, she no doubt began hammering on the door and kicking it, all the while still gripping the financier crumbs. When she succumbed to the gas a moment later, they were still there, in her grasp."

"Then it was a coincidence?" asked Madeleine, happy that we had cleared up this talk about her killing Elsie. Not to mention, everyone calling her baked good a cookie.

"I don't believe it was a coincidence," responded Hutton. He hadn't spoken for a while and probably thought it good to remind everyone he was still here and on the case. "Whoever mapped out this murder knew about Nancy and Sluggo's plans for their 'prank.' Arnold Bernard wished to augment that crime, transforming a simple, cruel stratagem into a simple, cruel murder. In doing so, he could also point the finger back at the crime's originator, leaving him and his accomplice out of it completely. It was rather efficient, really."

Cesar agreed that he hadn't seen a more efficient, augmented murder in months, maybe not ever. What did Vivian think? Vivian supposed it was well done, in its way, but the killer took a huge risk believing everything would fall into place. No pun intended.

Murderers are always audacious, Hutton pointed out. That's how they're caught. "And the crime was not as risky as you might believe. As Fleet said, the killer did not even have to be present."

Ditters called foul again. He had said the part about the killer not being present. Why didn't anyone ever give him any credit?

Hutton went on, unconcerned, "If anything went awry, the prank would take precedence. Even the feasibility of employing the backup generator as a murder weapon could be tested ahead of time."

"Is that why the lights went out?" asked Betty.

Hutton was certain of it. "The killer killed the lights for two reasons. One, to give him or herself time to turn on the generator. Two, to see if anyone saw him or her doing so. If at any time he or she was noticed, he or she could explain his or her behavior perfectly. The murder was an ambitious undertaking, but it either came off perfectly or failed without notice."

Vivian supposed that you could say that. She withdrew her criticism in the face of so many dazzling personal and possessive pronouns.

"It would appear that Arnold Bernard chose his accomplice well," said Fleet, taking back the detective's baton. "Unmasking him should prove no easy task."

"You know," said Madeleine, "there are more women here than men. You might as well say she. It's more likely a woman."

Fleet acknowledged this with another bow. I frowned at him. What was with all the bowing all of a sudden? People were going to start believing he really was a Romanian count.

"Speaking of our female contingent," he proceeded, "has anyone seen Ms. Norris lately?"

Evelynn went rigid. "I forgot all about her! You don't think the killer—oh man!"

"Perhaps we should spread out and find her," Hutton suggested, not quite snatching back the detective's baton, but certainly pawing at it in the other's grasp.

We all agreed to fan out. Hopefully, for Zoe's sake, we would have better luck with what we discovered than we did the last time.

Happily, we located the waitress safe and sound and completely un-monoxide-smoked.

I was the one who found her. She was sitting on the floor in Ditters' drawing room upstairs, her white-rim specs up on her bun and her face pressed down on her knees. She looked a wee little lass, hunched over like that. Not Nancy Mortimer wee, but wee.

She peered up when I entered, but soon went back into the fetal position.

I told her everyone had been looking for her.

"Why would anyone look for me?" she asked her ankles. It was a forlorn and pathetic comment to make. No wonder her extremities refused to respond.

"They've been worried about you," I insisted. I know a little about psychology and knew that it's always good to tell the batty individual that they're appreciated. It's a much better option than giving into your baser instincts and kicking the person in the keister.

"Were they really," she said. "I doubt that."

"Well, they were," I argued. "Everyone was very, very worried." Not enough to notice she had been gone for twenty minutes, but still worried.

I turned to see Enescu Fleet standing in the doorway. "You found her, Johnny. Good."

Yes, I had found her. *Good* was a relative term.

He knelt down beside her and employed a tactic I never would have considered. Then again, he had raised a daughter, so he should have a few tactics up his sleeve. "I don't think anyone realizes why you were so upset," he remarked.

"I'm sure they all realized," she said. "They've known all along, haven't they?"

Fleet disagreed with her. "You'd be surprised how little anyone notices when it doesn't apply to themselves. Take young Hathaway here. Why do you think Zoe was so upset, Johnny?"

"Not a clue."

"And there you have it. If it isn't about Johnny, then Johnny couldn't care less."

I wasn't sure how much I loved this approach, fueled as it was by a lot of Johnny bashing. But if it breathed some life into those scrawny limbs of hers, I was all for it. We had a murder to solve and the less time spent coddling alienated waitresses, the better.

She raised her face from her legs.

"You care very deeply for your employer, don't you?" he asked her.

"There's nothing I wouldn't do for him. Nothing!"

I had to interrupt here: "We're still talking about Ditters, right?"

She stared at me wide-eyed. "Of course we are."

"Right. Just checking."

"Come," said Fleet, offering her his hand. "We'll join the others."

She took it willingly, no doubt wishing her own father had been so kind and sympathetic. As she passed by, I whispered to Fleet, "She's in love with Ditters?"

"So it would appear."

I couldn't understand it. Another notch on my little friend's belt. It couldn't be his aftershave. From the thickness of his beard, he hadn't used any in years. Perhaps he played a musical instrument I wasn't aware of. He'd mentioned the kazoo. That had to be it.

"How long have you known?" I asked.

"For some time. Her defense of Ditters' removal of Elsie's body was very telling, but there were clues before then. The way she looks at him, hangs on his every word. Then there is the speech pattern."

"What speech pattern?"

"You haven't picked up on the nuances that have crept into her speech? She has spent so many close hours around this man, drinking in everything he says, that she has incorporated little British figures of speech into her own vernacular."

I hadn't noticed. But I had been incorporating Britishisms into my speech for decades.

"I thought at first that she had lived abroad, or that she had lied about her citizenship. But it's simply Ditters. He's become her obsession."

She wasn't the first to have one. "What do you think she meant by *do anything for him*?"

"What indeed," said Fleet, and strolled past me to where the waitress was waiting for us in the hallway.

He paused at the top of the steps. A door was ajar on our left. "That wasn't open before, was it?"

Zoe squeaked at the oversight and flung herself on the knob, pulling it shut. "Bollocks, I thought I closed that!" Okay, there I saw the speech pattern.

Fleet watched her with growing interest. "What's in there, if you don't mind my asking?"

"It's Mr. Dittersdorf's room. His special room."

"I thought the Dittersdorf bedroom was down the hall?"

Fleet's sense of direction, even in a series of rooms he couldn't possibly have seen before this evening, was as stunning as ever.

The mention of her dream man's bedroom made Zoe go weak in the knees for a moment.

"No, it's not his bedroom. But it's—it's special. He doesn't like anyone going in there."

Come to think of it, I did recall him skittling past the door during our prolonged tour earlier. Everywhere else he showed off in endless detail, but that door—his very special door—he just skittled past. I'm pretty sure that's a word. *Skittle.* Doesn't sound right.

"So what's in there?" I asked.

"You can't go in!" she uttered. That wasn't what I had asked, but now that she had laid it out there, I wanted to go in. I had to go in. You know how it is.

Fleet and I took a step closer. Zoe stood strong.

Before her mettle could be put to the test, Ate came bounding up the steps below us. "You better drop everything and come here. Oh hi, Zoe."

"I told you nobody cared if I was okay," sighed the waitress.

I was beginning to agree with her.

We followed Ate back down the steps and into the dining room. "There," she said. We followed her finger to an envelope, propped up on the middle table.

It was an expensive grade of stationery from the looks of it, the lettering on it practically calligraphic. (Pretty sure that's a word.) It read, "Enescu Fleet." A true Romanian count could hardly have received a correspondence more lavish.

He picked it up. "No one else has read it?"

I noticed the entire staff and guest list were gathered in the back of the room.

Their appointed spokesmen, Ditters, said, "It wasn't addressed to us, was it?"

Fleet agreed that it wasn't. He tore it open. "Interesting."

I asked him what it said.

"It's from our old friend Arnold Bernard."

That wasn't what I asked him. Why didn't anyone listen? "Yes, but what does it say?"

"It says that it took us long enough, mostly myself, to figure out who the true host of the evening was."

"Is that all?"

"No. It says that we have"—he consulted his watch—"forty-eight minutes to solve the riddles from dinner."

"What, the plate puzzles?"

"Yes."

I sneered. "Oh, we do, do we?"

"We do. He says that someone went to a lot of trouble to provide these and it would be rude not to give them a go. He never thought of the extraordinary Enescu Fleet as rude. His word—extraordinary—not mine."

"And if we don't give them a go?" I asked.

"We die," said the extraordinary Fleet, handing me the letter.

17 — Off Menu

My dearest EF, you marvelous and sedate old relic,

How nice it is to match wits with you again. I must confess, though, I thought you would arrive at your conclusions a little quicker. Age is a cruel mistress, is she not? No matter. Your Mental Acuity has withered on the vine long enough. Now that you have identified your true host, I will dispense with the inane formalities of that office—the drudges DD and wife can attend to that—and present you with your first challenge. Someone went to a lot of trouble to arrange a parlor game for you tonight, and this has been rigorously ignored. I've never thought of the Extraordinary Fleet as rude, and certainly not rigorously rude. You shall discover the first riddle in the last place a man of your magnificent superego would think to look (or was asked to look).

Enjoy, and please note, you have until the top of the hour to unlock the final solution. Fail, and the evening shall come to a close with a bang. (You may recall how I brought certain aquatic festivities to a conclusion before. I still had some of that PE leftover.) Have a blast, and all that sort of thing. And, please, don't walk out on your host. I've already taken certain precautions to insure that you don't consider such an action (and have put in place certain rewards if you stay put). Until later (one can only hope).

Yours, though separated by great distance and iron bars,
AB

I finished reading the message a second time and peered up to discover the whole of the *Cornichon*'s guests and staff huddled around me, trying to get a look at its contents. I could barely move, to say nothing of figuring out what the hell the psycho Bernard was blathering about. Also, Pixie's and Phillip's claws were digging into my ankles, and someone smelled like radish.

Adwick spoke first. "Kind of homosexual, isn't it?"

It's interesting what a person's mind fixates on. A certain type of person's mind anyway.

"Do you think it is?" asked Betty. She seemed surprised to hear him say that.

"I do. Very homosexual. Practically perverted. All those *dearest* and *things withering on vines* and *yours fruitily* and so forth. Bleck!"

"People's obsessions are often seen as perverse," sighed Zoe Norris. She sighed everything now.

Dom Jacobs agreed with her assessment. "The man is clearly obsessed with you," he told Fleet. Fleet nodded and said he had picked up on that himself.

"So am I DD?" wondered Ditters Dittersdorf.

I answered in the affirmative. Arnold was playing on Fleet's own nickname. Enescu Fleet's oldest friends—and occasionally his newest enemies—called him "Ef," spoken in one syllable, like the letter *F*. I guess that would make Arnold Bernard's initials pronounced *Ab*, like the stomach muscle, and Ditters' initials—well, how would you pronounce the letters DD together? *Dee-dee? De-de?*

"So he's calling us drudges?" asked 2-D.

I stared at him. That was what he took from it? Name-calling?

"How about the murder threat?" I said.

"Oh right." He read over the highlights again. "Where exactly is that? Damn thing's so frigging cryptic. I don't think I like this half-eagle, half-lion man at all."

Eagle and bear, I corrected. Eagle and lion was a griffin.

Ditters said he didn't like griffins either—to hell with all these endangered species.

"The murder threat is contained in the other abbreviation," Fleet explained.

"PE?" asked Vivian. She didn't get it. "If EF is Enescu Fleet, and AB is Arnold Bernard, who is PE?"

"I believe Pe is a thing not a person," suggested Dom Jacobs—or "DJ" as Arnold Bernard might call him.

"*What* the hell is PE, then?" asked Vivian.

Dom looked at her with his most snooty scowl. "I believe Pe is the symbol for lead."

"You mean the metal?"

He inclined his head.

"I think you're thinking of Pb," Ate inserted. "Pb for lead."

Hutton endorsed this. It was definitely Pb, short for its Latin name, *peanut-butter-um* or some such thing.

"My mistake," nodded the not-so-scientifically-inclined Dom—and apparently also not economically or legally inclined. The man remained a snooty enigma.

"You bet it was your mistake," snorted Vivian. "Mistakes like that could get us killed. We go running around like dingbats searching for a bunch of lead, and this Arnold Bernard person picks us off one by one." She turned to the crowd. "So what is PE, people?"

"PE stands for plastic explosive," answered Fleet. It was not the official abbreviation.

"Oh. I thought they called that C-4."

"They call it C-4 when it is C-4. There are different varieties. The first time Mr. Bernard and I met, he used a portion of it to sink a yacht."

"And now?" Madeleine Abrams asked.

Now, it would appear, he intended to use a portion to sink a restaurant.

Everyone stepped slowly away from the table. They kept still and silent. No sudden movements. I wagged my head at them. It's not like the C-4 (or whatever it was) was in a casserole dish or something. Some people just don't think.

"You mean—" blustered Sven violently, and if the explosive had been in the crockery, we would have all been dead right then. "You mean, he intends to explode the party?"

Well blurted, Sluggo, I thought. Well blurted.

"I'm getting the hell out of here!" exclaimed Vivian, and she had the spirit of the people behind her. Already I could feel another collective hiking fad mounting. The participants were limbering up.

Fleet held them in place with an emphatic command. He also brought his fist down on the table, Hutton style, spilling some mixed olives in the process.

I cringed. I know I said the C-4 wasn't in the casserole dishes, but I wished he wouldn't smack things about like that. I mean, it could have been in the olive dish. You don't know.

"You read the message," he said. "Arnold has taken steps to insure we remain here."

Evelynn's eyes went wide. "You mean this person, his accomplice, would blow up the bistro with themself inside? It's insane! Completely insane."

Nancy laid a hand on her arm. *Themself* was not a word, she pointed out. Even facing death, one could always speak properly.

"I highly doubt this individual would kill themselves, would they?" said/asked Adwick. It had started as a statement and ended as a question.

"The obsessed mind is a dangerous thing," offered Dom Jacobs. "The person could have a death wish. Or they could have made provisions to protect themselves from the explosive."

It was Hutton's turn to snort. "So we should be looking for an obsessively minded individual in fire-resistant underwear?"

Dom didn't appreciate the levity. "Of course, the exits could simply be wired to blow."

Hutton frowned suspiciously. "You seem to know a lot about what it could be."

Dom didn't appreciate the implication. And he didn't agree. "A deranged personality is difficult to gauge," he replied simply.

"And I would prefer not to try," concluded Fleet.

"So you think the exits are wired?" asked Vivian.

"No. Something far more insidious." He peered down at the paper again. "Did anyone happen to notice the postscript on the back of this page?"

We had not. Hadn't AB said enough without any damn PS's?

"I'll read it to you. It's very short. It says, *Look down, Socrates.*" Fleet—or Socrates, if you prefer—lowered his eyes toward the table. "I'm fairly certain that we have all been poisoned, ladies and gentlemen."

The room took it hard. "I knew I shouldn't have eaten that nasty pâté!" said Vivian. "It was in the pickles," gasped Nancy—"I ate a ton of them in the kitchen!" (I guess she couldn't eat *anything* she wanted, after all.) "Someone get a stomach pump!" demanded Adwick.

Fleet told them they had misunderstood him (again).

"We've not been poisoned?" asked Cesar hopefully.

"No, I'm fairly sure we have. But not with food. Someone help me move this table, please."

Three of us helped, revealing a large grate in the hardwood floor. Think of the one Ms. Monroe famously stepped on in film, though nowhere near as sexy.

"What the hell is that?" I asked Ditters.

"It's a grate, Hath."

"I can see that. Why so large?"

He didn't know. The previous owner liked air, he guessed.

Unfortunately, it was not air we had been getting. Fleet knelt down and pried it open.

He came up again holding a canister, about the size of a small fire extinguisher.

He read the label to us: "*Caution, contents—and participants—under pressure. May—and, indeed, will—cause poisonous, odorless vapor. Should you find yourself exposed to this, consult your nearest puzzle-solving private detective immediately. Operate no heavy machinery and seek an antidote within two hours. Antidote sold separately. Not harmful to dogs.*"

He set the canister down on the table. At least the harmless-to-dogs feature was a relief. "This is how Arnold insures our cooperation. No doubt the antidote—the reward he mentioned in his letter—will present itself after we solve all the riddles."

"What is it?" asked Zoe, hyperventilating. "What did we breathe?"

"It's difficult to say. It would have to be a slow-acting but no less deadly compound. Whatever it is, it would take far too long for even an expert to identify it exactly—that is, assuming we could get somewhere in time to consult such a medico."

"But there is a cure?" asked Adwick.

"There must be a cure!" yelled Sven. "We can't allow ourselves to be slow smoked." Finally, he could appreciate how Elsie Farmer had felt.

"I believe the antidote is here, yes," said Fleet. He had already stated as much.

"Then we should tear this joint up looking for it," suggested Nancy, very un-PR-like.

"Hey!" said Ditters. They'd just gotten this place nice.

Fleet supported that view. "I believe our time would be better spent focusing our attention on the task at hand. The antidote could literally be anywhere, disguised as anything."

"Just like Arnold's accomplice," I remarked.

Fleet said indeed. "As galling as it is, we have to play Arnold's game."

Ate stepped up on his left, Hutton on his right. "We've already wasted five minutes," she commented. She spoke calmly and collectedly. I've said it before, and I'll say it again, he had raised a good one there. "Where should we start? He said something about your ego?"

"Not my ego—my superego."

"I've always wondered about superegos," babbled Betty. She spoke haphazardly, the way a person does after spending two hours sucking on a pound of poisonous vapor. "Is it like an ego, only *super*?"

No one bothered to answer (except for Dom, who said no).

I thought it was an interesting question. If a superego were simply an ego with the strength of ten egos, Enescu Fleet would be the man to have one, alright.

"When we first sat down," Fleet continued, speaking to Betty, "you excluded your father and myself from the game. As a result, I never looked under my plate." He went to it now and pulled up the rim, smiling. He showed us a page stuck underneath. "This wasn't here before."

"Are you certain?" Hutton asked.

"No." Fleet wasn't certain of anything just now.

> *There once was an old man named Enescu* [it went]. *He went to sea, like old men do, but it was no meager fish he would engage. He fought a mighty blaze upon the waves, emerging, as always, with nary a scratch upon his skin. But shouldn't some portion of him be lost? Do the rigors of battle count for nothing? No, he remains intact. What the world has sliced away, the old man grows back. But is he a man at all? Or just really old?*

After reading that, I didn't feel so bad about my personalized riddle. Mine might have been insulting, but Fleet's was more personal. And anti-geezer.

It also wasn't much of a mystery puzzle. At least mine had a murder in it—my murder.

"Are we supposed to determine a killer from this?" I asked.

"There is no killer," Hutton said. "Only the old man and the sea."

"It seems almost mythological," Cesar mused. "Maybe we should look there."

"Perhaps the answer rests with Hemingway," said Ate.

"I knew there was someone you reminded me of," added Vivian, peering at Fleet. Her stare was censorious and desperate, though still strangely fascinated.

"Do you think of him as Hemingwayesque?" wondered Cesar. "I would have thought more Admiral Byrd or one of those old-timey naval guys."

"You're only saying that because he's called Fleet. And has a naval-looking beard."

"I don't think Admiral Byrd had a beard."

"Well, neither did Hemingway."

"I think he did sometimes. Or maybe I'm thinking of Victor Hugo or someone."

"The text," said Fleet, calling their attention back to our mortal struggle with a madman, "is a reference to my first interaction with Arnold Bernard. I had said we first met a month ago, at which time he sank a yacht. That wasn't strictly true. We were both passengers on a ship many years before then."

"And what did he do that time?" asked Vivian.

"He sank it."

She said ah. Good consistency there.

"The flames refer to the explosion he caused, and which I survived. But they might be making a reference to something else. Something ancient. A creature, not a man, who can emerge from fire without harm."

"I know this one," said Zoe. "It's a bird. No, not the admiral kind. A pheasant. The pheasant that rises up from the fire unharmed. That must be it."

Vivian wasn't so sure it was. She had eaten many a roasted pheasant in her day, and not a single one of them had risen up from her plate.

"Grows back portions of himself," Hutton muttered, "portions sliced away."

Suddenly, both he and Fleet turned to a painting on the back wall. I was already acquainted with it. I had faced it throughout most of the dinner party and was secretly glad for the murder, as it gave me an opportunity to get up and look at something else for a change.

It was a hideous painting for a dining room, depicting a hapless-looking lizard getting slow roasted over flames. If that didn't put you off your corn beef quiche sprinkled with fennel pollen, I don't know what would.

Hutton sprang to the portrait, with the old man only a length behind him.

"The salamander," they said as one.

While Hutton pried the pic off the wall, Fleet explained, "As many of you may know, the salamander was once believed to be resistant to fire. The actual creature, meanwhile, has the ability to regenerate lost limbs. I am the salamander, therefore, both modern and ancient. Or I am, according to Arnold Bernard anyway."

Turning the painting over on a table, Hutton was immediately rewarded in his efforts. A small scrap of paper was tacked to the back of the canvas.

The reward itself left much to be desired. "*Wrong one*," he read. "That's all it says."

Someone gasped. I thought it was simply an audience member out of sync, but it wasn't. Madeleine had an idea. "The salamander," she exclaimed, "it is also a grill. A broiler!"

Chef Sven swore under his breath. Shown up by a mere baker. "I knew that!" he protested, and off we went again—to the salamander!

On the way to the kitchen, I considered this salamander's backstory and frowned. In ancient folklore, the salamander was believed to emerge from fire unscathed. Fine. But why would a broiler be a salamander? The ancient bugger didn't create the fire; it resisted it. A kitchen-themed salamander should have been an oven mitt or something. That would have made more sense.

I didn't find it a very prepossessing device when we arrived. It was large and boxy with a stainless steel body and a long, narrow maw of (sometimes) flame. It wasn't flamed up now. Even still, I wasn't crazy about poking around inside it. In this place, where the most basic backup generator could kill you, I would just as soon stand clear of a device designed for sizzling things to a crisp.

Ironically, as I learned from Chef Sven while we jogged, most modern salamanders had adjustable tops. According to him, you raised this top up and placed your food inside, and Bob was your uncle (or, in Sven's case, Edvard or Gustav or someone). It would have made examining its interior an easy task.

Sadly, the salamander Ditters had provided his staff must have been excavated from the *Titanic*. It looked a hundred years old, if a day. It had no adjustable top, and the look on its stainless steel mug more or less dared you to stick a hand inside and see what happened.

Fleet didn't hesitate to do so (when did he ever?). We were running out of time—and besides, if the metallic beast did burn off a limb, he could always just grow it back again.

He reached inside it, but his brawny guns had too much girth around them. Show-off. The search began for a volunteer thinner-of-limb.

I smiled wryly. This was where my slender physique and refusal to work out landed me in the bouillon. It was strengthist, that's what it was.

I lucked out. We needed a build even more svelte than mine. Several eyes fell on Lesley. "What?" she said. "I'm not reaching in there." She looked to Zoe, who looked to Evelynn.

"I'm not doing it," said the hostess.

"I'll do it," sighed Ate. I didn't object to her sighing. She was a gamer, like her dad.

"Wait," he said.

"It's okay. We don't have any time to waste. Look at Zoe. She's already showing the effects of the poison."

Ate was right. Zoe wasn't looking too good. The waitress had gone a sickly pale, and her pasty brow was covered in sweat. Even her bun drooped listlessly.

"I don't feel so well either," said Nancy Mortimer. Her complexion also looked gray, but her brow wasn't all that sweaty. Maybe because it was so small. Less pores.

Adwick came to her assistance. "Here, sit down," he said, offering her a stool. Who knew that he could be so gallant? "Enough of this shillyshallying," he rasped, and went to jam his arm in the monster's mouth.

This also wouldn't do the job. Too stubby.

Fleet pulled him back. "I'm being stupid. There can't be anything inside the salamander."

Adwick wondered why not. He glared back at the thing. He was "this close" to getting the bastard on the ropes.

Fleet thanked him for his help but insisted we try another way. "The killer couldn't risk placing the next clue inside the salamander; it might have gotten burned up. It must be somewhere else."

He sidled up to the device. He looked like a man about to wrestle an alligator. Putting those brawny limbs to good use, he dragged the appliance out from the wall.

"There!" said Adwick. "Something fell to the floor. A paper."

I picked it up. It was probably just the instruction booklet—and in Chinese.

We lucked out again. It wasn't the manual, and it was in English. "It says, *All hail, the culinary emperor.*"

A short pause, and we had it. "Cesar's plate!" said the assembly. Ho, for the dining room!

Once there (again), the culinary emperor expressed some serious doubt. He couldn't figure out an ounce of his puzzle at dinner. We were never going to make it.

Pleasantly encouraged by this pep talk, Fleet presented us with our new challenge.

> *Far outside the limelight, the forgotten chef Cesar stands over a bubbling broth, a freshly made dagger Hole in his chest. He does not Fret, for the death of his fame has already preceded his Body's. With a mighty fist he throws in the Head of a fish and the Neck of a goose, garnishing it all with a dash of Nutmeg. What a strange Stock this is. The strong and silent chef says nothing about his killer. But perhaps he has demonstrated an even finer method for preventing other deaths.*

Okay, these riddles were just getting creepy and weird now. Not that the whole process wasn't creepy and weird to begin with.

Ate asked for the page. She appeared unfazed by its creepiness. "I think I got this. Hole, fret, head, stock, neck—"

"Haggis," I guessed.

"Nut, body—they're all musical terms. They relate to a guitar, I bet. Does that mean anything to anyone?"

It didn't mean anything on my end. Anyone else?

Hutton stepped up. "It's not talking about a guitar. It's talking about a mandolin."

"Alright, a mandolin, then." He always had to mince words with her. "Got any lutes or mandolins, Ditters?"

Ditters didn't think he did. Did a kazoo help?

"A mandolin isn't only musical," said Hutton. "It's also a device for slicing. *A finer method.* You slice veg fine with a mandolin."

We hurried back to the kitchen. I guess I was wrong. I *was* getting a workout. I always seem to get in the best shape when I'm about to be murdered.

We found the infamous mandolin, and Hutton pulled out another morsel from it. "Ouch! Damn blade." He read to us, sucking on his knuckle. "*Long live the flourishing Birch tree.*"

"I'm it!" shouted Vivian. Back to the dining room we went. It was 8:50.

I led the way this time. These dinner-party sprints really got the blood flowing—hopefully not literally. It occurred to me that we might have saved a lot of time, and effort, bringing the plates with us to the kitchen.

I was ahead in the last lap, but got tripped up (literally) by Pixie and Phillip. They were obviously in Arnold Bernard's pay. The rest of the gang had already piled back in through the doorway when I limped into the room.

There was something wrong. "What now?" I asked.

They moved back from the table and showed the place setting across from Vivian's chair. Her plate had disappeared.

18 — Key Ingredient

I knew we should have carried our plates around with us. All that exercise, running back and forth—it turned out to be no good to our health at all.

I was appalled by this Arnold Bernard's behavior. I realized he had tried to kill me before—and that still stung—but this took the prized gourd. It's one thing to poison your guests and make them run about like idiots for your demented pleasure, but to spike our guns like this? It wasn't gentlemanly. Arnold Bernard, and whoever he had helping him, was a dickhead.

"So that's just it," said Vivian. "We're going to die."

Cesar Bloom guessed so. He was highly critical of this denouement.

"Can't you remember what it said?" Ate asked her. "You said you had solved it?"

"Did I?"

"You did. Over dinner. Now try to remember."

Vivian tried. It wasn't going to be easy. Usually she had "people" for remembering things. "Uh, it had something to do with a fish market, I think. Lobsters were part of it, I'm pretty sure. There might have been a flounder mentioned at one point."

"We're going to die," said Lesley.

That seemed to be the consensus.

Zoe and Nancy, the worst off among us, sat over to the side, looking pale and sickly. Adwick seemed especially concerned with the latter. Her mousy companion might have been a bespectacled mannequin in need of a good manufacturer's overhaul for all he cared.

I don't like to brag, but I didn't feel the effects of the poison at all. I didn't think this was my rugged constitution. I didn't have a rugged constitution (although, I had been known to take a punch pretty well). Maybe it was good that the "game" had kept me distracted throughout this. I was trying not to think about it.

"I believe this might be a blessing in disguise," Enescu Fleet was saying.

Someone in the audience, not sure who, said *Oh yeah?* Someone else, I think it was Zoe, grumbled *You suck.*

He ignored these hecklers. The plate had disappeared for an excellent reason, he argued. Whoever was working for Arnold Bernard was trying to help us.

The audience didn't see eye to eye with him on this. The *oh-yeah* speaker said *Are they really?* while Zoe—I was certain it was her this time—muttered *Get off the stage.*

Fleet stood firm. "We're running out of time. We would never have gotten through all of Arnold's challenges before the explosive went off. His accomplice must have anticipated that. They are showing us a better way. We need to cheat."

"Arnold Bernard is the only cheater here," I said, and I wanted his accomplice to hear it.

"Thank you, Johnny. There are four puzzle plates remaining. Whose plate were we meant to solve last? That is the one we must focus on."

We all considered our plates. There wasn't a whole lot of enthusiasm.

I had a sudden inspiration. I still thought Arnold a scoundrel and a slime and an unworthy candidate for Fleet's chief nemesis—not to mention a dickhead—but much of this indignation was wiped away in one giddy realization. "It's got to be mine. I'm the key."

Hutton, Ate and Lesley reacted to my statement with some skepticism. Everyone always thinks their puzzle plate is the key. "Look," I said, showing them the goods, "it talks about a key. Mine has to be the final challenge, the challenge that must be *unlocked.*"

Hope began to dawn. Fleet said excellent. Hutton said sterling work. Zoe said something about my face that she didn't care for. Fleet took charge again.

"We'll decipher the puzzle. While we do, someone should search for the explosive."

"What about the antidote?" Adwick asked. He peered back at Nancy.

"We find one and we find the other," said Fleet.

Ate and Betty took this in hand. Betty was the obvious choice, since she knew the layout of her restaurant. Ate was the obvious choice to accompany her since she knew what to look for—and had a brain. (Sorry, Betty.)

While we were on the subject, I was a little disappointed that Pixie and Phillip hadn't sniffed out the plastique, but apparently dogs need specialized training for that.

Everyone else gathered around the puzzle. I stepped back and gave them room. I had gotten the gist of it before.

> *Poor Johnny lies dead in the middle of the farmer's market, his foolish head split asunder with a meat cleaver. In his hand sits another foolish head, made of romaine lettuce. Not a very discerning selection, Johnny, we must say! But, alas, could our intrepid victim have an agenda? Could this ingenuous/ingenious device unlock the identity of a killer? Johnny lies dead. But where does the key lie?*

"It does talk about a key," said Vivian.

"But what does it mean?" asked Cesar.

"It must have something to do with the romaine. Romaine, romaine—Roman!" She turned on her secret lover. "It's you, *Emperor* Cesar!"

Cesar looked pretty appalled himself now. "Why would it be me? Do you really think I'm a killer with a death wish?"

"I don't know what to think. You could be a death-wishing killer. How should I know?"

"Well, I'm not," he replied. "If you wanna know the truth, I don't even like the idea of eating animals anymore. There's too much killing in our business. I was this close to becoming a vegetarian last year." He held up a tattooed hand and showed us a unit of measure with his thick, heavily ringed fingers. It was pretty close.

This, more than anything else, shocked and disturbed Vivian. "Vegetarian? You mean no pork, no duck—"

"Especially no duck," said Cesar, who wanted to know why everyone had it in for these fine feathered friends. Suddenly everyone is foie gras crazed, he said, and cooking things in duck fat all over the place. He and his soon-to-be ex-wife had ducks at their lake cabin, and he had always found them charming and pleasant critters. In fact, he liked them a lot better than his soon-to-be ex. "I've cut out veal from my bistro's menu."

Vivian turned away in anguish. "I don't know who you are anymore!"

Cesar heaved a burly sigh. He addressed himself to Fleet. "You first met this Bernard on a shipboard poker game, right? Have you considered the possibility that he is bluffing?"

Fleet said he had considered it, yes.

"Do you think he's bluffing?" asked Madeleine.

"No."

The analysis and discussion continued. No one had any ideas. Not constructive ideas.

Instinctively, I looked to Hutton, who usually did pretty well at these things, but he only shook his head. "I'm done," he sighed (not as burly a sigh as Cesar's, but pretty well charged). He had nothing to offer us.

Nancy Mortimer did. In a far-off, nearly inaudible voice, she mumbled, "You're not *done*, you're *finished*."

Hutton asked her to repeat that. He glared as he said it.

She looked up. Her sweat-covered brow was determined, her expression bare. "A well-cooked Cornish hen is *done*. A person completing a task is *finished*."

We were minutes away from dying at the hands of a lunatic, her more than anyone, and she was babbling about verb usage.

I looked into her face, into that insipid, blank expression, and finally understood. Her stupid little comments, her insistence on appearing superior—it was a defense mechanism. This was how she coped. The poor woman was scared stiff. I pitied her. (I also scorned her, but I was doing my best.)

Hutton wasn't feeling as generous. "First of all," he said, "I'm not *done* or *finished* with Arnold's task. Arnold's task has finished me. And secondly, we don't need lectures from the likes of you, thank you very much. We're the ones who gave you your language—I think I can handle speaking it without assistance. And just so you know," he went on, blowing off more steam, "language is organic. It moves with the times. People used to pronounce the 'k' at the start of words. Now they don't. That means some brave soul had to step up to the *Royal Panel of Language* and say, 'Begging ye pardon, ye Royal Highnesses, but the villagers and I have been discussing it, and we no longer wish to call the most gracious Sir Goofus a *ka-night.*' 'Not call him a ka-night?' the panel gapes. 'What is this that ye serfs are saying?' 'We just think it ridiculous,' the brave soul speaketh on. 'From now on, he and those like him shall be called a *knight*, pronounced *night*. And the same goes for knife. It's not a *ka-nife*, your lordships—it's a *nife*.' 'Not a ka-nife?' asks the panel. 'Odds bodkins, I guess you scurvy *ka-naves ka-now* best.' And that morning," declared Hutton, "language began to develop for the better."

It was a stirring speech. He did the voices and everything. My favorite was the third royal panel member.

Nancy blinked at him throughout and said nothing. She just continued to gaze blankly. I could almost hear an oompah band playing mindlessly behind her glossy stare.

"There are exceptions to this progressiveness, aren't there?" I asked him, glancing at my watch. We were going to die in about five minutes. "Using *literally* to mean *figuratively*, for example?"

"Of course there are exceptions," Hutton replied. "People can't descend into total chaos. *Literally* is *literally*, not *figuratively*. A guy I know burned his 'updated' dictionary over that distinction—which was difficult to do, given that the dictionary was on a laptop at the time."

"Wasn't that guy you?" I asked.

Hutton nodded. It was him, and proud of it. The laptop wasn't his anyway. "And don't get me started on using *infer* to mean *imply*," he said.

No one got him started.

Fleet was gazing at the page. He still had our well-being in his sights. "I think we should be focused on the *lettuce* in the clue."

"Money!" said Vivian, snapping out of it. "That's a use for lettuce. *Get me ma lettuce.*"

Fleet shook his head.

"It's a pun," offered Zoe. " 'Let us' in?"

Fleet frowned.

"In French," said Madeleine, "lettuce is *la laitue.*"

Fleet patted her cheek.

Cesar bounded up from a chair. The closet vegetarian had had a brainwave. He grabbed the sheet from Fleet and said, "I got it. I think I got it. Follow me to the kitchen!"

The kitchen. How original. We hadn't been *there* before!

While we went, Betty and Ate searched. They searched the basement, the dining rooms, the kitchen—we must have just missed running into them—the bathroom, and ended up in the reception room at the front of the house: where it had all started.

Betty shivered as she searched. "Brr! It's cold in here, isn't it? Now, look at this! Who turned off the fire?" She might be fatally poisoned and about to get exploded, but a good proprietor could still concern herself with creature comforts.

Ate had paused to gaze behind a curtain in the corner. I'm not sure why. Apparently, she was leaving no stone, or drape, unturned. She twirled around. "Freeze!" she yelped.

Betty nodded. "Yes, it's downright frigid in here. Give me just a second."

Ate wouldn't give her half that. She rushed to Betty's side and virtually threw herself between the restaurateur and the fireplace. "You didn't turn off the fire?"

Betty was startled. "No. No, of course not. But somebody did. If you would just—"

Ate wouldn't. Bodychecking her out of the way, she shined her phone light into the fireplace grate. "Now, what do we have here?" she asked the mantel.

Betty drifted forward. "I don't know, dear. What do we?"

In the kitchen, Cesar Bloom was a celebrity chef on a mission. Give him a few more men, and a couple dozen elephants, and he could have crossed the Alps in a cinch. Or at least met Hannibal halfway.

He went straight for the refrigerator. He took out a carton of milk. It seemed like a weird time for a refreshing snack, but with three minutes left before our evening ended with a bang and/or we succumbed to a mystery poison, why not indulge? He had never mentioned anything about becoming a vegan.

"It's here," he said. "I know it's here."

"In the milk?" Adwick asked, and I had to agree. Did Cesar think the antidote was vitamin D?

Fleet, however, commended him. "Well done. I knew the clue was in the lettuce. I should have figured it out right away. *Milk.* That's what *lettuce* means."

"Milk?" repeated Evelynn, and I had to agree with her even more than I had agreed with Adwick. I knew English could be pretty goofy, but I never figured it was *that* goofy.

"I should have realized it after Maddy translated *la laitue* for lettuce," said Fleet. "In both languages, the word comes from the same word as lactose. And lactate."

Okay, okay, I thought. We could still keep it clean. I got enough of that talk from Lesley. "So the answer's in the milk, then. Show us, Cesar."

Cesar showed us. He shook the container. Feeling this wouldn't get the job done, he opened it and poured it out on the counter, then the floor, and eventually his shoes.

"I'm not cleaning that up," said Zoe, leaning on Lesley for support.

Nonplussed, Cesar went for the soy milk. Then the almond. And finally the buttermilk.

"There's nothing here," he said. He was incorrect. There was lots and lots of milk.

Ate came shooting into the room just then, skated across one of the pools—I think it was the low-fat variety—and plunged into Hutton's arms.

"You better come quick," she said, pirouetting back out of his clasp and down the hall again.

Ditters barreled after her. Pixie and Phillip trailed behind him, Pixie detouring to sniff at the soy puddle and snort at it.

We followed Ditters and the dogs. As usual.

Betty was still standing by the fireplace. She was emitting an odd sort of noise. Kind of a low humming. I could best describe it as "d-d-d-d-d." Perhaps she was trying to pronounce DD.

Her husband came to her side. "What is it, darling? What's wrong?"

"D-d-d-d-d-d."

"Yes, but what's the matter?"

"D-d-d-d-d-d," she added, pointing to the fireplace.

We looked. There, strapped in the grate, was Arnold Bernard's other calling card. A wad of plastic explosive, or PE if you're writing chiding letters to semiretired sleuths—which I wasn't.

"Well, we've found it," said Ate. "You can see there's a box connected; it must have the antidote in it. So what's the key code?" She looked to her father. Not feeling confident with what she saw there, she looked at me. We both looked back at her.

She was right. It was all very straightforward. There was a number pad on the PE. I could see it from where I was standing. This pad needed a code. All perfectly reasonable.

The countdown on the screen was at thirty-nine seconds. Thirty-eight. Thirty-seven.

There was only one problem. "The thing is—" I began.

"You mean you haven't found it?" She stomped her foot. "How could you not have found it?" She had kept up her side of the bargain—what was wrong with us?

"I—think—we—need—to—get—the—hell—out—of—here," said Vivian Birch.

Ate refused to move. "It's strapped around the gas pipe. If it goes off, it's taking everything here with it."

Great, I muttered, more gas. At least it was a new variety.

"Pull it off the pipe, then!" snapped Adwick.

"I would certainly advise that," said Dom Jacobs. It was nice to have his input.

"You can't disconnect it without cutting the wires," Ate told them. "I looked at all this. Besides, the antidote is in the box. Aren't you listening!"

Fleet started moving people back. He had no doubt that his daughter was correct, but we didn't need to stare the thing in the face to prove anything. We could still attempt to survive, even without the antidote. "Everyone down to the basement. Now!"

I didn't see Hutton among the participants. I knew he wouldn't have skipped out, not when something was due to make a hell of a mess, but I did pause to wonder if he had been trampled in one of our many movements to and fro the kitchen.

I spotted him at last. His unflappable features bobbed up in the entranceway above the back of Adwick's head. He was coming in as everyone else tried to go out. Typical Hutton.

Squeezing through finally, he walked briskly past Fleet, Ditters and Lesley. In each arm was a dog, scooped up in the confusion in order to prevent one of those senseless Maltese squishings you're always hearing about. He handed Pixie to Ate, shoved Phillip into my arms, and went to the keypad. With four seconds to go—it wasn't like it was one or two or something—he typed in 6455. The countdown froze, and the box popped open.

"Sorry for the delay, folks," he said. "Phil is a lot heavier than he looks."

"Six-four-five-five?" I managed to ask. I was having a little trouble speaking.

"*M-i-l-k*," he replied, and I said of course. "It's like most keypads. Six for *M*, four for *i*—"

"Yes, yes, I get it."

"Knew it!" said Cesar, disentangling himself from the horde. He pumped his fist. If I had been a network executive, that gesture alone would have been enough to bar the man from all prime-time programming.

We were happy he was happy.

All except Fleet. He was holding a tray of vials. There was a bunch of them, one dose per customer.

Except there wasn't. "There are only fifteen," he said.

Vivian did another quick count. "Balls! There's sixteen of us." Such was Fleet's point.

"Arnold miscounted?" asked Lesley.

Fleet didn't believe so. "He meant for us to choose. Leave one person out."

I could feel my ire rising. Like I had said earlier, the man was a dick.

"Leave me out, then," said Ditters, now playing the magnanimous host.

Cesar Bloom said no, he should be the one. As long as Vivian got hers.

I said they might as well skip me; I never liked mystery drugs anyway.

Madeleine Abrams offered to exclude herself. She had never believed that part about the poison not harming dogs, and without her little buddy, what did it matter?

Ate and Hutton began arguing about which one of them was less important. Hutton, who said he was, insisted that he could do this all day, and no one was going to beat him out at it.

The discussion continued for the next thirty seconds. Eventually, nearly everyone ended up throwing themselves on the exclusionary altar. You could tell who really meant it, and who did it merely for the look of the thing.

Fleet spoke up over all of us. I noticed he hadn't offered himself yet, which surprised me a little. I figured it out soon enough. He had already decided he would be the one to go without the antidote. For men like Fleet, there is no point in discussing or giving anyone a chance to talk themselves into nobility. He simply acted, not acted like he was going to act.

"We can decide all this in due time," he said. "I think we can all agree that Zoe and Nancy need their doses most of all."

He approached the ladies with two shot glasses. "I thought you might enjoy imbibing the drug in a more refined manner." He handed Zoe her shot first, then Nancy. They downed them.

Adwick asked the latter how she felt.

"Okay, I guess. Am I supposed to feel any differently?"

Fleet said the effect varied according to the patient. "Zoe?"

The waitress stood. Almost at once, she looked better. Her skin had returned to its pale rosy state, rather than just pale. Her bun was alive with renewed energy. "I feel great!"

Fleet nodded. "It's amazing what a placebo can do."

She stared at him. "What?"

"You just gulped a shot of pure mountain spring water."

Immediately Nancy stated that she didn't feel so good.

Zoe sat back down and looked paler. "So we're still poisoned?"

"We were never poisoned. Arnold Bernard simply wanted to keep us all here. Keep us playing. Your reactions were purely psychological."

"He's right," said Hutton. He had turned out the box of vials and showed us a paper. "It says, in essence, *only foolin'*."

I examined the sheet with him. "So what was in the vials?"

Dom Jacobs took up one of the units and opened it. He sniffed the top.

"Unless I'm mistaken—" He finished with a long, technical term I couldn't have pronounced in a million years.

"Is that anything like pure mountain spring water?" I asked.

It was not. Had we taken any of the "antidotes," we would have been dead in seconds.

Fleet explained, "Arnold not only wished to see who was the most selfless among us. He wished to reward that person by allowing them, and them alone, to live."

"Well, we fooled him," said Ate.

No one spoke for about a minute. I assume it was a minute. We no longer had a handy countdown screen to keep track.

During the silence, Phillip came over and poked his nose up on the table containing the plastique. *Now* he sniffed it out.

At the end of that minute or minute and a half—call it a hundred seconds—Zoe said, "Hey, has anyone seen Sven?"

We looked among ourselves. No Sven here. Emissaries were sent to the kitchen and the dining room, and they all came up empty.

Sven had skedaddled.

19 — Cook Off

I shook my head. First a perfectly good Arnold Bernard commemorative plate, and now a basically useless Scandinavian cook. Everything was disappearing out from under our noses.

"Looks like he took an extra pair of my mukluks," reported Ditters, "and a spare parka."

"Where could he be headed?" asked Madeleine. "You said it yourself, Nessie: there is nothing out there."

Fleet inclined his head. "Perhaps the chef knows something we don't."

But what? That was the question. Or the implied question, at any rate (maybe even inferred). Perhaps Sven had known something all along. Perhaps a lot of something.

With that in mind, we formed up groups so we could search him out and ask him.

It was always possible, Fleet added, that the man had panicked, due to his involvement with Elsie Farmer's death.

"Either way, he couldn't have gotten far," Hutton suggested.

The foodies rolled their eyes. That's what people always say!

Before we ventured out into the icy tundra, Fleet took a minute to congratulate Cesar on his ingenuity and sangfroid.

"Oh, it was nothing," smirked the conquering hero, "nothing at all."

I may have already mentioned the extraordinary sportsmanship—and sportswomanship—of the celebrity chefs. They knew how to roll with it. Peering over at Cesar Bloom's smiling, egg-shaped face, I was beginning to think that they rolled with it a little too well.

"You saved the day," said Fleet.

"Oh, it was a team effort. That tall guy is the one we really should be thanking."

He was damn right we should thank Hutton. I don't often sing the praises of my lanky friend, but the man deserved it. Cesar might have started us down the path, but it was Hutton who guided everyone across the chasm. (I'm guessing there was a hole in this path, with a footbridge or something strung across it—possibly with a tarp covering some kind of a hole, like on Ditters' balcony. I'll be honest, I didn't really think the metaphor through.)

I took a look at the pad on the explosive, and the keys didn't even have letters on them. The 6455 was all off the top of Hutton's head. Pretty amazing. I can't even match up the letters properly on a phone keypad. 1-800-Yay-Pizza always ends up as 1-800-Yak-Pizza, which isn't nearly as good. I could see why Ate liked him. He was a good boyfriend to have.

In all the hubbub, my thoughts about those two crazy kids had been shifted to the back of the stage, but I had not forgotten about them (the crazy kids or the thoughts). If I was correct and she was with child at Hutton's hand—well, maybe not his hand—Fleet should be glad to have him as the father of his grandchild. (I doubted he would be, but he should.)

Having given credit to Hutton, Cesar now proceeded to give some to Fleet. "You would have arrived at the same conclusion eventually," he said.

Vivian couldn't help inserting a comment of her own:

"If this doesn't catapult us into some prime-time consideration, I don't know a prime-time catapult when I see one."

A mildly quizzical gaze from Fleet prompted Cesar to explain, "Viv and I were talking, and as stressful as this has been, it might actually help us in the long run."

"A little publicity never harmed anyone?"

"Exactly."

Fleet nodded again. "You may be right. It seems like a hard way to go about it, but I suspect you're correct." He paused. "By the way, I meant to ask you—how did you know Arnold Bernard and I had encountered each other during a shipboard poker game?"

The smile dropped from Cesar Bloom's face, and he went a touch green about the gills. He resembled a pistachio more than ever, a split-open one. "You told us."

"I said a yacht. I said nothing about a poker game."

The celeb shifted uncomfortably. "I could have sworn you said something about it." He looked around the room, searching for a figurative life preserver, much like the preservers we had searched for the night of our onboard poker game—a game he should have known nothing about.

He looked my way. I don't know why. I wasn't about to help him.

Or maybe I was. "It must have been Hathaway's book."

"Oh, you've read Johnny's output?"

"Just the newest one. I haven't finished it. Too bad, since you've already revealed that Bernard was the killer." With that explained, he and Vivian quickly exited.

Lesley and I were alone with Fleet and Madeleine now. It was almost like a double date. A double date with a little murder, poisoning and near pyrotechnics thrown in.

"He thinks fast on his feet, that one," said Fleet. Somehow, I didn't think he was speaking of the milk clue anymore.

"You think he really bought my book?" I asked.

"It's possible. Or he may have downloaded a sample."

I nodded. Ebook samples were an excellent way for people to act like they had bought your products when they hadn't.

"That leaves two questions. Did he really read anything in the book at all, or did he know about Arnold Bernard through some other source? And, if he did read about him in your book, why did he?"

"Yes. Why bother," I agreed. So few did.

I got his point, though. It wasn't a well-known book (yet). Why would Cesar choose it of all things to read before coming here tonight?

Fleet offered no answer to his two questions. (It was actually three, but who's counting?)

"In either event," he said, "whether he bought your book or not, he missed out on a treat not finishing it. I enjoy your stories very much, Johnny. Though I do tend to think I come off as a touch too all-knowing in your narratives. If you realized the chaos and uncertainty that churns about in my mind during every case—well, I'll just say I don't regret retiring at those times. This is one of them."

He left now. Madeleine, Lesley (in search of her mittens) and Pixie followed in close formation behind him. He always got the girls. Phillip, as the dispassionate male, yawned and tagged along for the hell of it.

I didn't attempt to correct Fleet about that all-knowing-persona thing. He should have known I never exaggerate anything in my narratives, nothing significant anyway (which I guess was somewhat ironic, since he didn't seem to know that at all). I never try to hype him or Hutton or anyone else—and definitely not myself. I just calls them as I sees them.

I was tickled that he was one of my readers, though. Between him, Cesar Bloom (maybe), Lesley and Hutton, that made four. Arnold Bernard was also probably good for a copy. That's five. Now all I had to figure out was who bought the other three, and I had my sales figures all worked out.

Now that we were no longer in any danger from Arnold's booby traps (hopefully), and no one had actually been poisoned, I thought Lesley might want to team up with Nancy, Zoe, Ate and Evelynn to search for Sven. A girls' night out, as it were. Alas, she had no interest in girls' nights, outside or in. She chose her husband. This was fine with me. As long as she didn't talk about babies the whole time.

"Oo, look," she said, as we crossed the covered porch from the restaurant to the greenhouse. "Wouldn't that tree branch make the dearest spot for a child's swing?"

I mushed forward through the arctic temperatures and didn't reply. I wondered if Admiral Byrd had to put up with this from his men. Probably not.

When the Sven-searching assignments were handed out, Lesley and I had taken the greenhouse. I chose this because I already knew the layout, and with three-quarters of the way protected by an overhang, it seemed to involve the least amount of snow and slush in our shoes.

I had delayed a moment when we reached the kitchen exit. All that talk of not walking out on our host and doors possibly armed with parting favors had given me the vapors (figuratively this time). I sucked it up, however, and across the threshold she and I had gone.

It was fine. If Arnold had anything else planned for our gathering tonight, it wouldn't be in the form of exploding doorways. We reached the greenhouse, and I showed Lesley in.

She shivered. "It's freezing in here. I thought greenhouses were meant to be warm."

"I guess Ditters has one of the chilly kinds." I switched on the lights. All the veggies beamed up at us in the fluorescent sparkle. "You take the high road, and I'll take the low?"

She nodded. "And I'll be in Scotland before ye."

Ten minutes later, we met back at the barley (the closest thing Ditters had to Scotland).

"Anything?" I asked.

"Nothing," she said. She peered down. "So this is Ditters' famous Golden Promise?"

"This is it."

"Dinky. What's down that aisle?" she wondered.

"Oh nothing. Just some haricot vert." And a dead food celebrity, I mumbled to myself. Damn that Ditters.

We decided to head out now. Lesley felt strangely unfulfilled by her first visit to Ditters' Veg World. "I hope the others had better luck than us," she said. "All except Chief Crap-Head. Hey, did he say anything to you when we left?"

I explained that Chief Crap-Head and I said as little to each other as possible. "Why? What did he say to you?"

"As we were getting ready to split up, he said don't think that he's taken in by this respectability act. Then he said something about criminal tendencies running in families, and how you and I had been upping the ante lately. What do you think he was on about?"

I hesitated. A deserted greenhouse on a cold winter's night hardly seemed the place for revealing Lesley's deep, dark family secrets to her, but I knew my wife, and I knew that she wouldn't let up until I said everything I knew.

What I wondered was how the sheriff knew about them.

"Well—" I began.

I was saved by the bell. Actually, to be precise, by a slam and a clang.

Frowning, I hurried to the door and jiggled the latch. "Someone just locked us in."

20 — Dangerous Liaison (It's also a Sauce Binder Made with Egg)

I would have to think I turned a little green about the gills myself at this point. Trapped out here, with everyone else scouring the perimeter for an AWOL chef—it struck me as an excellent way for our wayward murderer to take care of another pair of victims. Kill the lights, sneak up behind, and there you had it. The murder practically committed itself.

For the first time since snagging this pleasant, undemanding assignment, I began to regret our selection. All this to avoid a little snow and slush. What was a little snow and slush when you came down to it? Not all that much.

With as much bravado as I could muster, I shouted, "Who's there?" through the door. It was a stupid thing to ask, really. It's like yelling "Come back!" to a thief as he sprints off with your wallet. He never comes back. And if someone locks you in a greenhouse so they can lay into you with their weapon of choice, they don't answer to "Who's there?" either.

Curiously enough, though, this one did. "Mr. Hathaway," came the reply—steady and unaffected. A stolid reply.

I was all over this paradoxical response. I knew I couldn't be the one out there, so there could only be one other person speaking. "Chief Adwick?"

"Mr. Hathaway."

I wasn't about to play this game again. If he wanted to resurrect vaudeville, let him do it on his own time.

I leaned in closer to the doorframe. It made my face cold. "Did you lock us in, Chief?"

"I did."

"Why?"

He made no reply.

I thought I may have stumped him, like one of Arnold Bernard's hilarious plate puzzlers, but he rallied after about ten seconds of silence. "I have a theory about you, Mr. Hathaway."

I rolled my eyes. Lesley crept up beside me, and she rolled her eyes as well. If he had been on our side of the door and could see all the eye-rolling going on, he'd have felt pretty silly.

"What theory?" I asked.

"I know your game."

"We don't have a game, Chief."

"I think you do. I think you've had one for some time now."

Lesley asked what he said. She wasn't getting any acoustics from her height.

"He said we have for some time now."

"We have what?"

"Had a game."

"What game?"

"I have no idea."

"Well, ask him."

I asked him.

After another moment of introspection, he answered mellowly, "I never should have let you two slip through my fingers all those years ago at Rangeley Manor."

I sighed. "Are you still on the Baccup caper? We didn't slip through your fingers, Chief. We simply left."

"And now it's come to this," continued the sheriff ruefully. "Murder," he muttered, and I could have sworn I heard a tsk-tsk-ing sound through the panel. "I know all about your young lady's father," he said.

"What did he say?" Lesley asked.

I didn't answer. There was no time. "Listen here, Chief, I don't know what you think you know, but he wasn't a killer. We're not killers either."

"That is not for me to decide. I'm just a simple public servant."

It seemed to me that the simple public servant was making quite a few decisions. It made you wonder what a complicated servant would do.

"If I'm right, they'll have you on a whole string of murders. You've been busy, Mr. Hathaway."

I staggered back, bonking my head on some sort of thermostat thingy on the wall. (So that's where it was.) I was certain now that the man had gone off his gourd. And his had never been much of a gourd to begin with. Nothing like Ditters' little fellow, lying tucked into bed on my right. "What the hell are you talking about, Chief?"

"I've read your books," he said.

It was a strange thing to say, out of context. Nevertheless, my mood lightened. I didn't think much of his methods, but I had a better opinion of him now. "You bought my books?"

"Checked them out of the library," he replied.

This wasn't as good to my bottom line, but I was still grateful. A reader was a reader. "But what does that have to do with locking us in?"

I felt my brow furrow on that last question. I hoped he wasn't one of those deranged fans who kidnap authors and do unpleasant things to them in the name of literary discourse. I didn't think I would care for that much adulation.

"I've been reading between the lines, Mr. Hathaway. I see what you've been doing with these narratives of yours. Very clever."

I still had no clue what he was talking about. Had I been doing anything with them? I was pretty certain I hadn't been all that clever.

"You're the one who killed all those people."

I reverse head butted the thermostat again. "I did what?"

"You killed all those people in Mr. Fleet's cases."

I gaped at the doorway. "You got that from reading between the lines?"

"I did."

"Well, they've been pulling your leg. I didn't kill anyone. I think I made that pretty clear when I reported what Fleet said and did. He always identified the killer. I'll have to check my math, but I'm pretty certain that not a single one of them was John P. Hathaway."

"That's what made it so diabolical, sir. You said one thing but did another. It's like that Hercule Poirot novel where the fellow had done the murder all along but acted like he hadn't."

I had to think about that for a second. Apparently, Cesar Bloom wasn't the only Agatha Christie fan at the *Crazy Pickle*. It wasn't the best book-club discussion I had ever come across, but I fancied I knew which novel Adwick was talking about. I won't identify it, in case you haven't gotten to it yet, but I would recommend you read all the Poirots—as soon as you finish with the rest of the Enescu Fleets, that is.

I paused a moment before continuing. I needed time to organize my brain. So, if I had this straight, the chief was saying I was the murderer, not just now but throughout all of Fleet's cases. My alibi? The verisimilitude of the detective's (incorrect) solutions. I had, in short, fooled Fleet, fooled my readers and fooled the authorities. I was a sort of murdering, literary savant, in other words, the likes of which Arnold Bernard himself could only admire. Wow, Adwick was right. That would have been clever.

Too bad it also wasn't correct.

I returned to the door. "Chief, I know you've been stressed lately. Retiring, having Ditters over for Thanksgiving dinner—perhaps someone has been hitting you in the head with a tuba again. I get it. But you have to understand, Lesley and I are not murderers. We are not thieves or traveling con artists. We're just a couple of crazy kids, trying to make our way through the world the best we can, with a private eye or two as friends, and the occasional corpse we have to deal with. But which—and I can't emphasize this part enough—we've had absolutely no part in corpsifying. Why don't you open this door now, and we'll talk about this like gentlemen?"

He didn't open the door. The clang on the other end had been a one-time-only sound effect.

I had hoped he might be considering my offer, but as the seconds ticked past and I heard no further peep from outside, not even the merest "Mr. Hathaway," I had to assume that he wasn't considering it. He'd gone.

As Ditters would say, it was too cheerful to think that the murderer had gotten him—the real murderer. No doubt he had simply gone to fetch some muscle to keep us in line until his backup arrived (possibly from Baccup). Then he could share his theory with the world.

He had obviously put a lot of thought into it.

Lesley had given up on listening halfway through and was now residing "comfortably" beside a bed of radishes. She tapped the earth playfully on her right and asked me to sit with her. "I turned up the temperature on that thermostat thing you kept smacking. The heat should be rolling in here any minute now."

She was right. If Adwick had his way, and the cell phones and roads cooperated, the heat would be rolling in any minute.

I sat. "Do you know that lunatic thinks we killed Elsie Farmer!"

Lesley wrinkled her nose in disgust. "Is that what he was saying? What an ass! Why does he think that?"

"Some cockamamie theory he's picked up reading about our adventures. He thinks, after we supposedly foiled him at Rangeley Manor with that stolen artifact—"

"Which we didn't!"

"Which we didn't—he thinks, now, we've graduated to murder."

Lesley couldn't abide that. International artifact thieves were one thing—it was almost gratifying to have someone believing that you could pull that off—but murderers, no. It was so common.

"What did he mean, he knew all about my father?"

I shot her an oblique glance. "It was nothing."

"He seemed to think it was something. You seemed to know all about it too."

I took a deep, slightly chilled breath. It was about time she knew. "Last summer, during that museum case, Enescu Fleet mentioned—in passing, you understand—that your father may have once worked as a sort of con artist and art thief in his youth. His name may or may not have been Gerome Lance, and he may or may not have been the head of a sort of gang. This was before he went respectable, of course."

I let it sink in a moment.

“Oh that,” she said. “Yes, I knew all about that. Jill told me about it last year.”

I smiled and rested the back of my head on the radish bed. That was one thing off my mind anyway.

“And this dratted inspector thinks that qualifies us as killers?” she asked.

“Like father like daughter. Only, in this case, the daughter is trying to one-up the old man with murder.”

“Ridiculous,” she shivered. “It’s not exactly getting balmy in here, is it? Do you think we should try to bust out? Maybe break a window?”

I hadn’t thought of that. We were in a house of windows, weren’t we? How hard could it be to break one of them?

I stood up and looked around. It’s weird. You always think that breaking a window is an easy task until you come down to doing it. I couldn’t find a single item capable of shattering our cell walls. No spades, no hoes, not even a simple garden trowel. It was almost as if Ditters had made his greenhouse shatterproof.

I picked up a radish and flung it irritably at the closest pane. Not even a dent.

“Okay, enough of this.” I slipped off my cardigan and rolled it tightly around my arm and fist. I stepped up to the windowpane, half-shut my eyes and let it have it.

Lesley rolled up onto her knees. “Johnny! Are you okay?”

I was not okay. My knuckles were in agony and so was the rest of my hand and my lower arm. My cardigan was fine.

I made even less impact on the pane than the radish had.

I stumbled away and swore harshly. Again, I don’t want to give away any spoilers, so I won’t reveal the ending. It began with “mother—” so Lesley probably liked it.

I slid the sweater back on my body—painfully—and sat next to Lesley again.

It was nice. I liked sitting. I planned on doing quite a lot of it for the foreseeable future.

“You should have worn a jacket,” she said, sharing the heat of her body.

Yes, I should have.

"It doesn't matter," she continued, nodding toward the undamaged window. "Someone will come along eventually, and then Adwick will have some heavy explaining to do. Locking people in. The very idea of it. He's insane."

Yes, I agreed. Insane. A man like that might even punch a window of reinforced Plexi with nothing but a ball of wool to protect himself.

Lesley examined my knuckles. "You'll be fine."

"Thanks."

"On the plus side," she reflected, "while we're locked in here, the murderer is locked out there and can't get at us."

"Yes, there's that."

"So who do you think did it?"

I rubbed my hand and said I had no idea.

Lesley didn't either, but that didn't prevent her from talking. "My money is on that Dom Jacobs fellow. I don't care if he is Adwick's gay lover, he's suspicious. Moreover, I feel like I've met him somewhere before."

"So you've said. Where do you think you've seen him?"

"I can't remember, but it was somewhere. Of course, that Cesar man is suspicious too."

I wasn't so certain about that. "Do you really think a celebrated food critic and chef would kill one of his own, pretend to poison a pack of people, and then nearly blow up a restaurant with himself inside?"

Lesley argued that there was no saying what a celebrated food critic would do. "And besides, we've never proven that he would have actually let the explosive go off. It might not have even been real."

"It looked pretty real to me."

"Perhaps. I think he had an out, though, an escape plan, all worked out with the fiend Bernard beforehand. That is, if Cesar's the murderer. It could be Nancy Mortimer. She would be more likely to be in league with someone like Arnold Bernard."

"Why?"

Lesley didn't know. "But Ate doesn't like her, and I trust her taste. And Nancy was the one working with Sven to do Ditters down."

"That's true. She might know more than she's saying."

Lesley gave me a look. "Don't you have any thoughts?"

Long association with Enescu Fleet has pretty much taught me to spurn my own thoughts. In the past, I reminded her, most of my theories had amounted to sofa lint, so why not leave them untheorized? I don't even try anymore. I just sit back and enjoy it while it unfolds. I was already sitting now.

"Well, I think you could take more of an interest."

I frowned. Were we talking about unmasking a murderer or getting her pregnant?

"But you're right about the sitting thing," she said. "It's nice to relax for once. Cozy almost."

I nodded. It was rather cozy—in a chilled, hard-turfed way.

She leaned her head on my shoulder. "Johnny?"

"Yes?"

"Is that a leg I see over there?"

I looked. I nodded again. It was rather a leg, yes.

"Elsie Farmer's dead body?"

"Yes."

She nodded. She thought as much. "Damn that Ditters."

21 — Different Pairings

I must have nodded off.

I dreamt my old friend Walter "Ditters" Dittersdorf had invited us to a restaurant gala, and there were lots of weird characters and pickle-laced entrées, and after that, a murder and disappearing chef of Norwegian descent, and then Fleet's arch-nemesis, Arnold Bernard, turned out to be pulling the strings—

Oh right.

"Johnny, do you have any interest at all in having a baby?"

Lesley was speaking to me. She was speaking calmly and unemotionally. The worst kind of speak.

I opened my eyes and blinked at her. I didn't know how long we had been conversing, or where this question had come up in the course of things, but I felt it best that I answered it quickly and well. "Of course," I said. "Give me a second to wake up a little."

She replied that she didn't mean now, and I said oh. That was disappointing.

"Do you have any interest in having a baby at all? Ever?"

I opened my eyes wider. "Of course. Sure. I mean, who wouldn't?"

"You don't seem like you do."

"Well, I don't know where you're getting *that*—"

"So you do or you don't?"

I paused, wishing there was a third option. I made up my mind. If I could tell the woman I loved that her father was once a no-good crook called Gerome Lance, I should be able to share my own feelings on fatherhood. "Well—"

"So you don't?"

"It's not that."

"Don't you think I'll make a good mum?"

"I think you'll make a fantastic mother!"

I still wasn't crazy about the "mum" label, but I assured her that she was aces in the mom department and full of nurturing potential.

"Don't you think you'll make a good dad, then?"

"I think you'll make a fantastic mother," I replied again.

"So that's it?" She wiggled closer. "You think you won't have what it takes?"

Of course I didn't think I had what it took! What a stupid thing to ask.

"What are you worried about? The responsibility? The commitment?"

Somehow, I felt like I shouldn't pick both of them. Once again, I wondered if there was a third choice. "It's like this," I said. "Do you remember the episode of *Star Trek* where Captain Picard got zapped by an alien probe and it allowed him to live a whole lifetime in an instant?"

"No."

"Right. Well, anyway, he did. This alien probe zapped him—"

"Why would it want to do that?"

"I don't know. It just thought it would. Anyway, he lived this whole lifetime in his head, the kind of life he never would have had himself—family, home life, etc—and then he woke up, and it was all just a memory. But a very pleasant, meaningful memory. That's how I feel sometimes. I see a cute little moppet run past and think, gee, that would be nice, wouldn't it? Having a little wiggle worm to take care of and love. Then I think about it again and think, gee, that's only the good part. The cute part. Then I start to dwell on how you can mess things up, and how your life has to change completely, and why would the kid like you anyway—kids never like me—and I get nervous. That's when I think that the Picard maneuver might be okay, because if it goes awry it would only be for a minute or two, and how much can you muck up in two minutes?"

I had an inkling that throughout this analogy I wasn't scoring any points with Lesley. Women so rarely understand the significance of good science fiction.

"So you're saying that you wouldn't mind starting a family, as long as you didn't have any responsibilities or commitment to it at all? That it would be a nice place to visit, in short, but you wouldn't want to live there?"

"No, no. That's not what I meant at all. And that's not what happened on *Star Trek*. Even though Jean-Luc got it done in a few minutes, that doesn't mean he didn't have any responsibilities. He probably had lots of recitals to attend and skinned knees to mend—it's just that they only occupied a microsecond of his time. It's all relative."

"I see. So you're okay with responsibility, in limited doses, just not the commitment?"

"No. I mean, yes. I mean, wait, what was the first one again?"

"Never mind, Johnny." She inched away.

"But I do mind," I told her, inching toward her. "I'm just tired. I do want a baby. Lots and lots of babies. We should make one right here. I think it's warm enough now."

"No thanks."

"Okay, we'll table the offspring for now. Maybe we should start with a dog. I understand Maltese are very nice. I think— Hey, did you hear that?"

"The sound of my heart breaking? I did."

"No, it was the door."

I stood up. Cautiously, I rattled the handle. It responded with a satisfying click, much better than a clank, and then it swung open. "I think someone just let us out."

I considered making an amusing callback to Zoe's quip about the lettuce—"lettuce out"—but decided it wasn't the right moment. Also, I couldn't think of an amusing callback.

I peered outside. Our guardian angel had vanished. I didn't care; I only wished to thank the person.

I came back inside, smiling. "Did you hear what I said, Lesley? It's open. We're free."

"That should please you," said my wife.

Outside the greenhouse we decided to split up (temporarily)—(at least, I hoped it was only temporary)—and try to locate Fleet. Only he could talk some sense into Adwick.

Lesley was dressed warmer, so she offered to take the perimeter of the *Pickle*, while I headed back inside and scoped things out there.

I didn't like the idea of her going alone, with both a deranged killer and a deranged police officer on the loose, but she was adamant. "I'm fine, Johnny. I need some time alone."

"Time alone to locate Fleet?"

"Sure, why not?"

I didn't like it. On a few levels. "Give me a second, and I'll grab my jacket," I said.

"It's not necessary. I want to be alone, I tell you. Besides, there's Ate."

I was confused. Did she want to be alone or not?

Strolling over to us, Ate asked if we had located Sven. We both shook our heads. If only we had, things might have been different. "Were you the one who let us out of the greenhouse?" I asked.

Ate said she wasn't. She was embarrassed to say that the idea never occurred to her. "Why, were you stuck in one?"

I said we were and explained.

She was as sympathetic as always. "This modern-day Javert has got to be put on a leash," she remarked. While she said this, I noticed Pixie and Phillip were in attendance with her. They weren't on leashes either.

"Well, I guess I'll head in," I announced, and Lesley said that was probably a good idea. "See you in there," I added, and she said sure.

But not why not.

I had told Lesley that it would probably be best if we avoided Adwick for now, or at least until cooler heads could talk some sense into him, but deep down inside, I secretly wished I would run into him, so I could wring his not-so-cool head right off his neck.

He might be a fan of my books (sort of), but I was no fan of his. Not only had he subjected me to the ordeal of sitting on Ditters' greenhouse floor for an hour, surrounded by the man's creepy veggies and a dead body, but he had forced my hand on the baby question. If not for him, I never would have babbled on about old *Star Trek* episodes, and Lesley would still think I was perfectly content to have a baby (sort of). Thanks to him, we had talked *openly*, and for that I wanted to kick him to Bar Harbor and back—which, if you know Maine, was a good distance.

I rounded the corner toward the kitchen and halted in my tracks. I could hear someone talking in furtive undertones. I crept closer and peered around the side of the house.

Dom Jacobs was there, without Adwick for once, and so was Nancy. The differences in height between Ditters and Sven had amused me, but they were nothing compared with Nancy and Dom. I couldn't decide if the contrast made her look more minuscule or him more giant, but whichever it was, they looked ridiculous.

I hadn't realized they knew each other. I wondered if they were friends, maybe even special friends. If they were, it would probably gash Adwick to the bone. At least there was that.

"I understand," Dom was saying. "This was not what I had planned, I assure you. But you must have understood my methods going in."

At this point in my eavesdropping, the busybody Phillip butted in. I hadn't seen him following, and he blended in so well with the landscape that I almost missed seeing him now.

A sensitive sort, and one who didn't appreciate people ignoring him, he re-woofed his greeting with a healthy helping of rebuke in his voice.

Nancy jumped. "What was that?"

Dom, unflappable as ever, said he believed it was a canine.

I hurried back inside.

"Oh, so there you are," said Hutton, greeting me in the hallway outside the foyer. He was examining his "beard" in the mirror. "We've been looking for you. Where's Lesley?"

Phillip nudged me in the leg. He was showing off what he had discovered and wanted there to be no mistake about who had found it.

I told Hutton where Lesley was. I also mentioned she was pissed and detailed our adventure in the greenhouse.

He nodded throughout my narrative. Like Ate, he was sympathetic. "You're right, Hath. That was a good *Next Gen* episode. Lesley didn't appreciate its artistic value?"

"She did not. And she won't let up on the baby topic. I wish she would find some other hobby. I'm sick and tired of babies, babies, babies."

Hutton said babies weren't so bad, if you caught them in the right context.

I sniffed at him and his context. He would say that—now.

He pulled himself away from his visage. "So why were you in the greenhouse so long?"

"I told you. Adwick locked us in there. He thinks we're the murderer(s)."

"Oh right. That is peculiar. Don't take this the wrong way, Hath, but you could never kill anyone. You're too disorganized. You would mean to pick up the murder weapon on your way home from the grocery store and would end up leaving it lying on the counter at the dry cleaners. You know how prone to amnesia you are."

"I am not prone to amnesia," I replied sharply. I had amnesia once. You would think I made a habit of it.

"Anyway, I wouldn't worry about the inspector," said Hutton. "He passed through a few minutes ago. Said he was taking a trek into town come hell or what-have-you and borrowed a pair of boots. Assuming he makes it down the hill unscathed, he'll probably get eaten by a wombat or snow leopard or something, so it's fine."

I nodded. I wasn't entirely sure that we had wombats and leopards up this way, but one could always hope. "Just in case he doesn't get eaten, we're trying to locate Fleet so we can get the sheriff's suspicions about me blotted from consideration. Adwick trusts Fleet, and Fleet wouldn't let the police mistreat his guy."

Hutton responded with a snort. I was that for sure. *His guy*. It was more than he could say for himself. "Which is somewhat ironic," he said.

"Why is it ironic?"

"Never mind why," he replied, and I snorted myself and asked him where everyone else was.

"I told you where the sheriff was. The chefs beautiful went down into the basement. Someone might have led them to believe that there was Napoleon brandy down there." He paused. "What? They were getting on my nerves. Ditters and Betty are inching their way down the east bank. They suddenly remembered having a neighbor on the far side of the ridge, and they're trying to see if they can make it to his property and use his phone. Evelynn and Zoe are preparing snacks, now that Sven is officially off-duty. I'm right here. Dom is somewhere being pompous. You're there. Ate is airing out Pixie. I'm not sure where Nancy is."

I told him I already knew where Nancy was. She and Dom. "What about Fleet and Madeleine?"

He snorted again. He and I were doing a lot of that. People might start suspecting we had a drug problem. "The genius is in the drawing room upstairs with his lady baker."

I found his tone suggestive and his use of the word *genius* full of snark. "You annoyed with him?"

A third snort. Or was that four? "Who—Fleet? No, not annoyed. Disappointed. I don't like his methods, Hath. In fact, I think they stink on a half shell."

"Why?"

"Why? He's not doing anything, that's why. He never does anything. And yet, he always solves the case in the end. It's irritating."

My expression brightened. Not to sound too Sheriff-Adwick-y, but was this professional jealousy I was hearing? It was clear that he was jealous of the old man's beard—could he be jealous of his successes as well? It seemed likely that he was.

In perfect alignment with my thoughts, he turned back to the mirror and smoothed the hairs on his face. "See how they pick up the light along the jawline. You can't teach that."

I said ah. Good to know.

I scowled. For all his criticism of everyone else, he didn't seem to be taking too active a roll in locating Sven. At least I had been out and about.

I pressed him on the matter, and he responded in very Hutton-y fashion.

"I don't need to leave the restaurant to search. I do my searching up here." He tapped his forehead.

"Find anything up there?" I asked, also tapping his noggin.

"Actually, I think I did. Or rather, not up here"—he tapped my head—"but in there." He tapped on a woman's purse, lying on a side table.

I'd had enough tapping. "What are you talking about?"

"I looked through Elsie Farmer's belongings. I found this." He showed me an article from a society page. It detailed how Sven had received some financial-wizardry award at some reception or other some years back. Also in attendance was his sister, Aileen Bernard.

I gasped. "Bernard? Holy crap, Sven's sister—"

"—is Arnold Bernard's wife. If that doesn't give us a lead on the mathematician's accomplice here, nothing will."

I couldn't believe it. And Elsie had this in her purse the whole time?

No wonder Sven had run. Maybe his role in her death hadn't been a prank, after all. It was the ol' triple bluff. The most obvious suspect was the answer all along.

"Hutton, this is huge—colossal."

He was aware of its size. He glanced toward the mirror and then back my way. "Do you like my beard, Hath?"

Blinking at him a moment, and at his irrelevant question, I said it was awesome.

He half-smiled, which was all you got out of Hutton these days. "I'm glad. Everyone else has been a real dick about it." He resumed his mirror examination, and I gave Phillip a look. The pup returned it with a wrinkle of his brow.

As Hutton turned, I noticed a sprinkling of ice and salt stuck to his back. The crystals caught the light of a nearby sconce and sparkled in it—which, I'm given to understand, you can't teach.

Apparently, I had criticized the man's shiftlessness unjustly. Not only had he discovered the smoking gun in Elsie Farmer's handbag, but he had apparently been out and about a lot more than I thought.

"Did you take a spill on the driveway, Hutton?"

"I wouldn't say that."

"So did you?"

"Yes," he said. He couldn't have done better if our host had littered the pathway with banana skins. Inspector Adwick wasn't the only gifted slapstick comedian in residence.

I brushed off his back. Then I brushed off Phillip. He was looking left out. "Don't worry, I won't mention the pratfall to Ate. I know how she admires you."

"Does she."

"And I wouldn't concern yourself with Fleet's methods." If he could buoy me up about Adwick and wombats, I could return the favor. "You'll think of something. He's not the only one who knows how to come through in the bottom of the ninth."

Hutton straightened up. Something had inspired him. Not that bottom of the ninth crapola—I really needed to work on my pep talks—but the first part. An idea had begun to gel.

He knelt down and picked up a few dibs and drabs of ice that had fallen. He went for the salt next. He sniffed it. Then, in a sudden stomach-turning impulse, he tasted it. Phillip, who didn't seem to find the notion strange at all, joined in, lapping from his palm freely.

Hutton stood and brushed his hands. "I should have realized why it wasn't melting."

"Why what wasn't?"

"The ice, Hath. What else?—Zoe Norris' fondue?"

Was that the snack she was preparing? I could go for some hot cheese about then.

"Be right back," he said, and dashed for the door.

I followed him outside and was disgusted once more as he and Phillip sampled a handful of driveway here and a handful there. First the area below the steps and then farther down along the cars. I supposed it beat Sven's cooking, but still.

"I've been an idiot!" exclaimed Hutton. "An absolute moron."

I was glad he could see it.

"Hath, do me a favor. If you can mince across the ice without splitting your skull asunder, check to see if there is a hose lying there."

I minced as requested. The porch was pretty slick, but my skull remained intact. I peered over the railing and spotted the item in question. A hose. Actually several of them, branching out everywhere. "You don't mean—?"

"No, not another murder attempt. Something much more basic than that." He skidded around the house, out of view, and then came back around again, moving rapidly.

"An absolute idiot," he repeated. He rounded the corner toward the stairs, slipping twice and taking another near tumble once. Finally reaching me, he said, "Keep everyone occupied for the next half hour, would you?"

"What if Adwick comes back?"

"Kick him in the gonads. In half an hour, it won't matter."

"Why half an hour?"

"Must you ask so many questions? Call it twenty-five minutes, if it makes you happy."

It didn't, but I called it twenty-five just to irk him.

"I have work to do," he said. He hurried past and went inside. I had hardly reached the door, when he hurried back out again, a sack in his hand.

"What's that?" I asked.

"Just go, Hath, I'm busy."

I went inside. And then I went upstairs. Maybe someone there could tell me what the hell was going on.

Fleet and Maddy weren't in the drawing room. Even if they had been, I doubt they would have shared their thoughts. No one ever shares.

I headed back downstairs.

I held up about halfway down. Ditters' "special room," the one off-limits to all but the most highly selected resident and/or pining-for-love waitress, stood invitingly on my left.

I tried to tell myself that I would look inside purely to check for Enescu Fleet and Madeleine Abrams. I didn't really believe they were in there—why would they be?—but for the two and a half seconds it took to creep back up the stairs and jiggle the doorknob, it placated my sense of right and wrong. Half a second more and my conscience might have gotten savvy.

The knob turned freely. The door opened.

Perhaps my guardian angel had been here as well.

"Hello?"

I didn't use any names. This was for a couple reasons. A) I wasn't honestly expecting anyone to be in there. B) I wasn't sure how I should address them if they were. Take Madeleine. "Madeleine," "Maddy," "Mads," "Ms. Abrams"? Which way would you go? Perhaps "Madame Baker" would suffice? As for Enescu Fleet, even now I still struggled with what to call him. The man was like a father to me, but what do you call a dad-like detective? Enescu. Fleet. Ef? The F-man? None of them sounded right.

No one answered, so it didn't matter. I stepped farther in. It was only natural at that point.

What I perceived inside was anything but. I stood in the entranceway, goggling at it.

It was a dark and woody room, much like any other in *Le Cornichon*. Hardwood floors, hardwood walls, a few rugs tossed here and there, and a certain mustiness in the air. But the decorative touch—it was like none other.

All along the walls, the panels were plastered with swords and axes of every description. I knew Ditters had always enjoyed antiques of a violent ilk, but this was taking things a little far.

In one section, you had your ancient ornaments: daggers, hatchets, broadswords, bodkins and various other jagged implements that had once given knights of olde pause on the battlefield. In another, more "modern" utensils flourished: flint pistols, revolvers, muskets, bayonets and a few vintage shotguns. I was beginning to think that I had stumbled into a murderer's paradise.

And that wasn't the extent of it.

On a wall straight ahead, blocked slightly by a giant beam, another assortment of doodads drew my eye. They were no ordinary knickknacks. On the left of the display hung a framed photograph of Lesley and myself taken outside the Wolf Valley Casino. I remembered it. It had accompanied an article in *People* about our first adventure with the world-famous Fleet.

On the right of the photo, another significant piece of memorabilia was nestled, this one of a naval variety: a wooden ship's wheel, split and hardened, as though it had been soaking in one of Ditters' pickling solutions overnight. I checked the plaque. It read: *The Stacked Deck*—the yacht Fleet and I had gone down on the night we had encountered Arnold Bernard. I had read recently that the yacht's owner, who had more money than any young, good-natured surfer lookalike could know what to do with, had auctioned off what they had salvaged from the wreck.

The proceeds had all gone to charity, and evidently the crown jewel had gone to Ditters. I guess he, too, had more money than he knew what to do with. And here I was worrying that he was strapped.

I gazed farther along the panel and spotted some sheet music on a nearby pedestal, carefully arranged upon a burnished brass stand. I didn't recognize the piece at first, but that wasn't surprising. Up until a few months ago, no one would have recognized it.

It was George Enescu's *Third Romanian Rhapsody*. Recovered by Fleet at the Pendleton Institute of Music last summer and later presented to the Romanian government for safekeeping, Ditters had somehow gotten his hands on it. I'd like to see him try that one on his kazoo.

And then there was the middle of the wall, straight across from the beam. There hung the flagship of the Fleet collection: a square canvas near and dear to my heart. It was Thomas McKnight's *Christmas in Connecticut*—the exact McKnight painting that had factored so significantly in our Ariadne Museum case the previous spring. It looked like the original. I had tried to purchase the painting awhile back as a Christmas gift for Fleet, but I could never track down the owner. Now I knew why.

I stepped back from the exhibit, and a shiver ran down my spine.

You might wonder what it's like to come face-to-face with a shrine to yourself. I can tell you. It's creepy. I suppose it's possible to encounter a non-creepy shrine, but I have to think that shrines, by their nature, have a hard time escaping that stigma.

I had pegged Sheriff Adwick as the sort of deranged fan who might kidnap an author as an act of twisted adulation. Examining the evidence, I felt I may have tabbed the wrong man in Betty D's life. Her husband appeared to be the real dangerous obsessive in the family.

What baffled and disturbed me the most was the deceit. Ditters had stated unequivocally that he knew nothing about my work the last couple years. So what was all this? If his lying didn't make his salute to the Hathaway-Hutton-Fleet team that much more disturbing, I didn't know a disturbing salute when I saw one.

I stumbled farther back from the wall, so much so that I drove my elbow into another of my host's mementos—a warrior's axe, hanging on the back of the beam.

As I stooped to return it to its hook, I noticed something curious, which took some doing in this room of the abstract and bizarre. One of Ditters' implements of carnage had disappeared. I recalled it had a sort of four-way chopper, like a canoe paddle gone over to the dark side. It had been hanging on a rack to the right when I passed, but now it had vanished. Plates, chefs, battle-paddles—they all flitted to and fro at the *Splendid Gherkin*.

I gazed around, just to see if I had been mistaken, and that's when I saw something else. There was an Indian *bhuj* mounted over the ship's wheel, and in the blade's reflection I saw a flash of movement careening toward me. It looked a little like a certain four-bladed oar, the likes of which would have made the local pond life think twice before flanking your canoe.

I ducked out of the way just in time and watched in awe as it pronged into the wall above my head.

Counting my blessings, and realizing that this would have been a pretty good way to split a skull asunder, I jumped up and staggered out into the middle of the room. There was no one there.

I surveyed the collection and all its trinkets, and on the third pass, I froze.

From beneath a heavy set of red velvet curtains—seriously, Ditters, you're not running a bordello here—protruded a pair of black boots. They were fancy and shined and very European. (Perhaps he *was* running a bordello.)

Sufficiently incensed, I stormed over and whipped back the fabric.

Of all the strange and otherworldly objects I had encountered here, this one took me aback the most.

I don't know who I expected to see lurking among the folds, but it wasn't Sven Hosten, leaning against the wall, a whole lemon jammed in his open mouth.

He gave me that sullen stare of his—the lemon flew out with a POP!—and he toppled forward onto the floor.

The man was deceased.

22 — Eighty-Six Sluggo

I should have known from the garnish. It was a dead giveaway.

I knelt down and checked the body just to be sure. It seemed unalive.

I could see the wound clearly now, smack-dab in the middle of his back. A lemon zester had been plunged into the gash. (A little over the top on the lemon theme there, I considered it, but who was I to judge?)

In Sven's left hand lay an old six-shooter. He must have grabbed for it during the struggle. They say the pen is mightier than the sword, and apparently a citrus grater does pretty well against a Colt. Not that I was willing to accept the former as the murder weapon just yet. It would have taken a mighty strong drive to pierce the flesh with that. Fleet could have done it—maybe my old friend Warren Kingsley, the bodyguard—but very few else. I couldn't have. No one would have argued that.

I stood up. I peered down at the dislodged fruit at my foot, and my blood ran cold. Ditters' argument with Sven—it had almost slipped my mind.

But surely people didn't kill their employees over an overabundance of rind in their cooking?—no more than they killed their ex-lady-friends to prevent those ladies from making things awkward with their wives and fathers-in-law. It was ridiculous. People didn't do that. Well, some did, I supposed, but Ditters didn't. Ditters was no killer.

He collected creepy weapons, yes, but lots of people collected creepy things. Granted, he seemed a tad obsessed with my detective work, an obsession that he had lied about. And if anyone could arrange the traps and challenges we had experienced tonight, it would be he. He had access, knowledge of the field and a grudge against at least three people present at the dinner party: Elsie Farmer, Sheriff Adwick and the oaf Sven. But did that make him a murderer?

I forgot where I was going with this.

The sound of a Maltese going bananas outside the door brought me out of my trance. It sounded like Phillip, but it could have also been Pixie throwing her voice.

I shook myself out of it. There was work to be done here.

The killer had made a run for it. If Phillip and/or Pixie had them cornered on the stairs, I could still do something about it.

I snatched the Colt out of Sven's grip—he fought me on it briefly (even murdered, he was an ornery cuss)—and bolted for the door. I threw it open, bounded out into the hall and immediately took a flying header over a small, furry roadblock in my path.

It was Phillip. (Pixie must have been otherwise engaged.) I raised myself off the floor and surveyed the scene. The person who had tried to impale me, and who most likely impaled Sven, could have gone down the stairs, but with the stoic Phillip there, they might not have risked it. They could have headed down the hall toward Ditters and Betty's bedroom, but then they would have chanced getting trapped. There were the upstairs dining rooms, including Ditters' future meeting room, but these were mostly small and sparsely accoutered, offering little by way of concealment. The most strategic retreat would have been two feet away.

The drawing room. Hide there and wait, and then slip back down the steps once Phil and I had passed along.

It's what I would have done. I got up and charged forward.

I didn't think to check the gun until I arrived in the entranceway. There was no reason why such an ancient piece would be loaded or even in functioning condition. Brilliant.

I looked inside. It was loaded and very possibly functioning. Happy about that, I despaired once again of my host and his careless habits. Leaving a loaded gun hanging on your wall. Not too bright.

Still, it benefited me. It would have benefitted Sven as well, if he had shot from the hip instead of just looking haughty and Norwegian at his killer.

I didn't plan on making that mistake myself, especially the Norwegian part. I crept across the threshold, ready to fire. Still no sign of anyone.

Phillip sniffed my shoe. My shoe was clear.

Something glinted in the moonlight. I swung around and saw it again. It was standing right there, straight ahead. Except it wasn't. I was looking in the mirror over the mantel.

I lowered my gat. No reason to start shooting up Ditters' place of business. Yet.

Phillip, perhaps remembering a date he had with some kibble, dashed off, and I was on my own again. I turned back to the mirror.

I nearly fired again. My nerves were that jumpy.

Once again, I relaxed my grip, and then it hit me. Literally. And when I say literally, I mean *literally*. (That one was for Hutton.)

All the nerves in my back went dead. The Colt slipped from my grasp, and slowly, dreamily, I tipped forward and onto the floor.

Sven had been a tough act to follow, but I like to think that I completed my belly splat with more panache, and without any extraneous fruit props.

I peered up from the floor. The maybe-murder weapon lay at my side. A meat cleaver. I figured as much when it struck. It felt like a meat cleaver.

I tried to move but instead just lay there, concentrating. Strangely enough, it was at that moment that I felt the most focused; energized, in a depleted sort of way.

There was something shimmering in the light on the sideboard. I pulled myself up, dragged myself across the floor (and the alpaca rug) and grabbed a bottle of whisky from the shelf.

Slowly lowering my face into the rug, I began to pass out.

But you knew all that before.

23 — Zest for Death

Enescu Fleet gazed into the mirror above the mantel. Those who knew him best would have recognized an intensity in his expression. His brow was set, his mouth hard, the twinkle in his eye sharp and penetrating. He was trying to make up his mind about something.

"I'll have the corned beef sandwich, I guess," he told Zoe, and the latter nodded and left. She resisted the impulse to curtsy. Ever since he had sussed out her love for her employer, the waitress had found herself in awe of this strange old geezer in tweed. She went out quickly and didn't look back.

Fleet turned around and faced the room's only other (human) occupant.

"I'm glad you're eating," said Madeleine Abrams, sitting in a chair by the window. Phillip had fallen into a contented sleep in her lap, while Pixie snoozed by her foot. The four of them were upstairs in the parlor, a.k.a. the most recent crime scene at *Le Vrai Cornichon*—one of three and counting. It was approximately midnight. "It's not your fault, you know."

"If not mine, then whose?"

"This man—Arnold Bernard. His accomplice—the real murderer. The weatherman. Anyone."

Fleet shook his head. "They were all fulfilling their real purposes in life, Maddy. Manipulation, murder, misapprehension about ice. Their roles are complete. What of mine?"

"It should all be over soon," she said. "This ordeal, I mean."

He was certain of that.

He returned to his far-off stare, this time subjecting the mountainside out the window to a careful scrutiny. He didn't really want to eat, but what did it matter? The authorities were expected in an hour, and he wasn't ready for them. He didn't want them here. He wouldn't have eaten anything had it not been for Maddy and her insisting.

She was a good woman.

"What could he have been trying to tell us?" he asked.

Madeleine shook her head behind him—he could see it reflected in the window.

"It was a clue," said Fleet—"that much we know."

"Do we?"

"I do."

She nodded slowly. "So this really is how your cases go. Victims leave these clues, and that tells you who has done it? Very useful."

Fleet agreed that it was certainly convenient. Lately, the victims had all done their part. He couldn't recall it going so smoothly in the old days, but you always believed things were tougher in your youth.

"Well, you would know how the young man's mind worked," she said. "What do you think he could have been trying to say?"

Yes, thought Fleet. He knew John Hathaway. As well as he knew anyone. Perhaps that was his own tragic flaw. He knew everyone, and therefore no one, individually, very well at all. He still knew next to nothing about Johnny's background, his family, his education, his views on adding a designated hitter to the National League. What did he know, really? Not all that much.

"So what do you think it could have meant?" Madeleine asked him again. "His clue?"

Fleet said he was stymied.

"Perhaps it was a reference to one of your previous cases."

Fleet didn't think so.

"A reference to something someone said tonight?"

Fleet didn't think that likely either.

"Perhaps he just wanted a drink," said Madeleine. "I know I could use one. And I hardly ever drink. You're a bad influence, Nessie Fleet."

He closed the gap between them, taking her hand in his firm grip. He hadn't gone down on one knee, so she had no reason to get too excited. Yet. "I wanted to tell you, Maddy, throughout this whole affair—"

Sheriff Adwick, in his trademarked way, interrupted right then. As Hutton might have guessed, the officer had given up about halfway down the driveway and come back almost as quickly as he had left. Just in time, too, for there had been more crimes afoot while he was gone.

"Well, it should all be over soon," he said, strolling in with Dom Jacobs, who—in his own trademarked way—maintained a thoughtful distance a step or two behind.

Fleet released Madeleine's hand. He greeted the retired officer with a nod and acknowledged Dom, the human owl, with a friendly smile.

That was how Fleet thought of the other man. Owl-like. He looked like a bird of prey, mostly around the face, but was Adwick his quarry or someone else? Were his intentions here natural, possibly even kindly, or did his imperturbable countenance mask a certain hostility? These were the sort of questions Enescu Fleet asked himself on a regular basis.

He cast another glance at the officer. The latter was peering down at Pixie with the knee-jerk suspicion of a man who would arrest a Maltese in a flash.

It was moments like these that Fleet regretted the light and charming manner he had cultivated for himself over the last fifty years; the manner—hell, the trademarked manner—which precluded him from exhibiting his true feelings about people. As far as the world knew, Fleet enjoyed the company of everyone he met. He liked everybody and respected them, and everybody liked and respected him. In reality, this was only half true. He did not like everyone, and he respected even fewer. Some people he positively loathed, and it was into this arena that Sheriff Adwick had essentially pole-vaulted from the moment the two had met.

"Any new details, Sheriff?"

Adwick sniffed importantly. "Nothing I can go into in the present company, but it's handy having the phones working again. They're sending Weston up from Portland. Good man, Weston, he'll get things done."

"You've worked with him before?"

"Westie? Only once—well, not worked with exactly. He was only passing through. But I felt I made my mark."

Fleet was glad Adwick thought so. "By the way, I wouldn't call him Westie to his face. You may have a history of good-natured mockery I'm not privy to, but in case you don't, it is Weston's wife, Sarah, the district attorney, who goes by the nickname Westie. Not he."

Adwick accepted the correction with a gracious nod and curled lip. He thanked Fleet for the update and said he would bear that distinction in mind. He was sure Westie—that is, Weston—would have appreciated the humor.

"Am I interrupting anything?" he asked, fixing the baker in a not-so-agreeable gaze.

Madeleine took her cue. Setting Phillip on the floor and tapping him encouragingly on the hindquarters, she remarked, "It's about time I got my little man a treat. He hardly had any supper tonight. Much like certain other proud men I won't mention."

She sauntered out, and then there were two. (Actually Dom Jacobs had never moved from his spot by the window, and neither had Pixie, so, in fact, there were still four.)

Fleet smiled at his "colleague." "Something you wish to discuss?"

Adwick glanced at Dom, who nodded. Yes, there was something they wished to discuss. "I know you're fairly close with these Hathaways, Fleet—"

"*Fairly* does not fairly state it, Sheriff."

"And I want you to know, I'll do everything I can to help. I don't know what Hathaway and his wife were up to here tonight, but I'll make sure Weston and his people go easy."

"Your consideration is commendable." Fleet paused. It wasn't necessary to pause very long in order to absorb the finer points of Adwick's thinking processes, but Fleet felt it was the polite thing to do. "You still believe he and Lesley were involved in the doings this evening? You think, perhaps, that Johnny hatcheted himself in the back with a meat cleaver?"

"No—" Adwick hesitated. He peered at Dom, who shook his head. No, they didn't think that. "I'd be willing to bet that something else was going on there. But I wouldn't put it past them to have their hands in *something*. You don't know them like I do, Fleet. At Rangeley Manor—that's where I first encountered the two of them—they were a slippery pair. She shows up under a false name. He sashays in, claiming to have an uncle who's a congressman—"

"Johnny's uncle *is* a congressman."

"And that's even worse," said Adwick. "Maybe that's why she did it. The uncle's got money."

Fleet cocked his eyebrow. "Do I understand you correctly—you believe Lesley was actually behind the assault on her husband?"

"I wouldn't put it past her. In my experience, it's frequently the wife who tries to do in her husband, and the husband the wife. If I had a dollar for every time my ex-wife—but that's not important," he said. "What I'm getting at is this. I feel sorry for them now."

Fleet fixed the officer with an indulgent eye. It was hard to hate the man when he had clearly gone insane. "You must be mellowing in your old age, Sheriff."

Adwick thought he probably was. "Now that my daughter is, for lack of a better phrase—*set up*—I've been considering taking some important steps in my own life." He glanced at Dom, who nodded. "You might feel like that yourself sometimes. Might I ask, how long has your daughter been married?"

Fleet frowned. "You're mistaken, Sheriff. Ate is not married."

Adwick said oh. He naturally assumed—the guy in the glasses—his mistake.

"Well, that's all I wanted to say," he concluded.

"I appreciate your visit," Fleet replied.

Adwick nodded and left. He, too, resisted curtsying. Dom Jacobs approved.

Downstairs in the kitchen, the ladies of *Le Vrai Cornichon* were discussing the various events of the evening. There were two camps at the moment, the "poor Sven" camp and the "poor-what's-his-name-oh-right-Hathaway" camp. Who were they sadder about?

Nancy was the founder and spokeswoman for the Sven camp. As a one-time colleague, both in and out of the culinary arts, she felt it was only right.

Evelynn also favored Sven, even if the man had the worst temper she had ever seen and rode the women ragged during all the practice dinners the previous weeks. Hathaway seemed nice, though. She was sorry he had to go and get himself cleavered.

Betty was staunchly on the *poor Johnny* bandwagon, as he was one of her husband's oldest friends and their guest. But as Sven's employer, she felt she should show him some support as well. It was so hard running a restaurant.

Zoe was all for—what was his name again? That's right—Hathaway. She liked Hathaway.

Ditters Dittersdorf, standing at the counter idly rolling a lemon under his palm, felt it did not befit his position as *Cornichon* president to attempt a tiebreaker. The women went on nattering, while he stared off into the distance—a smaller, less adequately bearded Enescu Fleet.

Like the sheriff, Ditters and Betty had not made it very far in their search for help. Roughly a third of the way down the slope, Betty had remembered that their neighbor's house wasn't on the east side, it was on the west; and Ditters had realized that this was just as well, since the family living there had moved away two weeks ago.

He looked up now, as Vivian Birch and Cesar Bloom came in to ask if they could assist with the food. It had been ages since they had helped out in a kitchen—really helped, not simply collected profits.

While they chopped and assembled, the feeling of the old days came rushing back. They remembered how it was, before semi-fame and (some) fortune had complicated things. They embraced these memories fondly.

"What you want to do there is slice the meat on a bias," instructed Vivian. "Wait, I can show you."

"These are damn good pickles," said Cesar, sampling some of their prep work.

All this, and still Ditters did not speak. Not even his favorite subject perked him up. It was all his fault, everything that had happened here tonight.

He knew what he had to do.

"It's not your fault."

Ate sat at the end of the three tables in the main dining room, while Hutton lay stretched out between them, thinking.

He did not agree with her assessment. "It's entirely my fault," he said.

Ate sighed. "It's thanks to you that the phones are working, and the police are on their way."

"Tell that to Hath. I never should have ignored him. I told him to go away. That was what I said to him before he went inside. 'Just go, Hath.' "

"Well, I don't even remember what I said to him. But it wasn't, 'Hey, watch out for cleavers in the shadows.' You can't blame yourself."

Hutton disagreed with her there too. He could blame himself, and he did.

"But you shouldn't. When the police arrive—"

"The hell with the coppers. This is personal now. What could his clue have meant, Ate? A bottle of whisky. Hath had to have a reason for grabbing it."

She had nothing to suggest. Her expertise did not lie in whisky. That had always been her father's thing. Scotch was one of the few items he collected obsessively. (She supposed it was better than the freak show she had seen in Ditters' room upstairs. She shivered just thinking of it.) "You ponder on it while I close my eyes for a second."

Hutton jerked up, sending a dinner roll careening into the shadows. "I'm a total wanker. I haven't even asked you how you are. How are you?"

Ate smiled and said she was fine. Just a little tired.

Hutton kissed her on the forehead and lay back down on the cherrywood top. "You're a good woman, Ate Fleet."

"And you're a good man—sorry, I'm going to keep calling you Hutton for now."

Hutton didn't mind. Hutton was his name. Sort of.

"Anyway, you just need to give yourself a chance," she said. "You'll figure it out. You always do."

This time he agreed. He would figure it out. He had to figure it out—for Hath.

"No one is going to stick a cleaver in my friend without an argument," he asserted. And he meant it.

"Have you seen my husband anywhere?" asked Betty Dittersdorf.

Fleet stepped down from the last step of the staircase and frowned. "No. Has he gone missing?"

"I don't know. He was looking very peculiar, and then I looked up and he had disappeared."

Fleet didn't like the sound of this. "Is there anywhere—"

"Come quick!" shouted Zoe Norris, flying around the corner. "I think Mr. Dittersdorf is going to do himself in!"

"What!" said Betty. "Why do you say that?"

"I just passed him in the hall, and he said he was going up to the roof and not to bother him. I think he's going to jump! Come quick!"

They came quick. Fleet. Betty. And everyone else within fifty yards of the waitress's squeaks.

It was the first attempt at a vertical climb for the *Cornichon* herd. Up until that point, their movements had all occupied a single horizontal dimension.

They got there well enough. A few members of the party nearly pitched over the railing. But they got there.

"This way," cried the waitress, "the door to the roof is just around the corner."

As they rolled down the hall, a single pretty head—brunette and attractively turned-out—poked out from Ditters and Betty's bedroom.

"Come quick!" exclaimed Lesley Hathaway.

The assembly paused. These contradictory *Come-quicks* confused them.

"If you're looking for Ditters, he's in here. It's Johnny. Come quick!"

For the second time in the last thirty seconds, the party complied. They came quick—or "quickly" as Nancy Mortimer was heard to whisper.

24 — Healthy Living

I awoke to an outstretched hand, a curious smell and a grinning Ditters Dittersdorf. In the hand was a pickle, some variety I had never seen before (and never wished to see again); on his smiling face the look of a mad preservation expert who had finally snapped.

When the chop fell earlier, I couldn't have told you who had wielded the cleaver, at least not consciously. I didn't like to believe Ditters capable of such a thing, despite his obvious obsessions and the need for him to clear up a few matters. If I had it wrong, however, and this was how he planned on finishing me off, I had every intention of giving him the fight of his life.

I strained against the blankets—apparently I was in bed—and that's when I saw Lesley standing over my bedside, choking back tears of joy. I also saw Enescu Fleet, Hutton, Ate Fleet, Betty, Cesar Bloom, Vivian Birch, Evelynn Brine, Zoe Norris, Nancy Mortimer, Chief Adwick, Dom Jacobs and Madeleine Abrams. I saw a lot of people that evening.

Phillip was sleeping on my foot, Pixie licking my face. At some point she missed my jaw and got a whiff of pickle. She growled mightily and nipped at Ditters' hand.

"Ouch, that smarts!"

"What—do—you—think—you're—doing?" I asked him. I spoke groggily, still wary of that pickle floating around my head.

"I was offering you a treat, Hath. Something to keep your strength up."

I informed him in no uncertain terms that my strength was fine; I didn't like it too high. "What is that, by the way? It smells horrible."

"It just needs to air out a minute," he said, shaking it like a pudgy thermometer. "It's one of my special concoctions. It's fortified."

"Fortified with what?"

"Alcohol. A grain spirit brine. It has Golden Promise in it. I went all the way up to the roof for it. It's good. Taste it."

I had no wish to sample any fortified pickles. "Why was it on the roof?" I asked.

"I have a special vat there, exposed to the sunlight. It's sort of a sun pickle."

Now I definitely had no wish to sample it. Fortified pickles, baked rancid in the sun, were not my cup of vinegar. "I appreciate the thought, Ditters, but no thanks."

"Okay, Hath." He seemed disappointed, but in good spirits. Possibly pickle spirits.

Lesley took a seat in the chair by my side. She had never moved from it the whole time I was out. "It sounds crazy, but I think the pickle might have revived you. I had fallen asleep, and when I woke up I saw Ditters waving the thing under your nose like a dose of smelling salts. I think it brought you back, Johnny."

I agreed with her. It sounded crazy. "What happened? What am I doing here?"

"Don't you remember?"

I heard Hutton cluck, and saw him shaking his head. "He's got amnesia again."

"I don't have amnesia!" I retorted. I remembered everything. Well, most everything. "How did I get here?"

"I carried you," said Fleet.

"You found me?"

"No, you got some help from the rest of the animal kingdom on that."

"Phil," I smiled. My new little buddy.

Fleet said not quite. "Pixie's the one who found you. She came running down the stairs, woofing her little head off and literally dragged us to the spot."

I looked into her shaggy face. Good girl. Apparently, she liked me well enough, after all.

"How much do you remember before then?" Lesley asked.

I glared at Hutton and replied, "It's coming back to me."

"You don't remember any of it, do you?" he said.

"Not at the moment, no."

He nodded knowingly. Amnesia.

I sat up in bed. My back was still sore and, from the looks of it, bandaged. "Who did all this?"

"That would be Dom," answered Fleet.

"Dom?"

"Dom Jacobs," he clarified, and I said thank you. I remembered Somber Dom just fine.

Lesley leaned in and whispered, "He was a marvel, Johnny." She went on to explain how he had stitched up the wound and filled me back to the Plimsoll mark after all the blood I'd spilt.

She was right; that did sound pretty marvelous. "How'd he do that?"

"We were very lucky," he spoke up. "The blade hit a bone, not an organ, and it turns out that Mr. and Mrs. Dittersdorf have a superb medical kit. The real key, though, was the person generous enough to donate blood."

I knew it couldn't have been Lesley. She wasn't the right type.

I looked around. It had to have been Hutton or Fleet. Either one of them would have given you the blood off their back. Not sure how medically sound that was, but they would have done it.

"It was Ate," said Fleet.

I smiled at her. In my semidelirious state, it was probably a pretty goofy smile. Before I could express my gratitude, she responded, "I was the best match. It's no big deal."

I had no wish to embarrass her. I said, "So I have Fleet blood in my veins now?" It would have been funny if it was AB.

"You have some, yes."

"Thanks."

"It's not as special as you might think," she replied.

Dr. Dom took charge again. He told the majority of visitors to move along. The man needed his rest. The police would be arriving soon.

Something in his smooth, commanding drawl seemed to spark a recollection in Lesley. "Now I remember where I've seen you! You're a psychiatrist, specializing in unusual phobias and fixations. I saw you speak at the local college one evening before my cooking class started."

Dom bowed to her identification but said nothing further.

She had another inspiration. "But wait, was Elsie your patient? She had a phobia."

Dom replied in the affirmative. She had a phobia. "As to the identity of my patients, I obviously cannot speak to that." He ushered the rest of the mob out of the room.

All that remained was Fleet, Hutton, Lesley, Ditters, Madeleine and Ate. It was still far too many for the modestly sized, though nicely decorated bedroom. Dom turned to Ate before leaving himself. "You should get some rest too, young lady."

Ate said she was okay.

I jerked up from the blankets, no doubt pulling out several of Dom's stitches in the process. "Good God, he's right! You had no business giving blood. Not in your condition."

The whole room, what was left, stared at me. I'm sure they put it down to the ravings of the recently cleaved, but I stuck to my guns. There was no reason for her to be a hero.

"I'm sorry, but you have to tell them," I said.

She stared at me. "I have no idea what you're talking about, Hathaway."

"You're—" I looked at Hutton. I had come too far to back away now. "You're pregnant, of course. I deduced it immediately."

The whole room, and it seemed strangely smaller now, turned to Fleet's daughter.

"Pregnant?" he asked.

She laughed. Not well, but there was a definite attempt at a chortle there. She coughed. "Of course I'm not pregnant."

The room said oh. They breathed more freely.

Ate was staring at Hutton now. I was glad it wasn't at me. I might have taken a slight misstep in my deducing. But I was so certain—

"As a matter of fact," she said, "we're married."

Enescu Fleet sat down on the end of the bed and began smoothing the fur on Phil's head. Pixie, weaving her way around my blanketed legs, bounded up on his arm, as if to ask, "What the hell?"

"Perhaps you'd better explain that," he told his daughter. Before she could explain—it remained to be seen if it would be better—he turned and gazed at Hutton.

I gazed at him myself.

"Hello," he replied brightly.

"It was a spur-of-the-moment decision," Ate began.

"Obviously," said her father.

"It was after Hathaway and Lesley had their ceremony last month. Hutton and I were hanging around town—you'd left—and I suppose I started getting a little depressed."

"You wished you were married too?" asked Lesley.

"Not at first. I mean, the idea didn't cross my mind then. I guess I felt lonely and left out, though. You see, it was my birthday."

Fleet slowed in his canine-massaging duties and peered up. His eyes fell on Madeleine. "That was always her mother's job," he whispered. Left to his own devices, he was lucky if he remembered Christmas.

"So anyway, Hutton suggested cheering me up with a trip to Vegas. We went, and had some fun, but I still felt, I don't know, empty."

"So you decided to fill the void with a quickie marriage?"

"You needn't make it sound so trivial, Dad. It—we—" She appeared to be struggling for a phrase more impactful than *it seemed like a good idea at the time*. "Oh, you wouldn't understand!"

An awkward silence loomed. I took a shot at lightening it.

"At least you won't have to change your name."

She flashed a glare my way, then just as quickly softened it. "No, I suppose I won't."

Ditters was confused. "I don't get it. Why won't she have to change her name?"

"Hutton's last name is also Fleet," I explained.

Ditters wore a peculiar frown. He looked like one of his sun pickle vats had gone off and the smell was drifting into the bedroom. "He's a Fleet too?" He lowered his voice tactfully. "You're not siblings, are you?"

Hutton told him not to be stupid. "I'm a cousin—an *adopted* cousin, that is. I have no Fleet blood in me at all."

"I do," I quipped, and then hushed up again. Perhaps I was still a little lightheaded.

"Oh, *cousins*," said Ditters. "My parents were cousins, second cousins, I think—or maybe just one of them was. Anyway, I turned out fine."

Hutton and Ate looked at each other. Those peculiar pickle frowns seemed to be spreading.

"So what's your name, then?" Ditters asked Hutton. "You might as well tell me; I've got half of it now."

Hutton sighed. "Enescu Fleet."

"I know that name."

"I am Enescu Fleet," said Enescu Fleet. "Hutton's parents named him after me."

Ditters looked at Ate. He was beginning to understand. "So you married your father," he remarked jovially. "I mean, in a funny sort of way, you did."

Ate blinked at him. I thought I detected a slight irritation emanating from the little woman regarding her husband's friends. They might have to have a talk about that later.

Ditters, meanwhile, couldn't have been more pleased. "So that's the deep, dark secret. It's not a bad name. So why did we call you Hutton?"

Hutton sighed again. He always found explanation tedious. "My initials are E. F." He gazed at his friend, waiting for something to register. The friend gazed back dully. "E. F. Hutton. See?"

Ditters didn't. Hutton went on sighing.

"E. F. Hutton was an important muckety-muck in high finance. Lent his name to a brokerage firm—" he prompted. "Very talked about when we were growing up—"

Ditters said ah. He'd never heard of the bloke. "Is that why you were so interested in the restaurant's financial reports?"

Hutton's third sigh put an end to the discussion. Ditters took the hint. "So we're all married? I'm married, Hutton's married, Hath too. All God's children are married."

I noticed Fleet wasn't showering anyone with rice. "The authorities should be here in roughly half an hour," he stated.

He stood up.

"Dad—" said Ate.

Madeleine spoke quickly, trying to prevent a schism in the family. "I think you'll both be very happy, Ate. Your dad married his wife, your mother, very abruptly. A whirlwind romance. It amazed everyone." She said the last part with a slight hitch in her speech. "And they couldn't have had a happier life."

Fleet glanced back at her. He wore a complex expression, equally mixed with gratitude and pain. He could not deny what she said, but he somehow regretted that she had said it.

"I have a question," I said.

All heads turned in my direction. Reluctantly, but they turned.

"Since when are the police coming? I thought the phones were down?"

"Hutton got the phones working," said Ate. She spoke absently.

"Oh yeah? How?"

He fielded that one himself. "There were jammers all over the property. That's why we couldn't get a call out on our mobiles. It had nothing to do with the reception."

I was delighted to hear it. "Will the cops be able to reach us, though? The roads—"

"The roads are fine. They've been clear for hours. The authorities are still a ways off—that's why we had to deal with your wound ourselves. But they're coming. Whoever killed Elsie and Sven wished to keep us here a little longer than usual. They turned on a series of hoses around the driveway. With the slope of the hill, and the precipitation already on the ground, it provided a nice moat of ice around the restaurant. After that, all they had to do was make sure it didn't melt too quickly. They did that by spiking the salt."

"Spiking it how?"

"They replaced it with rock sugar."

I was astounded. The old Elsie Farmer maneuver. Her original prank against Sven back in cooking school.

I began pulling away the covers. "Sounds like we have half an hour to solve the thing, then."

No one else stirred. It had been a long day.

Even Hutton regarded me blankly.

Slowly, the rock sugar of his mood began to transmogrify back into salt, melting away his frozen reserve. "Hath's right. We have a little more than thirty minutes here. We can do this. We've never failed before, and I don't plan on starting now. It's like I said earlier—"

" 'No one is going to stick a cleaver in my friend without an argument'?" I quoted.

He stared at me. "Yes. That's right, Hath. How did you—"

I dismissed my sudden clairvoyance. It was not important how I knew. Besides, I had no clue how. I just knew.

"I have a few ideas I wish to discuss," I told them. I gazed around the room. "Perhaps Hutton, Fleet and I can have a moment alone?"

I didn't like leaving Lesley out of it, not after she sat by my side the last couple hours, but I couldn't exclude Ditters alone without attracting his attention. I gave her a wink, and I thought she understood. If she didn't, she would be sure I understood her displeasure later.

Madeleine was gracious as always. "He probably wants to discuss his clue."

I blinked at her.

"The clue you left after your stabbing," Fleet explained.

I was still baffled. Then it began to come back. I had left a clue; they were right.

Now, what was it?

"When we found you," said Hutton, "you were grasping a whisky bottle."

I knew that. "Why a whisky bottle?" I asked.

"We were hoping you could enlighten us," said Fleet.

I frowned. "Well—"

"You don't remember why you grabbed it?"

I shook my head.

Hutton muttered something. He had his diagnosis, and he was sticking to it.

"It is an unusual situation," agreed Fleet. "We're no strangers to murder victims leaving a 'dying clue.' As Maddy has pointed out on several occasions, it seems to work out that way an inordinate number of times for us. This is the first time, however, that the victim has left behind a dying clue without actually dying."

I nodded. I appreciated the advantage I had provided by living, and wished I could help them out, but I had nothing.

"Maybe it was planted," said Ate. "Like the cookie thing and Elsie."

Fleet didn't believe it was. Not this time. "There may be another explanation why he doesn't remember why he did it."

"Amnesia," muttered Hutton.

"No, not amnesia. He may not have observed the killer, but his unconscious mind did."

Hutton said it was an interesting theory. We should bring it up to Dom Jacobs sometime.

"I'm not sure we require his expertise in this instance. We can do it ourselves."

Lesley was on board. "All we have to do is figure out what his unconscious mind was saying, and we'll have the killer?"

"Precisely."

"So we don't need Hathaway at all," Ate remarked.

"Not so you would notice," said Hutton.

"Thanks, guys," I replied.

Madeleine made a broad gesture. "Perhaps it was the label on the bottle. I know with wines, there is often quite a story behind each vineyard."

Fleet considered the idea, then reluctantly rejected it. The label was from a nondescript distiller and was very faded on the bottle. "I don't think Johnny could have seen it from that far across the room. Based on the trail of blood—"

"Please!" said my wife.

"—he would have dragged himself a considerable distance before he could make it out."

"It's something to do with the hootch itself, then," said Hutton. "He wanted to tell us something scotch-related. That had to be what he was thinking. He was scotch-minded."

"I'm still right here," I said.

Madeleine tried again. "Maybe he was—no, never mind it. I'm still thinking of wine."

"Maybe he meant to grab wine," chimed in Ate. It seemed the sort of thing he/I would do, she said.

Lesley had to confess that there might be something in that. "I remember once he went all the way down to the corner store for some soy sauce, and when he came home, it was Worcestershire."

Hutton recalled the resulting stir-fry was very beefy.

I also remembered the incident. I brought home Worcestershire because Lesley had asked for Worcestershire. The soy canard was a complete frame-up.

"Seriously, people," I insisted.

Madeleine waved another meditative hand. "It would have been much easier if he had reached for the wine. There is so much history in wine. Each vineyard, each family name. It is the life's blood of France." She looked up and frowned. Fleet and Hutton were staring at her. "And Californian wines are also very fine," she added. Always the culinary diplomat, that Madeleine Abrams.

Neither stare ebbed. It was not vintner chauvinism that compelled their bad manners. Something had occurred to them.

Fleet stared at Hutton, Hutton at Fleet.

"It couldn't be," said Fleet.

"Or could it?" asked Hutton.

"It's so simple," said the elder PI.

"Simple as they come," agreed the up-and-comer.

Fleet stepped briskly across the room, took Madeleine's tender face in his hands and kissed her quickly on the lips. "You're brilliant."

Hutton thought she was brilliant too. Newly married, and with his wife standing right there, he merely gave her an enthusiastic OK-sign with his hand.

I tried to speak, but he cut in before I could. "We need to figure this out," he told Fleet.

"I believe I have it mostly mapped out now," said his new father-in-law. "The pieces are falling into place nicely."

The pieces were falling nicely for Hutton as well. "Five minutes?"

"Call it ten," Fleet replied.

Hutton smiled. He could have done it in five.

Fleet put his arm around Ditters. He had to stoop slightly. "Would you mind assembling everyone upstairs in ten minutes?"

Ditters looked as baffled as I was. "What, in here?"

"No, no. Somewhere more expansive."

"The drawing room?" Hutton offered. "You don't mind, do you, Hath? Returning to the scene of your axing?"

"I think perhaps the drawing room is too on the nose," said Fleet. "Also, there are not enough seats, and Betty is currently soaking the hearthrug in various solvents. I think I saw a meeting room down the hall—"

Ditters said the meeting room was A-okay too. What were we talking about?

Hutton and Fleet had no time to explain. The denouement would take place in the meeting room, ten minutes from now.

Fleet kissed Madeleine again—both times I noticed an interesting look on her face—and then he went out with Pixie.

"Come on, you little booger-head." (He was speaking to the dog.) The little booger-head came.

Hutton followed right behind, pausing to give the baker a friendly fist-bump. No sense getting overly personal with Fleet's bird. He'd done enough of that already.

And then there were just the four of us. Ditters. Madeleine. Lesley. And myself.

"Seriously, what are we talking about?" I asked.

25 — Clearing Away

I never did get a chance to tell them about Ditters' secret shrine and how it made me feel. I guess I would have to schedule a session with Dr. Dom on that.

I noticed Ditters hadn't left with everyone else. Madeleine had excused herself soon after. If she had been my murderer, I wouldn't have minded at all. A charming woman, and one who knew never to overstay her welcome. I liked that in a murderer.

I couldn't say that about Ditters. And, yes, I realized it was technically his room to begin with, but who had put me there? That's what I kept going over in my head.

Perhaps to relieve some of that brain friction, Lesley pushed her fingers through my hair. It was then that the man finally took his cue. "Well, I won't horn in on you lovebirds any longer. See ya in ten, folks."

I followed him out the door with my stare. Maybe it was the pain relievers Dom Jacobs had administered, or my natural distrust of men who wake me with pickles, but I couldn't help suspecting my old friend still. It pained me to do it, but they don't make relievers for that.

I hadn't liked the look of relief on his face when it was revealed that I couldn't remember who had tried to murder me. I thought it was a look of relief. It could have been a daydream about dill, I supposed.

The clue I had left could have pointed to him. Who was it that mentioned they were thinking of making whisky? Ditters. Who was it that had the market cornered on Golden Promise barley? Ditters.

It gave me food for thought.

Of course, there were other parties privy to the GP. And if my unconscious mind really wanted to indicate Ditters, it could have directed my hand to any number of pickle-related knickknacks in the parlor.

I just didn't know what to think. It gave me food for confusion.

"—don't you think?" Lesley asked.

I wondered how long she had been talking. I really had to work on that.

"Don't I think—?"

"That's it's wonderful that Hutton and Ate are married?"

Oh, that. "Absolutely," I said.

"And it turns out she wasn't pregnant at all. You probably didn't notice it, but I was sort of wondering if she might be, from the way she was acting. But she wasn't."

No. Apparently not even a little. "That's a job for more experienced couples," I replied.

Lesley frowned. "I wanted to talk to you about that, Johnny."

I was expecting she would. My bandages were still a little restrictive, but I could probably make a go of it if I leaned a certain way—

"I don't want to push you into anything," she said. "We have our whole lives."

Yes, our whole lives. I recalled Madeleine's words. Fleet and his wife's life together. That wasn't that long, from what I understood. What if they had waited? What if they had skipped it entirely? It wasn't a pleasant thing to think about. I liked Ate.

I had made up my mind. "I don't think we should wait."

"No?"

"No."

"What changed your mind? Almost dying?"

"It helped."

"Is that what happened to your captain Picard? He almost died and then—"

"Never mind Captain Picard," I said. I was sorry I'd ever brought him up.

"But you're sure you really have changed your mind?"

I was sure. "We'll just have to teach the little lass how to watch out for danger. We don't want her coming home looking like a pincushion like her old man."

"Lass? You don't want a son?"

Son, daughter, lass, it was all good. I supposed I leaned a little toward a daughter. Not that it was up to me. A little Lesley. How adorable would that be? More adorable than a little Hathaway, that was certain. I'd had my fill of that guy for years.

"We'll just have to strain both our brains to keep her safe. Neither one of us is exactly responsible. But if we knuckle down and really concentrate, it might be okay. You remember Warren's friend, Mahrute? The quality bodyguard? Maybe he could help out for a few years—"

A look of alarm had crept across Lesley's face. "You don't really think our child would be in danger, do you? I'm sure Fleet can deal with this Arnold Bernard—"

It had nothing to do with Arnold Bernard. "Kids need constant watching. When I think how negligent some parents can be—"

The alarm turned to realization. She finally understood. "You were never balking at having children out of selfishness, were you?"

"No. Who said I was?"

"I did, I guess. But you weren't being selfish at all. You were being obsessive. It's not that you couldn't love; you were worried that you would love too much."

"Something like that," I said. Why, was that weird? She was acting like it was weird.

"But, Johnny, you can't love your children too much. And you don't have to worry about keeping them safe. Lots of people a lot stupider than us manage to get the job done."

I supposed there were some people stupider than us. And I was in possession of *Special F* in my blood now. That could only help.

I took her hand in mine. It looked cool whenever Fleet did it. "We'll just take it as it comes. Hopefully, the child won't inherit all my traits, such as not knowing when to duck when someone swings a meat cleaver at them."

Lesley agreed. She also wouldn't mind if she skipped out on inheriting the Darlington family's giant hippopotamus feet.

She jumped up (she didn't look like she had big hippo feet to me. The hostess Evelynn, but not her). "What do you think the guys have planned in the meeting room?" she asked.

I had no idea. "They seem to have something figured out."

"You still can't remember who tried to kill you?"

"Nope. Not sure I ever knew."

"Not your conscious brain anyway?"

No, not him. My conscious brain was an idiot.

Lesley said she had a few things to do before they got started. She must look a wreck.

I wouldn't say a wreck, no (except for her feet). She went to freshen up, regardless of my insistence that she looked fine, and almost at once, Ditters took her place. He appeared thoughtful and disturbed, which was not a good look on him.

I think it was the beard. He looked like an Amish hitman who had just been shunned.

It seemed fitting, in a way, that my wife's vanity would lead to her husband's premature demise. Once, while attempting to adjust her makeup in the passenger seat of my car, she had turned the rearview mirror toward herself, almost causing me to swerve into the path of a convoy of dump trucks. She maintained that the rearview had nothing to do with my swerving, while I maintained that she was a little fathead. We can laugh about it now.

This time she had left me alone with Ditters Dittersdorf, and I wasn't laughing.

He walked up and down the room, the tips of his fingers pressed together in concentration. "Are you comfortable, Hath?" he asked.

I said I was comfortable enough.

"Nothing I can do?"

I said nothing I could think of, no. There were a couple of things I would rather he didn't do, but other than that—

He nodded slowly. He released the tips long enough to pick up a pillow from a side chair. He fluffed it idly. "Hath, is it my imagination, or are you acting a little distant toward me lately? Almost like you're afraid of me or something."

I said it must be his imagination. I wasn't distant or afraid. I asked him what he thought he was doing with that pillow.

He set the murder linen down again. "I know you've been sliced and diced and that couldn't have been pleasant— By the way, I haven't been able to locate one of my meat cleavers. They think that's what got you. Adwick must have it for evidence or something, but I'd like it back. Anyway, did I do anything to offend you?"

"No."

"Did I not do something, and that offended you?"

"No."

"Did you do something I ignored and that caused some offense—"

I said no. I wasn't offended. I was fine.

He took out a revolver. It looked a little like the revolver I had found in Sven's hand, only longer in the barrel.

I was less fine. Where was Warren Kingsley's friend Mahrute when you needed him?

Ditters explained himself. "Don't be alarmed. Just checking the hardware. Until the old man and/or Hutton reveal the murderer among us, I've taken to packing heat. It's not comfortable in my pocket, though. Keeps chafing me."

I leaned up. The time had come for plain speaking. Maybe, just maybe, if I got in his head before this went much further, I could talk him down. "I know you're not right in the noggin just now, Ditters. It's not your fault. But you don't want to do this."

Ditters blinked at me. "Do what, Hath?"

"Shoot me."

Ditters blinked some more. "Shoot you? Why would I shoot you?"

Exactly. That's what I wanted to hear. "Give me the gun, Ditters."

Ditters gave me the gun. "You're not going to shoot me, are you?"

That was a stupid thing to ask. "Of course I'm not going to shoot you!"

Ditters said good. We were in agreement, then. He wasn't going to shoot me, and I wasn't going to shoot him.

We stared at each other in confusion.

"I saw your shrine," I told him.

"Shrine?"

"The mementos from all our cases."

"Oh that!" He plopped down on the bed. Phillip woofed. Neither of us had seen him lying there, lurking. He was like a canine Dom Jacobs.

Ditters got more situated. "I was hoping that would be a surprise."

I didn't know what he meant. "Surprise how?"

"I've been collecting all that for months. That's why I pretended I didn't know anything about your business. It was all part of the surprise."

I nodded. I was beginning to pick up that the theme here was a surprise.

Ditters went on, "They were gifts. Well, one for you and one for Hutton. And then I was going to give one to Lesley and one to Fleet's daughter. I was thinking you might like the sheet music, and Hutton the painting. Do you think Fleet would like the wheel?"

I said I would prefer the wheel, as long as he was asking. "So wait. You collected all these tokens of our cases as a surprise gift for everyone? Where'd you get the music?"

"Oh, I just bought that off a guy who knew a guy who worked for the Romanian government. Not certain it's authentic, but his accent sounded right."

I agreed accents were important. "So you weren't keeping these items as a deranged shrine to your old friends—friends you secretly hated and were planning on murdering in your restaurant?"

Saying it, I could see how it might have sounded a little less than gracious. I felt bad about that.

Ditters did too, apparently. "You thought I was the killer?"

"I didn't really *think* it. It just crossed my mind once or twice."

He went on gawking. "Then you must have thought I killed Elsie and Sven."

"Well—"

"Hath, how could you?"

"I wasn't happy I thought it, Ditters. But the evidence was stacked against you. Elsie was an old girlfriend, likely to make things awkward for you and Betty. Sven used too much lemon zest, and he was found with a lemon in his mouth."

Ditters hadn't heard about the lemon. He thought he had been a fruit short at last count.

As for the evidence stacked against him, he had a response to that too. It was coarse.

"In case you have forgotten," he continued, less crudely, "Betty was okay with my past with Elsie—you saw that yourself. Not that it was that big a thing anyway. And who kills a person over citrus zest? Maybe I would have come to like it—who knows? As for trying to kill you, Hath, you're one of my closest friends. I bought a ship's wheel for you, for God's sake."

He made a strong argument. I apologized for thinking he was a killer. What more could I say?

"So how did you afford the wheel?" I asked him. "It couldn't have come cheap."

He furrowed his brow. I don't think my apology had been one-hundred percent accepted. "I didn't actually buy it."

"You stole a ship's wheel?"

"No. Betty and I went to this charity auction from the sunken yacht you were on. I just thought I'd pick up a plank of the boards or something to add to my collection, but then they ended the auction with a raffle, and I won the wheel."

"Nice," I said.

He thanked me for the compliment. It had been nice, yes. It was more than he could say for me.

I apologized again. I'd had a pretty hard day, I reminded him.

Ditters supposed I had. He slid down from the mattress.

"I guess we should see what the rest of the detectives have to say. Hopefully, they won't try to railroad me like you did."

I agreed that one could always hope.

I laughed lightly, bringing out another rigid glare from my old friend. I was glad we had established that he wasn't a killer. He could have a real dark look about him when he wanted. "I was just remembering the last time we saw each other. I thought you were trying to kill me then too, remember?"

Ditters remembered.

"That's when I hired Warren Kingsley as my bodyguard. What a lark that was."

Ditters said Warren wasn't so bad. "I bumped into him last year. He gave me a fantastic recipe for fish chowder. You had it at dinner tonight."

I mused on this after he had left me to dress. He had a point about Warren.

That soup had been pretty dynamite.

26 — Bold Flavors

Since meeting Enescu Fleet, I had attended my share of dramatic reveals and denouements, and even an unmasking or two. It had become pretty routine. That said, I couldn't recall taking part in any of them while pumped full of drugs in order to dull the effects of a butcher knife in the back.

That was a new sensation, and one I could do with experiencing just the once.

The narcotics, coupled with the late hour, were causing a touch of drowsiness. I would nod off now and then, Lesley later insisting that I had also been muttering in my sleep.

I don't know how Fleet and Hutton decided who would address the populace. Perhaps they played rock, paper, scissors for it. Maybe Hutton had simply deferred to the old man. As Ditters could tell you, there was nothing wrong with buttering up your father-in-law.

While my eyes periodically drooped shut, then shot open, then drooped closed again, Fleet provided a tight and well-told synopsis of the evening's goings-on.

He detailed these, not as we had experienced them, but in their actual sequence as he understood it. He explained how Arnold Bernard, arch-villain and notorious scamp, had worked from afar to accomplish his goals. Unknowingly, Ditters and Betty had opened their doors to a dozen or so guests, some of whom were pawns in Bernard's diabolical dinner theater, others coming in purely as a side dish.

These people, Fleet argued, played no role in Bernard's drama and could be considered human hush puppies of a sort—fillers without any real nutritional value.

Several of these persons, seated around the table, frowned and muttered to themselves.

The purpose of this charade, Fleet told us—or so it would seem, he said—was to put the semiretired detective through his paces. Make him jump through hoops. Watch him dance. Fleet repeated the phrase: *or so it would seem.*

In order to accomplish this outrageous entertainment, Arnold required the assistance of someone at *Le Vrai Cornichon*. This person would agree to this for one of two reasons. Insane devotion to Arnold Bernard or some ulterior motive that coincided nicely with Arnold's plans.

Fleet took the second proposition first. Among the party, plenty of folks had motives for wanting Elsie Farmer out of the way. Take Cesar and Vivian: the secret lovers who resented Elsie Farmer's success.

It was Elsie, Fleet had since discovered (after making a few late-night calls), who had recently been offered a prime-time hosting gig, a gig now open to other candidates. Cesar Bloom and Vivian Birch were those kinds of candidates—which explained why Vivian had professed her sorrow over Elsie's death "now of all times."

That made for a pretty good motive. The couple also disliked Elsie for what she held over them. She knew of their relationship and could, on a whim, use that information against them. No, Cesar and Vivian would not have minded at all if someone had gotten Elsie Farmer out of the picture. But were they killers or just ambitious, adulterous snobs?

Cesar looked at Vivian, Vivian at Cesar.

Next up there was Ditters Dittersdorf. He had once had a relationship with Elsie Farmer. The woman's indiscreet manner and flare for vindictiveness could have complicated his newest business venture and his happy marriage. But was inconvenience and awkwardness a sufficient motive for cold-blooded murder? That depended on how awkward and inconvenient Elsie wished to make it.

Then there was Zoe Norris, Ditters' waitress.

I saw Zoe stiffen in her seat.

There was Zoe, Fleet proceeded, who was deeply in love with her employer. Zoe, the unprepossessing employee. Zoe, whom no one noticed and who would do anything for the man she secretly cared for, a man compromised by this vamp from the past.

Zoe had gone completely rigid and was making a strange, deflating noise from between her lips. It might just be my opinion, but I don't believe she cared for having her secret love revealed.

The board glared at her from their various spots around the table, none more glary than Betty Dittersdorf. Ditters barely looked at her himself. He was used to having women adore him.

Zoe continued wheezing, while Ate leaned in and said, "Try not to sweat it too much. He always does this."

It was true. Fleet never seemed to mind carting out people's skeletons from the closet. He was all about thoroughness.

She might not believe it now, but it was a good thing that he had spilled the beans. It was good to clear the air. She couldn't go on harboring this devotion. Give her a few more months and she would start her own shrine to the D-man, and it wouldn't be an amusing misunderstanding like his had been to me. It would be the full megillah, complete with X's through photos of Betty's face and pictures of Zoe cut out and pasted next to Ditters in group shots. No one wanted that.

"So whom have I left out?" asked Fleet.

"The human hush puppies," muttered Nancy Mortimer snarkily.

He thanked her. Not only for the prompt, but for a reminder about another pair of interested parties. "There are a few more non-fillers. There are Nancy and Sven, investors in a distillery that would only come to pass if Ditters' restaurant failed."

"I told you, I knew nothing about that."

"Nothing of the 'prank,' perhaps, but you knew of the proposal. Sven most certainly knew about it. He planned Elsie's accident. The question is, how far did he intend to go with it?"

"You would bring that up," Nancy hissed—"since he's dead and can't defend himself!"

Once again, Fleet thanked her. "The very point I was going to make myself. Sven is dead, murdered. This murder was done to make a statement, or so—again—it would seem. On first blush, it would appear this bold statement was spoken, figuratively, by Ditters Dittersdorf. He hated the chef—hated him even more when he learned of his scheming—and after killing him, it would seem that he couldn't resist showcasing the deed with a nod to one of their popular culinary disagreements. I refer to Sven's adherence to citrus zest and Ditters' hatred of it. Had this been the case, it would have been indicative of a man with a deranged killer instinct and an even more deranged sense of humor."

The deranged one looked up from a fingernail that appeared to be giving him a problem. "What? I wasn't listening."

Cesar Bloom approached the conundrum from a technical angle. "What don't you like about lemon zest?"

"It's yucky," said Ditters, chewing off the nail and spitting it on the floor.

Vivian Birch shook her head in disapproval. "It's a necessary piquant addition, my man. Absolutely necessary. End of story."

Hutton came to our friend's defense. "That's enough with the foodie-talk, you two. You set yourself up as these culinary gods, but you're not the be-all and end-all of good taste. I mean, you—Birch woman—you don't even like cinnamon. What sort of monster could hate cinnamon?"

Vivian stared at her accuser in disbelief. "How did you know that?"

I've mentioned how Hutton disliked revealing his methods and giving explanations (nearly as much as Vivian disliked the bark of the cinnamon tree). But in order to move things along quickly and get back on point, he replied, "I saw it on your Twitter feed once."

"But that must have been three years ago: a slip-up during an interview. It cost me a job on *Dig Dem Desserts*. I haven't mentioned it again since."

Hutton, who had a near eidetic memory, didn't know what that had to do with it. Didn't everyone remember everything they saw on Twitter?

Fleet, placing his hand on the shoulder of the first chair and thanking him for his comments, continued, "Ditters was meant to look like the culprit behind Sven's death—and therefore Elsie's murder—but it didn't fit. It was sloppy. Overly theatrical."

"Isn't everything this Bernard does theatrical?" asked Madeleine.

"It is. But it isn't haphazard. The murder of Sven was. I tried to put it in context of everything else that had occurred here tonight, make it fit, and I couldn't. Our attention had already been directed to Sven as the likely perpetrator of Elsie's murder. And then, the key evidence to that effect came to light. Sven Hosten was related by marriage to Arnold Bernard. The case would appear to be closed. Sven was Arnold's man, and shortly before we discovered this, Sven disappeared. It was open-and-shut.

"But who, then, had killed Sven? If Sven had committed suicide, I might have understood. That would have been tidy at least. But Sven had not killed himself. Was it possible that Arnold Bernard had more than one accomplice here? Perhaps, but I had not known him to work that way before. Last time, one accomplice was more than enough, and even then the latter was shortly dealt with. Until Sven's death, everything here had the appearance of a carefully constructed play for Arnold's and our entertainment, mostly Arnold's. But this was different. It was almost as if two scripts had gotten mixed together after the dress rehearsal. Once the footlights had gone up, the actor was defying the director's instructions."

Fleet took a break to let everyone absorb what he had said. If it were possible to be both baffled and riveted, the detective's board members were that. The analogies to the stage were a little beyond most of them—their bag was food (except for Cesar Bloom, whose bags were both)—but it sounded like good stuff, and they wanted to know more.

Fleet satisfied their appetites. "Fortunately, we don't have to rack our brains too much about the killer's motivations. Not yet anyway. We have a shortcut to that person's identity. In short, we have Johnny."

The board turned toward me. I shook more fully awake. I had heard every word.

"Johnny saw the murderer," continued Fleet.

I nodded drowsily. Saw the murderer. Yes. Wait, had I?

"He might not recall seeing his assailant consciously, but his unconscious mind did see. His clue proves that. As George Bernard Shaw tells us, *the unconscious mind is the real genius.* Isn't that so, Dom?"

Dom Jacobs perked up. He was starting to look a little like a depressed boa constrictor. Fleet's question uncoiled him. "Shaw did indeed. He actually had many fascinating insights on the topic—"

Fleet cut him short. No one likes a blabbermouth. "The genius of the unconscious mind. What was Johnny's unconscious genius trying to tell us? What of his 'almost' dying clue?"

"The whisky," said Hutton. "The bottle he snagged just before passing out."

Adwick said ah. That had bothered him as well.

"But what does it mean?" asked Evelynn Brine.

Fleet smiled. He loved it when people asked him things like that.

"As many of you already know, Johnny and Lesley have been toying with having a child. This involved—well, I don't need to tell you everything it involved—but it did entail picking up some new knowledge. Johnny has been hitting the books pretty steadily over it."

"They needed a book?" Vivian asked.

"The book of baby names," said Fleet. "He mentioned it before. Thanks to his studies, there isn't a name origin that eludes him now. For, as many of you *don't* know, Johnny actually has an excellent memory and attention for detail."

I sniffed. Try telling that to Hutton.

"He's a lot smarter than he looks in other words," Fleet concluded.

Or something to that effect. My attention to detail had gotten distracted for a minute.

I appreciated the kudos, but I thought I should probably clarify one thing: "I've got *A* to *Z* on the girls finished, but I'm only up through *B* on the boys."

Fleet accepted the amendment. "*A* to *Z* on the girls will be quite sufficient."

The ladies in the room all looked at each other.

"Toward the end of your studies, you will, no doubt, have come across the meaning of a name under *Z*. The name Zoe." The ladies in the room all looked at Zoe.

I nodded. I did remember the origin for Zoe. Zoe, from the Greek *Zoë*—note the bing-bongs. (Ate had that decorative touch too—*Atë*—but she refused to use it. These girls today—)

"The meaning, Johnny?"

"Oh right. It means life."

Fleet nodded. "Life. How apropos in a discussion of death. How apropos in a discussion of whisky. Does anyone here know what the word *whisky* means?"

I raised my hand, but Fleet shook it off. "I had overlooked the answer until Madeleine mentioned how wine is the life's blood of France. Most alcohol is viewed that way by its respective culture. A connection to life. There are several translations from the Gaelic for the word, but they all essentially mean one thing. 'Water of life,' or 'lively water.' "

Everyone in the room, not just the ladies, stared harder at Zoe—the life of Greece. She didn't look Greek. Or lively.

The waitress had resumed her leaky inner tube impersonation.

"But, curiously enough, Zoe is not the only name meaning life among the ladies here tonight. Johnny?"

I peered up again. I hadn't realized I would play such an important role in his presentation. Good thing I had gotten some shut-eye first.

"No, you're right. Lots of names mean life. From what I can gather, about half of them. *Life* or *brave*."

"Examples?"

I thought for a few seconds. "Well, Vivian is the obvious one."

"You bastard," she muttered.

"And—" I paused, looking around the table. There was another one. But it eluded my consciousness for now.

Fleet picked up where he had left off:

"We know Johnny must have gotten a glimpse of his would-be murderer before the cleaver landed—perhaps in the mirror over the mantel. We also know he grabbed for the whisky bottle at the nudging of his unconscious mind. Whisky. *Water* of life. That's the key point. We've been leaving out the water."

He peered around. "Nancy's name relates to water. Her last name, that is."

The Mortimer straightened up. "Does it? I just thought it meant death."

The room shivered.

"What?" she asked. "Everybody's name has got to mean something."

"It does," Fleet agreed. "And yours does relate to death, you're correct. But technically it doesn't just mean death, it means *dead water*."

"Oh." She went pale.

Fleet held his stare on her a moment, then let up. "But it's unlikely Johnny would have known that. It would not have appeared in his studies."

He was right. I didn't, and it hadn't.

"And it would have only related to the clue in an ironic way. Men with knives in their backs are seldom so fanciful. So, once again, where does that leave us?"

"A name meaning life," said Ate.

"And water," added Lesley.

I finally remembered. I was just about to speak, when Fleet lowered the hammer. "What do you have to say to that, Evelynn?"

The hostess glanced up. Her face had gone bright red. "What do I have to say to what?"

"Your name—it has a rather unusual spelling, does it not?"

"Does it?"

"It does," said Ate. "You've got an extra *n* in there."

Evelynn—with the double *n*—sniffed. "Well, maybe you can borrow one."

Ate said another *N* would make her *Nate*. Not a bad idea, she supposed. Her father always did want a boy.

Frowning, Fleet continued his dialogue with the hostess. " 'Evelynn.' By itself, the name means—Johnny?"

"Something youthful, lively. Oo, *lively*."

"Yes, lively. But it gets better. Let's look at the names apart. *Eve*—another variation that means life."

"They all do," I said.

"And *Lynn*, which means lake, or body of water. Add them back together, and there we have it. *Life water*. Or *lively water*. Water of life."

Evelynn "Lively Water" Brine laughed hysterically.

27 — Nothing Too Savory

Her guffawing continued well into the night. That's how it seemed anyway. I knew she was a cheerful girl, but this was getting ridiculous.

She finally wound down, and Fleet proceeded sternly, "There's no point in saying we have no proof. Johnny will have remembered everything by now. Johnny?"

By golly, he was right. I did remember everything. The creepy parlor, the shadows dancing in the moonlight. A face in the mirror. My face, as it happened, but something beyond it as well, just over my right shoulder. Evelynn Brine. That hunted stare in her eyes. Then a look of determination, icy resolve and, yes, enjoyment. She had gaffed me, and she had liked it.

I remembered it all.

Fleet appeared uncertain. "I can hypnotize you if you need some additional oomph recalling."

No additional oomph would be necessary. "I got it. The whisky. The *Eve* plus *Lynn*. It was exactly as you said. When I hit the floor, the whisky was the first thing I saw, and something seemed to urge my hand toward the bottle. It just made sense."

Fleet turned back to the culprit. His manner was grave. "So you can see, there's no point in protesting."

Another faint chuckle escaped her. I wondered if she was going to argue a frame-up, as Ditters had. Fleet probably wondered this himself. He continued to increase the heat on his stern look, raising it all the way up to dour.

"I wasn't going to argue," (she argued). "It's true. I killed all three of them."

I cleared my throat.

"Sorry, two. I keep forgetting, you didn't die."

I thanked her. It was an easy mistake to make. "You're Arnold's accomplice?"

She gave her melon a reverent dip. "I love him. And he loves me."

As a man of the world, Fleet tried not to roll his eyes. Instead, he asked, "How did you first encounter each other?"

"I was doing some volunteer work, helping criminals make plans for life after prison. I didn't get to speak with Arnie long. As a restricted prisoner, he wasn't even supposed to be on our list. But we made a connection then and there. We started writing to each other after that. And that was it. I would do anything for him, Mr. Fleet, just anything."

I couldn't resist some eye-rolling myself. How was it that all these grotty little men—sorry, Ditters—had all these hot women worshipping them? Well, lukewarm woman in the case of Zoe Norris. (Sorry, Zoe.)

I was beginning to feel left out. I mean, seriously, what did a guy have to do?

I peered over at Lesley and saw her glaring at me. I really believe that woman can read my mind sometimes.

"So you fell for each other?" asked Fleet.

"Fell hard."

"And at some point Arnold asked you to commit murder for him?"

"I wanted to help," she said. It was what a hostess did.

"And that's when you took the position here?"

"That took some cajoling. They weren't hiring. But I wheedled my way in. After that, it was smooth sailing. It's amazing how you can manipulate people if you set your mind to it. I practically arranged this evening single-handed. No one ever realized; they didn't have a clue."

"Really!" sniffed Betty Dittersdorf. "*Never had a clue.* It's not easy juggling all the responsibilities here, you know?"

"Oh, I know. We were lucky everything else fell into place. Arnie and I were. At first, I thought the weather wasn't going to hold up—"

"And by 'hold up,' " Fleet clarified, "you mean not hold up?"

"Exactly. It wasn't absolutely necessary that the storm trapped everyone here. Arnie and I had other plans if it missed us. Just like I had different notes to leave out from him, depending on how fast you all solved things or didn't solve them. The weather *was* a little tricky, though. Once we had our plans in place, it had to be bad enough that it kept people here for a while—long enough to get Arnie's message on the 'poison' and all—but not bad enough that anyone canceled outright. It was nearly perfect for that. The near-perfect storm."

"And what it lacked in perfection," said Hutton, "you augmented with your own special touch?"

"Yep. The hoses took some arranging, but they really did the trick, didn't they? The landscape here is ideal for it. It's like those sledding hills you used to scope out when you were a kid, home from school on a snow day. The rock sugar I thought of on the fly. Just like that." She snapped her fingers by way of demonstration. "It's funny, too, because Sven later mentioned how Elsie played her prank on him, switching out the salt, and I said to myself, *Hey, we girls think alike*. I don't know how much it helped keep the ice frozen, but it was hilarious watching everyone slip and slide all over the place. You all kept adding salt, or so you thought, and you were just making the driveway a tasty dessert. Ha-ha."

Fleet subjected her to a not unkindly stare. "This is all a game to you, isn't it, Evelynn?" He glanced at Dom, who nodded slowly. That would be his professional assessment.

"Are you kidding? It's been the best game ever. Hard work, though. Whew!"

Fleet said whew was right. "Would you have had time to disarm the explosive if we hadn't entered the proper code? I assume you had a remote control of some sort?"

"Arnie wanted me to have a kill switch, but I didn't want anyone to see me fidgeting with anything in my hand, so I tossed it."

"So you would have perished?"

"Probably," said Evelynn Brine. She didn't seem to fully understand the question. "But I didn't. And what a thrill it was experiencing it with you all. It was practically—well, I don't want to say what, because I'm a lady. But it made me go all funny in the nether regions. You have no idea—or maybe you do. You were there."

Fleet assured her that his regions had preserved an icy detachment throughout.

Evelynn continued, "I didn't think it was right, us getting Cesar's help, but I suppose people do play these things with their friends. It was lucky we did. Lucky I helped you figure out to cheat. You were never going to finish in time."

"And what of the victims who weren't so lucky in our game?"

"Them? That was just part of it."

"You feel no remorse?"

"Not really. Sven was a nasty old crumb and a slave driver. He deserved what he got."

"And Elsie?"

"She wore too much rouge."

She peered my way. I hoped she didn't think my cheeks were amiss. I always strive for the natural look.

"I was sorry about Johnny there. But he was breathing down my neck. Anyway, it turned out okay."

I was glad she thought so. My back felt like it had taken several passes under the salamander, but otherwise I was dandy. Good of her to feel bad about it, though. It's always nice when a demented killer has a moment's regret after trying to take you out.

"The stuff with the shed was my favorite part. All we had to do was piggyback on the plans Sven already had in place, and it was done and done. You see what I meant when I said he was a nasty old crumb—Sven was."

Fleet saw. "What went wrong in the collection room?"

Evelynn smiled. "You noticed that, didn't you? It was like you said before. It was meant to look like Sven had killed himself. But he didn't cooperate. I took him aside while everyone else was wiping their brows and congratulating each other over the disarmament. I showed him the article about his sister—it didn't start in Elsie's purse, by the way. Elsie knew nothing about it. I said I felt sorry for him and told him to hide in Mr. D's secret room while I found a way to get him out of here. He took the bait perfectly—just like Elsie had taken his—but then when I came upstairs later, he was very short with me. Downright rude, really. I guess he'd been thinking about everything and realized, if he was innocent, why was he hiding? And why was I helping? I had already planned to slip one of the revolvers off the wall—I made sure it was cleaned and in working condition first—but he must have seen me coming. We struggled a minute, and that's when he whipped out the meat cleaver of all things."

"Hardly sporting of him."

"I know, right! Anyway, he made a slice at me—nearly caught me in the arm, too, the animal—and it made me let go of the gun. He took another slash, and that's when he accidentally let go of the cleaver. So we were even. I made a dive for the gun, he made a dive for the cleaver, and the hilarious thing is, I wound up with the knife and he the gun. Luckily, I got the blade in his back good and firm before he could turn around and fire. So, you see, it was self-defense, really."

I looked to Hutton, who professed to know something about the law, and he shook his head sadly.

Fleet had enjoyed hearing Evelynn's story. It had a little of everything. Love, mystery, adventure—meat cleavers. The one thing it lacked, he said, was a motive. "Did Arnold—"

"I call him Arnie."

"Did Arnie ever explain why you were doing this? Did he try to make sense of it?"

She went reflective again. It seemed like another odd question to her. Why would Arnie have to explain? Did Clyde explain to Bonnie? "You already know why. You said it yourself. Arnie was getting his revenge on you. You can't say you didn't ask for it, Ef."

Fleet wouldn't say that, no. He'd asked for it the instant he didn't kill the man when he had the chance.

The hostess was aghast. "Don't say that! It's not right."

But Fleet had said it. And as far as I was concerned, it *was* right. "You're correct about one thing, Evelynn. I did say that Arnold had done all this out of revenge."

"Arnie!"

"But that was not Arnold's motive here. That's where I went wrong."

The room gasped. I figured they had one more left in them.

"What do you mean? You're never wrong. You're Enescu Fleet, Arnie's arch-nemesis."

It's funny. You never think of it that way. I always thought of Arnie—sorry, *Arnold*—as Fleet's arch-nemesis. But I suppose Ef was as much AB's nemesis as AB was Ef's.

"What do you mean?" she demanded again.

"I mean, I allowed Arnold to feed my ego. I accepted his taunts and believed that I, Enescu Fleet, was the motive for the crimes here tonight. I never was. Had things gone as planned, we would have assumed that Sven Hosten was Arnold's accomplice because of their familial connection. Arnold had married Sven's sister, so it would follow that Sven had the motivation to kill. It was actually the other way around."

"Sven married Arnie's sister?" asked Adwick, confused.

"No. The marriage was exactly as I stated. But that didn't give Sven motivation to help Arnold kill Elsie. It gave Arnold motivation to kill Sven."

The room gasped. Okay—now, they were just milking it.

"It was the age-old motivation of money. Sven was very wealthy. I knew that as soon as I heard that he had given up a seat on the stock exchange. Exchange seats do not come cheap. Only the most influential companies and prominent families can afford them. Sven's family has always had plenty of money, and after the various members had passed away in recent years, so too had Sven."

"The old skinflint," snorted Ditters. "And he was going to do me down on that distillery deal and all the rest of it. Hell, he even made me give him a raise last week."

"The thrill of the chase," said Fleet. "Sven enjoyed making money—almost as much as he enjoyed making food."

Ditters guessed so. It was all that financier guy E. F. Hutton's fault, he supposed. Bad influence.

"Sven's sister did not have her sibling's love for finance. She had not gone into the family business. She had married a mathematician against their wishes. (I read up on her when the mobile phones came back online.) She has very little means herself. But Sven wasn't quite the monster his staff pegged him as. He never offered any of his family money to his sister, but as the last living member of that family, he *had* left everything to her in his will."

"Now you're just making stuff up," said Hutton. "How could you know that?"

"I put a call into their family lawyer," Fleet explained. "He owed me a favor." Apparently, the retired PI truly did have friends everywhere, even in Sweden or Norway or wherever Sven hailed from.

Hutton was shaking his head again. "But it would never work. You can't benefit financially from a crime."

"Arnold wouldn't be the one benefitting. His wife would."

Hutton confessed there was something in that. He'd have to toss it together and see if it made salad. "They might try to prove she was in on it."

"And likely fail. Not after it was assumed that Sven Hosten had committed murder, ostensibly to assist Arnold with his revenge, and then committed suicide. The authorities would be suspicious of Mrs. Bernard's connection perhaps, but they would be compelled to believe I had been the motivation behind the crimes. Just as I had been compelled to believe it. And that's where *you* had gone wrong, my dear." He was speaking to Evelynn again, not Hutton, whom he was probably not ready to call dear. "Arnold needed Sven to appear to die at his own hand. Your improvising has complicated things for your dream man and his wife."

"So you think the wife was in on it?" asked Lesley.

"It's hard to say. She was Sven's sister. But no one marries a man like Arnold Bernard without knowing what they're getting themselves involved in."

The various couples around the room shot furtive glances at each other.

"You're wrong!" uttered Evelynn Brine. "Wrong!"

Now she thought Fleet *could* be wrong. I wished she would make up her mind.

"His wife doesn't care a fig for him. And he doesn't give a damn about her!"

Fleet begged to differ. In the Bernard household, he would argue, there were plenty of damn figs to go around.

Evelynn didn't have to sit here and listen to this. She sprang to her feet and rushed for the door.

No one blocked her exit. This was partly due to our sympathy and understanding when it came to the poor young woman's disappointment in love. But it was also due to the large, glinting meat cleaver she had produced from under her sweater.

"So that's where it went," said Ditters. It was always the last place you looked.

I mentioned earlier how my association with Enescu Fleet had earned me a seat at quite a few juicy denouements in our time together. (Like exchange seats, these don't come cheap.) And while that was certainly true, there was actually one denouement I had attended before I ever met the detective. That was at Sir Roger Banbury's place. Ditters was there, as were Lesley and Chief Adwick, and after we had unmasked the criminal involved, the latter cast a pall on our rejoicing by snatching up a gun Ditters had left lying out on a nearby table. (Even then, the man was negligent with his firearms.)

I bring this up because it seemed like Ditters was always arming murderers.

I guess I couldn't blame him for the butcher knife, though. It wasn't he who had misplaced the hatchet. I suppose, if we were going to get real technical about it, I was one of the last ones to see it.

One thing I could blame him for, however, was not having one of those firearms lying around now. He had showed me a perfectly adequate specimen not twenty minutes ago. Where was that gun now? I'll tell you where it was. Not in his pocket.

Peering across at him, I'm pretty sure I saw him mouth the words "too chafey."

But that was neither here nor there. The hostess at *Le Vrai Cornichon* had the floor—and the knife—and she was waving the latter like a woman possessed. I flashed back to Ditters waggling his special breed of pickle over the bed and felt roughly as I had then, though slightly less appalled.

There are lots of things that can call a board meeting to a close. One of the more effective ways involves a finely honed blade of menace whisking about in your vicinity.

Evelynn had made it to the door. She turned around and instructed everyone to stay back.

The minute she disappeared, Fleet did not stay back. Neither did Hutton. And, with a sigh, neither did I. She had already stabbed me once. What more could she do?

We hurried to the door, and out we went after her.

We could see she was making good time down the hall.

And then she wasn't. She skidded to a halt at the top of the stairs, just as an authoritative voice carried up from below. It sounded like the voice of the law. "You up there, Ef?" it asked.

I didn't know who it was, but I liked their timing. The voice repeated the question, approaching steadily closer on the incline, while Evelynn dashed to her right and into the parlor. "Our" place.

A great smashing sound followed. We reached the entranceway and saw her clearing away shards from the window with one of Ditters' antique chairs. Then she jumped.

"This is why I wanted to have our meeting in the executive room," sighed Enescu Fleet.

We reached the opening alongside the law—a pair of them. I didn't catch their names.

I figured Evelynn would be well on her way by now. An easy drop into a snowdrift, and off she would be to meet the crazed mathematician of her dreams (who would explain that she had screwed up his plans royally and he would just like to be friends now).

But Evelynn Brine wasn't well on her way. She wasn't well at all. She was lying sprawled out on the ice below, her leg evidently broken and her spirits dampened.

"I'm very cold," she called up to us.

28 — Cordial

An hour later, I sat in the dining room, eating a sandwich. Fleet was there, and so were Lesley, Ate, Hutton and Ditters. There were no snarky plates, no exploding fireplaces, no food celebrities. It was just as nature had intended.

I wasn't wearing a watch, so I couldn't tell you what time it was. I'm not sure it mattered. The case was solved, and we were enjoying a well-earned meal. Fleet was finally eating the corned beef sandwich he had ordered—well, it was there on a plate anyway—while I tried the brisket with horseradish and mayo on some freshly baked Maddy Abrams rye.

"This is damn good," I told Ditters. I chomped on a pickle. Even that was pretty tasty.

"Thanks, Hath."

"Why the hell don't you just serve this? Drop all that Frenchy crap."

"You mean turn my Français deli into a plain deli? You know, you might have something there. I'll have to run it by my new partner."

"Huh?"

"Cesar Bloom wants to open a restaurant with us. He'd been looking for a menu for his new restaurant, and he's fallen in love with the food here."

"Really?" I asked.

If Evelynn's affections had taught us anything, it was that some folks did have strange tastes.

"Turns out he loves the pickles. He also likes scotch, so it's a win-win."

"You can't call it scotch," Hutton said. "Not unless you're planning on moving your enterprise to Scotland." He was getting as bad as Nancy.

"New England whisky, then," said Ditters. He wasn't picky.

"You said new restaurant," I pointed out. "You're giving up on *Le Vrai Cornichon*?"

Ditters nodded. "I'm not sure where I stand with it, since Sven owned the land and Sven is dead. I don't want Mrs. Arnold Bernard as a landlady. I'd just as soon start fresh somewhere new, just Betty, my pickles and a fistful of Golden Promise barley."

It sounded like a Judeo-Scottish spaghetti western.

I looked to Fleet. "Is Arnold's wife really going to inherit the Sven millions?"

Fleet said he may have something to say about that.

I nodded approvingly and picked up the second half of my sandwich. I congratulated him (and Hutton) on another case well done.

"It all came down to you, Hath," Hutton replied. "You're the one who took one for the team this time."

"He's right," said Fleet, pointing out once again how my not-dying clue had paved the way to the solution. "Although—"

"Yes?"

"You could have made it a little easier on us."

"How so?"

"The woman's name was Brine. There were no end of pickling items in the room."

"Well, yes."

"He's got something there," said Ditters. "One of the books would have been perfect."

"What books?"

"Cookbooks on the science of brining. There was one right there, titled *Brine.* You probably should have grabbed that."

Fortunately, before I had to endure any more of this uncalled-for abuse, Cesar and Vivian came in to say they had finished with the police and were heading home. Cesar had my last book tucked under his arm, so I guess he had bought it, after all. In hardback!

Fleet stood to offer his best wishes on their future endeavors, both personal and professional.

"One final question, if I may?" he asked Vivian.

"I guess you've earned it."

"You've stated that your last name isn't Birch. In all my investigations, I can't find what it is. You've hidden it well. Would you mind indulging an old man and telling me?"

The corner of her mouth twitched upward.

"Vance," she said.

Vance. It wasn't a bad name.

"Vivian Vance," she emphasized. "As in Lucy and Viv—*I Love Lucy*. I had Ethel Mertz's name!"

"And that wasn't good?" I asked. It had always worked okay for Ethel.

"Not for me. I've got nothing against the girl, but I couldn't go into showbiz like that. Vivian Vance! The whitest woman I've ever seen."

After she and Cesar had gone, I leaned into Ditters, who, like his namesake, knew something about plant life. I asked him to refresh my memory. Weren't birch trees frequently white in color? He was pretty sure they were.

Adwick was the next one to leave. His consultation with the authorities had run its course, and they wished him the best—somewhere far away.

He shook Ditters' hand. The two men looked into each other's eyes and nodded contentedly.

"I've never liked you," said the sheriff.

Any other man would have followed this up with some gracious qualifier, explaining how people can change and so on.

Adwick did not. He simply said, "Good luck," and that was it.

"I think he's warming to me," whispered Ditters, as he resumed his seat. "Of course, it's no wonder. I had an ace up my sleeve this time."

Before I could inquire into the nature of this ace, Fleet stood and congratulated the officer. This baffled me—although, like the authorities, I supposed we were all happy he was going.

"The sheriff is shortly to be remarried," Fleet explained.

Adwick raised his palms modestly, as though to discourage anyone from making a fuss. We weren't planning on it.

I exchanged a look with Lesley, who exchanged one with Ate, who exchanged one with Hutton.

Ditters alone spoke. "Married to a—"

"Nancy," answered Adwick.

"Nancy Mortimer?" we all asked.

"Of course." Evidently, the ex-sheriff didn't mind that she had nearly been an accessory in a murder case. It must be love.

Ditters still wasn't grasping the matter. "But we thought you and Dom Jacobs were a couple," he blurted out. Now, why didn't Adwick like his son-in-law? There had to be a clue somewhere.

Adwick stared blankly at the assembly. Suddenly, unexpectedly, he burst out in laughter. I had never seen the sheriff laugh before and could definitely add it to my list of one-offs. It was like watching a porpoise with the bends.

"Me and Dom, ho-ho. No, I don't have any of *those* feelings about him." He wiped back a tear from his eye. "No, it's me and Nancy, alright. I love that little lady. We met during my visits here the last few weeks and, well, just fell for each other. I could gobble her up."

I nodded sullenly. I did have another half a sandwich to eat. I would appreciate some consideration. "If you need a good place to honeymoon—"

Adwick showed me the palms again. He had that all worked out. Dom had recommended a place.

I'd had enough of the Dom Jacobs mystery. "So who the hell is the doc to you?" I asked. "Just a friend? A colleague?" Like Fleet, I had to know.

"He was my therapist," said Adwick simply. "He was helping me with something. In a way, I was helping him too." And on that cryptic note, he left.

Fleet, once more, came to my confusion's rescue. "I've spoken to Dom. It seems he was trying out an experimental therapy, whereupon the patient, Adwick, faced the source of his fixation in the real world. All under his doctor's supervision."

"And this fixation was?"

"Ditters. According to Dom, Adwick was having recurring fantasies about beating the young man to death with a giant gherkin."

I nodded again. I could see that. "Wait. Dom told you this? What about patient confidentiality?"

Fleet couldn't speak to that. He supposed he just had the sort of manner that encouraged people to open up.

I shook my head. It was either that or roll my eyes. "So Dom isn't the man of Adwick's dreams. Too bad. I saw him talking with Nancy, you know—Dom Jacobs, I mean. Was she in on this special therapy too?"

"Very much so. But when she saw Adwick locking you and Lesley in the greenhouse, she felt the therapy was only diverting her fiancé's anger and confronted Dom about it."

"So it was Nancy who let us out?" I might have misjudged the pip-squeak. There was some good in her, after all. "And Adwick isn't gay. Who would have thunk it?"

Fleet said not he. Nor, as it turns out, did Dr. Dom. They had several sessions wherein Adwick admitted to an inexplicable physical attraction to Ditters, an inexplicable physical attraction that both intrigued and repelled him. But Fleet couldn't go too deeply into that. Doctor-detective confidentiality.

I slid my sandwich aside. That had done it.

Next in the parade of exits came Betty. She wasn't really leaving, just going to bed. She didn't look so good.

Ditters told her about Nancy, and she smiled wanly. Her father had spoken with her on his way out the door. She couldn't be happier. (She sure looked like she could be.)

Ditters stood and squeezed her around the shoulders. "We actually have some good news of our own," he announced. "Betty is pregnant." And there was Ditters' ace. The grandkid. I knew he would find a way.

Betty smiled weakly again, and then excused herself.

The pickles were making her queasy.

I noticed Lesley looking a shade perturbed. I asked her about it later, and she wondered if maybe we should wait a little longer on the pregnancy thing. She hadn't liked Betty's look. If that was the face of motherhood, she would just as soon give it a few months. Or years.

Why the rush?

It was just the five of us in the dining room now. And Pixie. I always forget Pixie.

"I've been remiss in congratulating you," Fleet told his daughter.

Ate smiled. "Sorry to leave you out of it, Dad. It just sort of happened that way. I thought for sure you would have figured it out."

Fleet smiled himself and said he supposed he hadn't been much of a detective lately. Even Sheriff Adwick had picked up on their bond.

He turned to his new son-in-law. "I can think of no one I'd rather have at my daughter's side. And no one I'd rather have pick up the baton as Enescu Fleet, consulting detective."

Hutton and Ate looked at each other.

"You don't mean you're retiring?" she asked. "I mean, *really* retiring this time?"

Fleet thought perhaps he was. "And I'll give you a word of advice about technique," he told Hutton. "I've heard you asking Johnny on occasion about my approach to solving crime. Your incredulous wonder about how I do it."

"I never meant—"

"It's fine. There is an obvious answer. Experience. You do a thing long enough, put in enough hours, and everything starts to become second nature. The fishy-sounding alibi sounds fishy because you've heard that ploy a hundred times before. The motive lurking deep down below in a respectable family reminds you of a thousand motives before it. You begin to pick up on these patterns when you get as old as I am. It's repetition, that's all."

"And knowing everyone," I added.

"And knowing everyone," Fleet agreed.

"Doesn't sound very grand," said Hutton, after a moment's reflection.

"It isn't. Although, someone with your skills can make it pretty grand, I'm sure. You should reach the pinnacle of this profession much quicker than I did. Just don't expect too many shortcuts. It's not often that you have a Johnny-on-the-spot, like we did tonight." He slapped me on the back as he said this. It was such a nice moment that I tried not to cry out in agony.

"I guess you'll be spending more time with Madeleine now?" asked Ate. She was making an effort to sound open and approving. I think she succeeded. It sounded genuine.

I could tell Fleet appreciated the thought, but he shook his head. "No, Maddy and I have parted ways again, at my suggestion. She said she knew it the minute I kissed her earlier."

"A woman always knows," nodded Lesley.

"But why?" asked his daughter, who didn't know. "If it was anything you were picking up from—"

Fleet assured her that it was not her. He took out a slip of paper. It was the first of Arnold Bernard's taunts, the letter. "If you look at the pattern in this message, you'll see why."

We all reread it. "I don't get it," said Ate.

Hutton didn't reply, so Fleet explained:

"The capitalizing of the *M* and the *A* in *Mental Acuity*—MA for Madeleine Abrams. Then there's the overall tone of the thing: a mock tribute to love. Bernard knows about Maddy. Until I finish things with him, I can't place her in danger."

"But that's crazy, Dad. He knows about all of us."

Fleet agreed with her. And that was why he had to focus. "I have work to do."

Ate chewed her lower lip. "You believe he has other stooges out there, don't you?"

"Stooges that won't be quite so easy to vanquish. Yes, I do."

She switched to the upper lip. "You're not retiring at all, are you? It's the other way around. You're coming out of retirement completely."

Again, Fleet couldn't speak to that.

"Arnold Bernard has always been one move ahead of me," he said. "I can't stand idly by and let that continue. I have to beat him at his own game once and for all. And that is what I intend to do. You might even call it a promise."

FURTHER READING

If you enjoyed *Fleeting Promise*, and have not already followed Hathaway's suggested reading order, you might want to have a peek at the first four Enescu Fleet mysteries: *Fleeting Memory*, *Fleeting Glance*, *Fleeting Note* and *Fleeting Chance*.

The other book he mentions, *Five Star Detour*, features his first encounter with his future wife, Lesley, as well as a complete buffet of misadventures with Ditters Dittersdorf and Sheriff "Chief" Adwick.

www.ingramcontent.com/pod-product-compliance
Lightning Source LLC
Chambersburg PA
CBHW020610310726
48979CB00008B/1411/J

* 9 7 8 0 9 9 1 2 3 2 4 7 5 *